Praise for
TIGER QUEEN

"From the beginning to end, *Tiger Queen* had me eagerly drinking in every page with great anticipation of what would come next and left me thirsting for more."

Brenda Drake, *New York Times* bestselling author of the Library Jumpers series

"A tumultuous tale of shifting sands and political pressure, *Tiger Queen* chronicles one warrior princess's high-stakes path to the throne. A compelling, all-consuming story of strength, duty, and danger. An absolute must-read."

New York Times bestselling author Alethea Kontis

"In a world where water is scarce and danger is plentiful, Kateri discovers that the most defining points in her history are not what she thought. But she refuses to back down. With its gripping characters and fascinating creatures, *Tiger Queen* will sweep you away on the desert sands."

Savannah Goins, author of *The Gwythienian*

"Annie Sullivan's *Tiger Queen* will grab you by the throat and not let go until the final, blissful word has swept past, leaving you captivated, satisfied, yet wanting more. I couldn't put it down. Walk—no, run—to your local bookstore to snatch up your very own copy. Best book I've read all year!"

Michele Israel Harper, award-winning editor and author of *Kill the Beast*

"An absolutely thrilling, action-packed adventure set in a richly crafted world with a fierce heroine you'll root for—*Tiger Queen* is impossible to put down!"

Kim Chance, author of *Keeper* and *Seeker*

TIGER QUEEN

ANNIE SULLIVAN

BLINK

Tiger Queen

Requests for information should be addressed to:
Blink, *3900 Sparks Dr. SE, Grand Rapids, Michigan 49546*

Hardcover ISBN 978-0-310-76877-7
Audio ISBN 978-0-310-72965-5
Ebook ISBN 978-0-310-76876-0

Interior design: Denise Froehlich

Printed in the United States of America

---

19 20 21 22 23 / DCI / 10 9 8 7 6 5 4 3 2 1

*Once again, to my family: Mom, Dad,
Katie, Pat, Michael S, Danny, John,
Maggie, Michael K, and James*

*Also to my middle school English teacher,
Mrs. Desautels, for first asking me the
question, "The lady or the tiger?"*

CHAPTER 1

I watched as two guards pulled a thin boy into the arena. His feet left trails in the sand as though two yellow-spotted sand snakes followed his path. The guards chained him to the short center post so he couldn't move more than five arm lengths in any direction. Then they retreated, leaving the boy and his puddled shadow alone to face the crowd.

The boy stood like a lopsided cactus in the sun, with his elbows away from his body to keep the thick metal chains from burning any more skin than necessary.

He couldn't have been more than eight or nine.

Now he'd come to my arena—my home—where I fought each month. And we all were waiting to see if he would leave it alive.

My father rose from his chair. The jeers and shouts of the crowd quieted, leaving only the sound of the breeze drifting in across the desert, shifting and remaking the far-off hills of sand.

My eyes darted back and forth between the two doors that stood shut before the boy. Which door concealed the tiger? It was impossible not to wonder while I waited for my father to speak.

"My people," he said, "we have before us an accused Desert Boy. One of the very same urchins who plagues our kingdom by stealing from our wells, forcing me to ration what little water we have." He let the cries die down before continuing. "This particular Desert Boy was caught leading a caravan of contraband goods into the city." He paused while the crowd reacted.

The boy couldn't even bring himself to face my father. He kept his chin tucked close to his chest. Probably to hide his tears.

I steeled my face. Let him cry. Let him return even the smallest fraction of water he'd taken from us, from our people, over the years. I wouldn't let the sight of him get to me. It didn't matter that he was so young. I couldn't let it matter. If this boy's only crime had been bringing in forbidden goods, it might be forgivable, even understandable. But he was a Desert Boy, a water thief. And that could never be forgiven.

The drought had hit all of us hard, and yet these boys thought they were above the law, that they had the right to take more than their allotted share. How many more people would live now that there was one less Desert Boy stealing our water? Sacrificing his life would save countless of my people's lives—people who fought to survive despite the number of times he and his kind raided the wells, people who were dying in the streets from thirst while he and his friends drank their fill.

I squared my shoulders. Justice needed to be carried out until the water returned and Achra could once again take its place as the thriving oasis it once was. It was the only way we would survive—and if there was anything Achrans were known for, it was surviving. We had turned the harsh desert into a sanctum for merchants, artisans, and caravans—at least until the water ran out and groups like the Desert Boys formed.

But we would rise again, and until we did, we had to do what was best for the people. That meant making this prisoner face justice.

"But," my father continued, "this boy claims he was out

hunting for moonstones and stumbled upon the caravan just as my guards arrived."

I scoffed and rolled my eyes, chiding myself for even thinking of giving the boy sympathy. It was unfortunate one of the ever-increasing sandstorms we'd been experiencing hadn't wiped him out in the desert and saved us the trouble. He may look young, but he was clearly a Desert Boy through and through—using the same excuse they all gave when we caught them. And as the sun rose higher—and the temperature of my blood along with it—heat radiated from the sword sheathed at my side, begging to be unleashed. This boy was clearly trying to slip through our fingers so he could run straight back to our wells and bleed them dry, bleed us dry, make us so weak we were unable to fight back.

We couldn't let that happen. As the future queen, I couldn't let that happen.

"We should never have brought him to trial," I turned and said to my father. When Rodric, my father's captain of the guard, hadn't been able to get the location of the other Desert Boys out of the kid, we should've kept him locked up. He would've broken eventually.

"Kateri," my father snapped, bluntly cutting off my name as the crowd roared around us. "Control yourself and your tongue." He pursed his thin lips—ones identical to mine—as he stared down at me.

His eyes said what his lips didn't. Be in control or someone else will take control. He'd drilled that phrase into me as my fighting trainer over the years. But it'd been a while since he'd scolded me like that. I crossed my arms and sank back into my seat, pulling my long braid over my shoulder. I tugged at the loose tail, twining the dark strands between my calloused fingers.

I *was* in control of myself. One of my mother's killers stood before me—was on the verge of escaping—and I hadn't leapt into the arena to make him pay for his crimes. I ignored the fact this particular boy would have been too young to take part in the raid that killed my mother and baby brother. He was still a Desert Boy. Leading the illegal caravan into the city was the least of his crimes.

"While the desert offers no justice, I do," my father said, turning back to address the boy. "Before you are two unmarked doors. Behind one is the cart of contraband goods, which will be yours to keep should you choose that door. Behind the other door is one of my pet tigers, which will be released into the arena within moments should that door be selected. The decision is yours, and yours alone. But fail to choose, and the tiger will be released." He let his words float around the arena.

For the first time, the boy raised his head and faced the crowd. His eyes held my father's for a moment before swinging to mine. There was a pleading weakness in them that made my stomach churn. How could he help bleed the Achran wells dry and then expect pity from those he caused to suffer?

He wouldn't find any pity here. I leaned forward and stared him down until he turned away.

The boy focused on the doors in front of him. The chains fettering him to the post clanked together as he lifted his arm and pointed to the door on the right.

I snuck a glance at my father's face. He always knew which door hid the tiger, and he couldn't hide the upturn at the edges of his lips that would curl into a smile when the accused picked that door.

No smile played about his lips. My heart flipped faster than a dune in a sandstorm. I bolted up in my seat. Hot afternoon air grew unbearable in my lungs as I held my breath.

The door creaked open to reveal a cart piled with earthen jars full of still-living spiral snails waiting for nobles to use their shells to flavor their water, bolts of spider silk netting fine enough to catch sand and keep it from coming in windows and doors, and clay containers full of nogen nuts and spiked rainberries waiting to be crushed into spices and perfumes.

"No," I whispered. And then I was shouting it over and over again. The cry was drowned out by the roaring of the crowd.

I shook my head in disbelief. The desert wouldn't do this to me. It couldn't. My heart pounded in my chest as my stomach twisted at the thought of the boy walking free. Free to raid our wells. Free to attack our guards. Free to cause suffering to those left in the city as water rations were cut more and more because of the never-ending drought that had started before I was even born.

The boy threw his arms into the air and stomped his feet into the sand in celebration, laughing uncontrollably.

It reminded me so much of my mother, of the laugh I would never hear again—the laugh the Desert Boys took away from me. And they would just keep taking things away unless we stopped them. Unless I stopped them.

I pulled my sword out of its scabbard.

I had one hand on the railing, ready to vault into the arena, when my father's hand shot out to stop me. His fingers wrapped around my arm in an iron-like grasp as he gave me a silencing look.

I ground one palm against the searing metal of the railing while the other gripped my sword's hilt. My chest shook with rage. "He's a Desert Boy," I said through gritted teeth. "We can't let him escape."

"Sit down." My father's eyes turned cold. When I was little, I couldn't imagine how anything that icy could exist in the desert.

And now I couldn't understand what my father was thinking. But I did know what happened when I disobeyed. Ripping my hand away from the railing, I slid back into my seat and dug the tip of my sword into the floor to keep from staring at the smile on the boy's face. Chunk after chunk of rock chipped away from the crumbling arena. I drilled the blade farther and farther until I couldn't feel the muscles in my arm.

"Justice has prevailed," my father shouted. "The boy is free to take the cart and go."

Guards moved forward to unshackle the boy. He whooped and hollered and kicked sand into a wide arc as he sped toward the cart.

My knuckles turned white around the hilt still in my hands. "There is no justice in this desert," I said.

"Perhaps justice has been kinder than we thought, Kateri," my father replied. He motioned, and a figure melted out of the shadows at the top of the arena.

Rodric sauntered down the steps, pausing to bow before my father.

"Your trap is working perfectly," my father extolled.

Rodric bowed again, but he couldn't hide the smirk sliding across his lips. He was only a few years older than me, but the tiny scars running up and down his arms and neck—left there by fire-legged flies—spoke to his upbringing. He hadn't grown up behind curtains of spider silk to keep the flies and sand out. No, he'd grown up at the mercy of the elements.

He'd adopted the closely shaven hair favored by most of the soldiers. Of course, that was after he'd shown up to one of their training sessions months ago, emerging from the tail end of one of the sandstorms as though the desert were depositing him on our doorstep. He'd looked haggard and windblown, with hair down to his shoulders. But appearances had been deceiving; he'd marched up to my father's then captain of the guard and stabbed him before the man could even get a word out. When the other soldiers brought Rodric before my father, he'd stood tall and said that if the head of my father's security was that easy to kill, he should find someone else to fill the job.

Someone like Rodric.

My father had seen something in Rodric and took him on.

But I'd never seen what my father had. My father had been a strict yet even-tempered teacher. When I got injured while training, he'd see to me himself—refusing to let the apothecaries do it. He'd bind up my arm or leg or whatever I'd injured while drilling into me what I'd done wrong. He'd say pain was earned by inattention and lack of skill, that it was up to me to avoid pain by doing better. After he'd bandaged me, he'd make me repeat the move I'd messed up until I could do it perfectly one hundred times in a row. It had been rough at the time—all those nights I wasn't allowed to go to sleep until I'd executed the move flawlessly again and again—but I knew my father did it for me, for us. He wanted me to win, and that meant I had to be the best.

Though when my father handed off my training to Rodric a few months ago, after seeing his skill with a blade, I learned what truly harsh training was. Sure, Rodric conditioned me in ways similar to what my father had, like building up my stamina and strength by having me hang above pits of raw worms that would bite into me if I fell in or tying me to a rope during the start of a sandstorm, making me run against the wind. Those I could handle. But unlike my father, Rodric didn't wait for me to bandage my wounds. He'd give me small cuts and then purposefully flick sand toward them.

And he thought everyone fought better when they were mad. So he'd do everything he could to goad me. He'd steal my sandals, making me fight barefoot in the burning sand. He'd shove my face into that same sand, one hand holding my face down while the other tried to bury it, suffocating me. He'd grab me from behind and pull my eyelids open, making me stare into the sun until I could fight free from his grasp.

I hated his methods, preferring a more calculated fight—one where I studied my opponents and found their weaknesses. That's what my father had always taught me. Look for a weakness and exploit it.

So while I couldn't see whatever it was my father valued in Rodric beyond his brute strength, it was obviously something exceptional, because my father had been turning to him more and more these past few months. And I was being left out of decisions. Like this one.

"A trap?" I scanned the arena as people emptied toward the streets. I didn't see any guards waiting to ambush the boy, so I studied my father. He'd seemed oddly calm—oddly indifferent—during the trial. My eyes landed on the doors across the arena. "You put carts behind both doors," I said, wishing it came out more as a question than a statement.

Rodric leaned against the railing and squinted down at me. "Of course."

Heat pulsed through my body. "You let him get away? You're

the captain of the guard. It's your job to catch him. He's not some water beetle you buy in the marketplace that the merchant swears will lead you to some underground spring. No, that boy is a scorpion—you have to squash him while you can so he doesn't crawl away and hide, waiting to sting you when you're not looking."

Rodric clenched his jaw before replying, "It's better to let one scorpion go when it'll lead you to all the rest, so you can kill them where they sleep."

I started to retort, but my father interrupted. "Rodric, send as many guards as you think necessary. I want their hideout found and destroyed." Once his order had been conveyed, he moved toward the exit.

Rodric turned and motioned for two guards to come forward. He gave them brief instructions before the men headed out after the boy.

I shook my head. If that child had any brains, he'd already ditched the cart and melted back into the desert like the loathsome creature he was. Those guards would never find him—especially since they were scared of venturing past the crumbling city wall. They'd seen too many of their comrades carried back in with the yellow-and-black veins that accompanied a bite from a yellow-spotted sand snake. Or they simply didn't return at all.

No. If that boy was to be stopped, it had to be someone who wasn't afraid of the desert. It had to be me.

I slowly backed away, tracing my fingers along the railing, hoping Rodric wouldn't notice my path took me closer to the same door the boy had pulled the cart through. Once I was far enough away from Rodric and my father, it would be an easy leap into the arena and a quick jog across the sand. I was calculating my chances of making it when a shadow fell across my back.

"I know what you're thinking," Rodric said. He was standing so close I could feel the heat radiating from him despite the afternoon heat. "You plan on following that Desert Boy."

I turned to face him, pushing my back against the railing. It shuddered under my weight, threatening to topple into the arena. "If you're not going to do your job, someone has to."

Rodric's eyes narrowed. "I've already found one of their old hideouts. It's just a matter of time until I find their current one." He had tried several methods to catch the Desert Boys, like setting traps around seemingly unguarded wells to tempt a raid in the middle of a deserted square. He'd also tortured the few suspected Desert Boys he'd caught. But despite being hung upside down above the tiger cages or put in boxes with hundreds of raw worms, the boys never spoke.

"You think your two guards are going to follow him into the desert?" I retorted.

"And you would? You're no Tamlin. You don't know what's beyond the city walls like I do."

I forced myself to meet his gaze. He stood a little more than a hand taller than me, and his body was thick with muscle. "The desert doesn't scare me. I am my father's daughter, and Tamlin's blood is in my veins just as it was in my ancestors'. He faced the desert and lived, and so will I."

Unlike anyone before him or since, Tamlin had survived traveling across the entire desert on foot, emerging from the sands to be crowned king when he saved the people from an approaching army. But even before his trek, the Achran people had believed the desert chose its rulers. Endless plagues of sandstorms, incessant droughts, and ceaseless scorpion invasions were signs of weak blood on the throne. Although my father blamed the increasingly awful drought and run of sandstorms on the Desert Boys, claiming even the desert itself was trying to rid them from its dunes. And things wouldn't get better until they were stopped.

"What was your plan if you found their hideout?" he continued. "Were you going to take them all on at once? I've taught you well, but not even you could take on Cion."

I rolled my eyes. "Cion doesn't exist." As far as I'd heard, no one had ever laid eyes on the Desert Boys' leader. He was more likely a myth made up to scare us. No one could be as good with a blade as the rumors made him out to be.

People said he could swing his sword through the gap in a snake's forked tongue before the snake could retract it. That tale was outdone only by the rumor that if you threw a grain of sand into the air, he could split it in half with his blade. But the people who spread such things were likely the same ones who said the sand parted for him, and that's why he could sneak up on the wells so quietly. Or that the dunes settled around him like a cloak, making him impossible to see. Some even claimed he was made of sand, and that's why the guards couldn't catch him. He would just melt away into nothing when they tried.

I didn't believe any of it.

But Rodric did. Especially the claims about his skill with a sword, which is probably why he sliced out the tongue of anyone he found talking about Cion's abilities.

That was why I didn't dare mention I'd tried to do the things Cion was rumored to be capable of. I'd snuck down to the kitchens and stolen snakes from the baskets before they were killed for feasts. I'd set them free in my room and tried for days on end to slip my blade between their outstretched tongues. All I succeeded in doing was scraping my floor and having to dodge endless numbers of bites. I'd even tried splitting a grain of sand in half. I could smack it and knock it away. But only one grain of sand ever hit the floor. It wasn't possible. None of it was.

Rodric's face darkened. "He exists." His hands clenched the bars of the railing, strangling them as he leaned his weight forward.

"If he's as good as everyone says, what will *you* do if you're the one to find him?"

"I'm the best swordsman this desert has ever seen. No one could beat me, not even you."

I scoffed, pretending to brush off the comment, but this time his words bit deeper into my skin than any cut he'd given me while practicing. He was right. I couldn't beat him. And I'd tried.

During our first lesson, he'd sliced three hairline slashes into each side of my neck. He'd said if he'd made them any deeper, I would have been like a fish on land, unable to breathe. Rodric called it a new technique, but he hadn't bothered to teach it to me.

In order for the desert to accept me as its future queen, there could be no one fiercer, stronger, or better than me in a fight. I'd pulled out my sword and rushed up behind him. Just as I was about to send my blade into his back, he turned, grabbed my arm, and flipped me over.

The next thing I knew, he'd pinned me to the ground and whipped out a knife, pressing the blade against my throat. "If you ever try that again," he said, his eyes wild, "I'll hang you from the tower of your father's palace." He eased off me and dropped the knife to the ground.

I'd lain there for a moment praying that sand hadn't found

its way into my new wounds and dealing with the stinging pain that swept through me every time I moved.

I wanted to pick my knife up to try again, but something in Rodric's eyes made it clear he'd follow through on his threat.

As these weren't normal training injuries, I'd started wearing a thick golden cuff around my neck after that to cover the scars. To keep my father from seeing, from knowing I'd failed to be the best. And it worked. My father saw me embracing my strength, not hiding my weakness, because he believed there was nothing stronger than metal in the desert.

But I hated how it choked me and slid like oil across my body when I sweat. It also fettered me to my father in a way that felt like I'd given up on my mother's beliefs entirely, that I'd lost another part of her.

The cuffs were typically worn by the rich nobles as a symbol of their wealth—a show that they didn't need that metal to bar their windows against sandstorms or to hold water buckets together. Some had ornate patterns scrawled across the metal with holes dotted across them like stars in the sky or depictions of flowers or thick, wavy grooves.

My father had given my mother many when she married him, but she'd never worn one because she said it weighed too heavily on her.

I'd always thought she meant its physical weight. It wasn't until years after she died that I realized she meant it was because it was a waste to wear gold merely as a decoration when it could've been given to someone who needed it.

It was a stark reminder she hadn't grown up in the palace. She'd been a poor but beautiful sand dancer when she caught my father's eye.

She'd made me promise once that I wouldn't wear one, that I'd look for strength in myself instead. I'd kept that promise until Rodric had made me break it, had made me so weak that I needed one.

My hatred for him burned brighter than the noonday sun.

As much as I wanted him dead, though, I needed him alive. He was the only one who'd ever been able to find a Desert Boys hideout. It'd been old and empty, but it was more progress than the old captain of the guard had managed.

And if Cion really did exist, I needed Rodric to help me fight. As well as to help me train for my final two bouts against suitors in the arena so I could secure my place as our next queen. Though once I became queen and the Desert Boys were destroyed, I'd send Rodric away. My father had been the first to teach me that you want strength to surround you, and Rodric was strong. But something about the way he'd shown up and killed the old captain of the guard made me uneasy.

He'd emerged too much like Tamlin from the desert, and I'd never gotten a word from him about where he came from or how he came to be so skilled. I was only grateful he wasn't nobility so I'd never have to face him in the arena. Because I was going to be the one to rule these people like Tamlin had done. Not him.

"Why don't we go after Cion together?" I asked.

"Because Cion is like a yellow-spotted sand snake. You'll never see him coming. The only way to get him out of his hole is to set a trap. I've got my two best trackers after the boy. Once they've followed him to the hideout, we plan our next move." He shook his head. "Besides, you should be focusing on your fight tomorrow." He crossed his bulging arms and stared down at me.

I looked to the door the Desert Boy had gone through and

groaned, knowing my chance to slip away had evaporated faster than spilled water. But there would be others. They couldn't hide forever.

"Come on." Rodric pulled out his sword and leapt over the railing into the arena. He motioned for me to do the same. "It's my job to make sure you don't lose."

Sighing, I unsheathed my sword and leapt down into the sand. He was right. Tomorrow I'd be fighting for more than my life. I'd be fighting for my freedom.

CHAPTER 2

I slipped two daggers into the laces of my high sandals while my maid, Latia, tied my breastplate in position. I'd never been considered tall, but Latia had to stand on her tiptoes to accomplish the task.

"Good luck, my lady," she whispered. She'd always been quiet, but whenever I put on my battle gear, she shrank into herself even more, as if putting it on turned me into a monster who might run her through if she forgot to double knot a fastener or polish the family crest emblazoned on my armor.

I ran my fingers down the crest. A roaring tiger's head with a scorpion on either side, their tails raised so they connected at the top of the emblem.

My father had added the tiger and kept the scorpions that had been placed generations ago because of Tamlin. Once, Tamlin had been nothing more than a caravan leader. But after his caravan was attacked, he escaped, and during his legendary journey across the desert, he had run across Scorpion Hill to bring news of the approaching Smorian army to the Achran people. No one had ever crossed the desert on foot before. And no one had since.

Tamlin's warning allowed the city to fortify against the impending siege, ensuring not a single Achran died, while the Smorian army perished outside the city gates from a mix of thirst, snake and sun spider bites, and assassin wasp stings. They hadn't understood the desert like Achrans did.

As a result of his heroic actions, the people clamored for Tamlin to be their king as much for saving the city as for not being stung while crossing Scorpion Hill. People said that the scorpions didn't sting him because they recognized him as the master of the desert. The legend that all Achran royalty is immune to the scorpion venom that kills everyone else originated from that incident.

And once I finally cemented my place as the next Achran ruler, I would venture out into the desert to hunt for the Desert Boys myself. I wouldn't be scared of the scorpions that hid in the sands. The desert would've chosen me, and I would show it my gratitude by ridding it of the gang of thieves that continued to bleed it dry and poison it with its presence.

I admired myself in the mirror once Latia finished. Behind me in the reflection, two dresses lay folded on a shelf. One was a thin, gauzy gown. The other was a traditional wedding dress. It was bright blue, like crystal clear water, and covered in dangling, multicolored ribbons. It was said that each ribbon represented good luck to the guest who tore it from the dress. It had been brought down on the chance I didn't win the fight.

I had no intention of wearing it. I'd already decided that when my seventeenth birthday came next month, I would burn it. Or maybe I'd hike as far into the desert as I could and fling it away to face the same future as all my failed suitors.

Next to the dress lay one thin gold bracelet. That I wouldn't discard. A swirling pattern that resembled dunes was embossed on its surface. It had been my mother's engagement bracelet.

Another Achran tradition. One bracelet worn on the left arm meant a girl was engaged. If I lost, I'd have to put it on along with the dress. And after the wedding, a second bracelet would be added to the right wrist as well.

I'd kept my mother's as it was one of the few things of hers I had, preserved for me only because mothers were supposed to pass down their engagement bracelets. But that didn't mean I actually wanted to wear it. I'd always thought of them more as shackles than symbols of love.

Somewhere through the ages, it had also become tradition for husbands to give their wives a bracelet for each year they were married. Some of the ladies could barely lift their arms due to the weight of their bangles.

That would never be me. I'd rather be incapacitated in the arena than by jewelry.

There was only one piece of jewelry I did want. My mother's crown.

I thought they had burned it along with her body almost ten years ago. My father had let me think that when, weeks after her death, I'd asked him for it, for another piece of my mother, because I'd wanted to wear it someday. But he'd surprised me before my first fight in the arena months ago, arriving at the gladiator prep area with the crown in his hands.

I'd gasped when I saw it. Its jagged metal peaks rose gallantly upward, sharp enough to prick a finger and strong enough to withstand almost anything. It encapsulated everything the desert was—sharp and unyielding but regal and strong—and everything I wanted to be.

I reached for it, but he pulled it back.

My distorted reflection showed a face not unlike my mother's, though clad in thick gladiator gear. A true mix of my mother and father, who would continue to lead the Achran people back to prosperity. I'd stood a little straighter.

"I brought this to show you what awaits you at the end of this journey," my father said. "Let it inspire your fight today."

I had nodded.

My father hadn't brought the crown out since, but it was because I'd won the first fight so quickly; my father knew I didn't need to be spurred on. I would uphold his legacy—my family's legacy—by winning the throne.

The memory faded as the door to the gladiator preparation room swung open, screeching as the joints ground against the sand caught in them. Rodric didn't wait to be invited in. To him, I was his pupil, not the princess. Latia lowered her gaze and backed away so quickly she nearly knocked a pitcher of water off the table.

Rodric smirked.

"Ready for battle?" he asked.

"Of course," I said, grabbing my helmet and shield and following Rodric out the door. The heat in my blood had risen with the sun, as though my body could sense the fight to come. My veins thrummed with life, coursing just beneath the surface, ready to respond when I raised my blade.

We emerged into the cool tunnel under the arena that stretched all the way to the gated entrance leading to the city streets. Past the contingent of guards who had escorted me from the palace, I could just make out the mass of scrawny arms clutching at nothing through the bars.

The guards used their spears and swords to keep back anyone who tried too hard to get into the stadium, although I couldn't fathom what they expected to find inside. The tunnel's only offshoots were the prep area I'd just vacated, which held little of material value, and the tunnel used to lead the tigers from the palace dungeons to the arena.

I ignored the crowd and pulled on my helmet, moving farther down the tunnel. The closer I got to the closed doors, the more claw marks lined the walls. My fingers had sunk past my first knuckle when I'd run my fingers down those grooves before my first fight. The wounds my sword left behind always seemed thin and shallow in comparison after that.

I stepped past the cage-like bars that kept the tigers in place when they were needed for arena judgments. The tunnel smelled like the cages, the heavy odor of sweat mixed with unwashed fur.

The door I stood behind now was the door that had concealed the goods won by the Desert Boy. I let the thought spread anger through me.

"Remember," Rodric said, banging my helmet to bring my attention to him, "he's got a weak right side, but he's big. Don't let him use his bulk against you."

I nodded as Rodric receded back into the darkness of the tunnel. Then, I was alone facing the wooden doors. In a few spots, you could almost see through the gouges the tigers had left.

I took a deep breath.

My mother had taught me an old sand dancer tradition; they used to sprinkle sand over their feet before every performance, asking the desert to guide their steps. I slid my sword from its scabbard and bent down and grabbed a handful of sand, releasing it over my weapon and offering up my own prayer to the desert. It was my way of keeping my mother with me, of asking her to help determine my path. And my husband.

Only two more fights until I earned her crown.

Outside, I could hear the crowd roar.

I moved my head from side to side, loosening the muscles in my neck. Then I jumped a few times, tucking my legs high up under me, making sure everything was in place and that my movements weren't restricted. I shook the tension from my arms and wiped my sweaty palm on my tunic before gripping my sword tighter. Then, I waited.

The doors creaked open, and the sunlight blinded me. I held my sword above my head as I entered. My heart rate drowned out the crowd, and I took measured breaths as I moved forward into the arena.

My eyes immediately went to the man entering through the other door to my right. It was Lord Hamic's son, Hardesh. He was tall. A good head taller than me, but he didn't have the amount of muscle Rodric had. His dark sideburns were visible under his helmet. He was about twenty-five years older than me. His first wife had died some years ago, after giving birth to two daughters.

Some said he'd killed his wife when she didn't produce a son. It was a practice whispered about in alleyways and at the wells, but never openly. Whispers that became more frequent after my father instituted a law allowing two children per family back when the drought began so we wouldn't deplete our water resources.

Some men still clung to the old belief that a man's strength was determined not only by his sword arm but by how many sons he had, because once only royal sons were allowed to fight in the arena against select male challengers when they turned sixteen in order to secure their right to rule. Thus, if a man had daughters, he was thought weak, that the desert wished to end his line by not giving him anyone to fight in the arena.

That changed with Tamlin. He had only daughters, but the people loved him and agreed that the desert had chosen him to rule. It was only fair to give his line a chance to continue. So when a son wasn't born, the oldest daughter was given a chance to claim the throne—as Tamlin's daughter Rainnina had done. She only had to beat one challenging opponent per month during her sixteenth year in order to claim the throne. But Tamlin had also insisted that if any opponent beat a royal daughter, the suitor would win the right to rule and would marry her.

But even if I married Hardesh, we wouldn't be allowed to have children together because of the rationing law. That's why I'd thought Hardesh was such an odd choice on my father's part. He knew the importance of heirs better than anyone. But I took it as a sign he knew I'd beat this challenger as I had the others.

Hardesh and I reached the center of the arena at the same time. Our shadows melted around our feet as though being swallowed by quicksand.

"Born of noble birth," my father shouted from his seat in the stands, "both are equals by blood in the arena. Only their skill will separate them."

The crowd erupted.

I studied Hardesh. Weathered hands fidgeted with his sword hilt, and his eyes kept flicking between my sword and my face. He had a chink in his armor close to the collar on his right side, which meant that Rodric had been right. That side was weaker.

"Should he win," my father called, "he will wed Princess Kateri at the feast this afternoon, but should he lose, he will be banished to the desert. Do you agree to these terms Hardesh, son of Hamic?"

Hardesh didn't take his eyes off me. He lifted his sword into the air, signaling his agreement.

I kept the smile off my face. When he'd lifted his arm,

he'd revealed several more scratches down the right side of his breastplate.

This would be easier than I thought—not like when I faced my third opponent during the middle of a sandstorm. I'd assumed we'd wait a day for the storm to end, but my father said we had to deal with whatever the desert sent us if we wanted to be masters of it.

But I'd won that fight easily, and this one wouldn't be half so difficult. I dug my feet into the sand, sword at the ready, and waited.

"Begin!"

The roar of the arena fell away. Blood rushed through my body.

We circled, studying the other's movements—the only sound the swish of the sand as it scattered beneath our feet.

Sweat dripped down my back.

Hardesh brought his shield up to cover most of his face. The other hand gripped and ungripped the hilt of his sword. Perspiration stained his brow.

He feinted forward but pulled back.

I watched Hardesh's eyes the way my father had taught me as a child. Hardesh looked down before rushing forward and swiping his blade toward my legs. Anticipating the move, I surged forward. I leapt over his sword and swung mine around, glancing off his shield and sliding across the armor on his back.

He cried out, staggered, but didn't fall. "You've been practicing since your last fight, I see. You're better than I expected," he said.

"You're not," I retorted. I brought my sword around and sliced through the leather cuff on his wrist. It snapped in half and fluttered to the ground.

He kicked the leather away. "You're not the delicate flower everyone describes," he said. "You're more like a cactus, prickly all over."

"That's right"—I let one of his blows slide off my shield—"because no one can touch me." I could have knocked him out with the edge of my shield right then. He'd left an opening in his defense when he'd gone for my legs, but I didn't take it.

The whole point of the fight was to show the world what I could do, that I was a force to be reckoned with, that I was my father's daughter, stronger than any man—strong enough to rule the desert.

I dropped into the sand and slid my sword across the cords of his sandals. They flopped away from his hairy legs, leaving his feet bare.

Hardesh hopped around in an attempt not to burn his feet.

The crowd roared with laughter.

I relaxed my stance and waited for him to regain his. What I didn't count on was how angry I'd made him.

Hardesh bolted forward. I parried his attack, but he kept pressing onward. His sword clanged against my shield with enough force to send me stumbling backward. I dug my feet into the cooler layers of sand to keep my balance.

The crowd booed.

I didn't have time to bring my sword up to block his next blow. I flipped my shield higher to stop his sword from biting into my thigh, but his weapon skimmed down the shield and cut into my calf. One sandal strap split in half. Blood spilled down my leg.

I gritted my teeth, refusing to cry out. Droplets of blood buried themselves in the sand at my feet. I was supposed to be untouchable. I wasn't supposed to take any hits. Any signs of weakness in me were signs of weakness in the monarchy.

And there were no weaknesses in the monarchy.

My father's eyes bore into my back.

Hardesh lunged for me again. I blocked his sword with mine and rammed the edge of my shield into his face. He tumbled backward, landing hard on his back. Thick blood squirted out his nose and pooled in the dirt around him. He rolled around, groaning and covering his nose with his hands, but he didn't get up.

I aimed my sword at his throat, proving to the crowd and my father I could've ended his life if I'd really wanted to. Then, I yanked it away.

My chest heaved from the exertion and from my own stupidity. I resisted the urge to hurl my shield into the sand by curling my fingers so tightly around my sword hilt that my nails bit into my palm.

I sought out my father in the stands. His squat, round eyes—so unlike the almond ones I'd inherited from my mother—stared down at me. Something sinister flickered in his glare. Something I recognized all too well. I shouldn't have let my opponent get close enough to hit me.

Back when my father had been my trainer, he'd collected dozens of fire-legged flies and locked me in an empty room inside the palace one night. He'd released the flies into the room, saying I'd only be let out when I made it through a night without any new burns. I had to be so fast, so aware of my surroundings that I was untouchable.

It had taken me three nights to succeed. But I could still remember the look on my father's face on the mornings he found new burns on my skin. His eyes would narrow, and his lips would thin. He'd straighten, pulling away from me. "Not good enough."

He'd dutifully rubbed a salve into the burns after I was released, understanding that injuries had to happen in order to learn. He'd tolerated my mistakes during training. But mistakes couldn't happen now, not when I was on display, not when my strength was a reflection of his.

I'd never gotten injured in an arena fight before. But now I'd disgraced him. I'd done the one thing I was never supposed to do. I'd made him look weak.

Beneath my breastplate, sweat slid down my skin. And in the middle of the desert, I went cold.

I searched for something I could do to show him I was good enough. I'd won, after all. But there was nothing. The damage was done.

I swallowed as my father rose from his chair. He looked oddly indifferent. Or maybe he was trying to control his anger like he'd always told me to do.

The crowd quieted.

"Hardesh has failed," my father said. "He is hereby banished to the desert. His survival will depend on his skills."

Guards came forward and picked up Hardesh under his shoulders and dragged him away, but not before the screeching of two young girls cut through the noise of the crowd. The girls attempted to scale the railing before being pulled back. I knew they were his daughters. I couldn't bring myself to look.

"My daughter is victorious and one step closer to proving she is strong enough to lead you. She will face one more challenger on her birthday next month," my father called, his voice hollow. He stared down at me, but I couldn't read his expression.

As my father exited the arena, I sheathed my sword and bowed as far as I could without causing pain to shoot up my leg.

I was already rehearsing what I could say to my father to try and make this right.

I slowly made my way to the door I'd entered by. I waved to the crowd as I went, walking as if I had never been wounded.

Inside the shade of the tunnel, I slumped against the wall. The stone was cool against my body. I closed my eyes and let the heat seep out of my skin.

"That was not the fight I was expecting," Rodric said, emerging from the darkness.

My eyes shot open at the sound of his approach. Instinctively, my body tensed as he neared, expecting an attack that may or may not come depending on his mood. Oddly, he seemed happy.

His eyes went to where blood ran down my leg. "You were faster than him."

"He was older and more experienced," I said.

"Is that an insult to my teaching?" he asked. "Or a testimony to how you should be training harder?"

I clenched my hands at my sides to keep them from going to my sword. I pushed past him down the tunnel, untying my breastplate as I went. He quickly caught up to me.

"Don't think I'll go any easier on you in training tomorrow because of it." He nodded toward my injury.

"I wouldn't expect anything less from you," I said through gritted teeth.

I quickened my pace until I reached the small prep area.

"Hurry to the feast," Rodric called. "I'm sure you can't wait to find out who your last suitor will be."

I shoved through the door and slammed it behind me.

Latia jumped when I barged in and bolted the door. She quickly rolled up the small parchment she'd been scribbling on and shoved it into a pocket of her dress. "I wasn't expecting you back so soon," she said. "That might have been your fastest match yet." Her hands smoothed over the fabric of her pocket.

I rolled my eyes. I'd caught her at this before. And when I'd demanded the small scrap of paper from her, I'd found a map of the rooms around mine. She'd sheepishly admitted she couldn't write and had found this to be the best way to leave notes for the soldier she had her eye on, informing him where they should meet. She always lowered her face when she spoke about it, but I could still catch the blush creeping up her cheeks and the tiny smile she tried to hide. I suppose they were the typical signs of being in love. Not that I'd know.

She'd once asked if I thought her weak for falling in love. I'd scoffed and waved her off. Her options were different from mine. If the arena didn't decide my husband, I didn't know how I would. How could I ever believe anyone was ready to rule Achra with me? My people would depend on me—just as my mother had always hoped—and I wasn't sure I could trust someone else to fight on their behalf.

No, with Latia I was more worried she hadn't told me which soldier it was, which made me think it was one I constantly complained about being unskilled or incapable of following directions.

She could do worse. At least soldiers had stable positions. And extra water rations.

When it was clear I wasn't going to question her, she relaxed. Her eyes went to my leg. "You're bleeding."

I let her rush over and undo the rest of the sandal straps and slide them off my legs. I collapsed into a chair and let her inspect the gash.

"It's not deep," Latia said, her fingers prodding my leg. "Why don't you take a bath while I look for something to put on it?"

I nodded and started removing my gear while she added a few more buckets of heated water to the bath before disappearing through the door. I slid into the water and winced as my cut touched the surface, but it was balanced by the instant relaxation of my muscles.

Latia returned with a jar of salve and dressed the wound when I emerged, wrapping it in layers of soft muslin. Then she spent several minutes rubbing thick lotion into my skin, kneading her hands across my arms and legs until the scent of coconut clouded around me. She never wiped the excess off her hands, instead discretely smearing it across her own face.

Once she finished, she wove colored ribbons—a different hue for each opponent I'd beaten—into my hair and helped me step into the white gown. It was my father's favorite color because it got dirty so easily, which is why most people in the kingdom didn't wear it. But after being dressed in my thick armor, it felt like I wasn't wearing anything at all.

At least it was better than wearing the wedding dress, and now I only had one more suitor to go. But first, I had to face my father and his disappointment.

I tried not to think about that as I exited the arena.

Six guards fell in around me as we walked toward the gate that led back to the palace. No air moved in the tunnel. The fabric of my dress clung to me as I began to sweat waiting for the gate to be thrown open. I wished I had my sword strapped to my waist or a dagger laced to my leg. Going through the crowd was always worse than facing the arena. Sweaty hands clawed at me, begging for money and water. Dirt smeared across my body.

Fingernails dug into my skin. Calloused hands tore out strands of hair and ribbons without discrimination. Others shouted insults and threats, as if it was my fault they didn't have anything to drink.

And I wasn't allowed to fight them.

They didn't blame the real culprits—the drought, the increasing sandstorms, and the Desert Boys. No one knew how many boys existed or where they hid between raids, but they were the ones dooming my people to a life spent with sand clogging their throats and not enough water to quench their thirst. I'd heard it whispered in the palace that they could drain a well in a single visit.

That's why the south well had been closed off for the past month and water rations dropped to two buckets a day. Yet, they still blamed me. Or, more accurately, they took out their frustration on me. But once I beat my final suitor, I wouldn't have to spend my days training under Rodric's watchful eyes. No, I would spend them scouring the desert for the Desert Boys' hideout. I would find them and finally set my people free from the terror and thirst they caused.

Then they'd stop treating me like they always did when I left the arena.

One of the guards pressed in closer. "Some fight today," he said.

I turned toward him. A pointed nose and graying hairs stuck out from under his helmet. Lost in my thoughts, I hadn't noticed Sievers was on duty. He'd been one of my training partners when I was still learning how to fight. He was more careful with his blade than most and had pressed me to try harder without threatening to injure me if I misstepped or swung too early.

"Thanks," I said.

"I was able to watch a few minutes," Sievers replied. "My children always want to know how our princess fairs in the trials." He had two young daughters, whom I'd caught a glimpse of once when they came to collect their father. They'd clung to his legs and pulled at his cloak to make him hurry faster.

If I pulled at my father like that, he'd say I was acting like a dog.

"Not as well as I should have this time," I said.

He casually leaned his spear against his shoulder and considered me. "Use some thicksteen oil on the leg," he advised.

I offered him a small smile. "Sorry you were placed on guard duty," I said with a nod to the crowd.

"They're rowdier than normal today," he said, shifting the metal armor plates on his shoulders. "It makes me nervous. I haven't seen them this agitated since the start of the great drought, when your father had to knock the water rations down to half a bucket a day."

I nodded but didn't get a chance to say anything more because the gates were thrown open, and we descended into the madness of the crowd.

CHAPTER 3

Bodies crushed against the guards, forcing my protectors to squash against me. Hands spread their fingers wide before raking toward my head. I'd dodge one direction and then be pulled back the other. My head arched back. Strands ripped from my scalp. Somewhere a child chanted he'd gotten a ribbon.

Another child grabbed the fabric of my dress. "Water," he begged, his voice hoarse. He wore no shoes or shirt, and I could see the outlines of his ribs running down his chest.

The guard ahead of me rammed the wooden end of his spear into the child, sending him spiraling backward into the throng of the crowd. "Move back," I yelled, hoping to keep the child from being trampled.

I turned my head to follow the path the boy's body took into the enveloping crowd. That's when something round and hard smashed against my temple. I staggered into Sievers.

He caught me before the crowd swallowed me. "You're bleeding," he said.

Jolts of pain shot through my head. My vision blurred. I saw four guards in front of me instead of two. I couldn't concentrate on moving my feet forward while the ache in my head spread.

I became aware that Sievers's arm was around my shoulder, pressing my head into the crook of his arm, protecting me from the rocks still being thrown while also guiding me through the gauntlet. "Get her to the East Well," he shouted to the other soldiers. "There will be more guards there."

He pushed me forward. Rocks glanced off his armor with more force and frequency. Their constant clink was what I imagined falling rain would sound like.

As we pressed on, my vision cleared and the tops of buildings appeared around us. The crowd thinned on the narrow streets. We burst into the East Square, where a line snaked away from the well. Six guards stood around it, monitoring how many buckets each family took by collecting their ration coins in turn.

The guards responded as they saw our approach, clearing a path. As soon as we got to the well, Sievers rested me on the ground nearby while the other guards held the crowd back.

He inspected the wound on the side of my head. "It's not as bad as I thought," he said. "Head wounds always bleed more than anything else." He lowered the bucket into the well and hoisted up fresh water. He gave me an apologetic smile before tearing a strip from my dress to use as a washcloth, then bathed the wound.

He wrung the cloth into the bucket and stared at the bloody water for a few moments before throwing it out.

"Just because you get extra buckets for being a soldier doesn't mean the rest of us do," someone called from the crowd. "Stop wasting our water and get back to your palace."

Sievers lowered the bucket back into the well, shaking his head. He and I both would've saved the water if we could've in this drought, but it'd been too bloody to salvage.

A shadow fell across me.

"These people would have killed to have the water you just threw out," a voice said.

I squinted against the intense sunrays to make out the figure as I scrambled to my feet.

A man about my age stood on the ledge of the well, leaning against the wooden frame. He wore thin pants and a woven shirt that had seen better days. He lifted his head, shaking long, unkempt strands away from his face. "But water doesn't mean the same thing to someone who's never gone without it."

Sievers pointed his spear at the man. "Back away from Princess Kateri."

The man scoffed, and a sly smile spread across his face. His eyes examined my dirty face and torn garment. "You'd think they'd take better care of the famed Achran Flower. Maybe they've been overwatering you."

I studied him as well. The untamed hair. The confidence to approach the well. A Desert Boy. He had to be.

"If anyone's overwatered here, it's all you Desert Boys. But I'll be putting an end to that." My hand went for the sword hilt that wasn't there.

He yanked the bucket up from the well and poured water into a container held by a small boy I hadn't noticed. "I'm not just any Desert Boy," he said. "I'm their leader. But you can call me Cion."

I didn't breathe. I didn't think. I reacted. I grabbed the sword from Sievers belt and leapt forward. My vision swirled, and the well hazed in and out of focus.

"The cactus's spines come out," Cion said. He drew his own sword. It was a blade unlike any I'd ever seen. Instead of one shaft of straight metal, this one had two that forked away from the hilt like a snake's tongue.

Maybe that's what had started those annoying rumors.

"Keep pulling water," he shouted over his shoulder to the

boy. Then he leapt up, somersaulting through the air above my head and landing in front of me. He again flicked his long hair out of his eyes with annoying confidence.

Sievers and another guard tried to leap between us, but I shoved them away. There was no way I was giving up a chance to face Cion in the flesh. I grinned. Bringing in Cion was exactly what I needed to make amends with my father.

"I didn't think you existed," I said, jabbing my sword toward his throat.

He easily sidestepped the blow. "That's why I decided to put in an appearance, keep you on your toes. Maybe if I'd done that sooner, you wouldn't have been so slow in the arena today."

I cried out as I lunged for him. He ducked out of the way, giving me a clear view of haggard boys taking up arms against the soldiers while another line of smaller boys pulled bucket after bucket from the well and passed it down the line and out of sight. Without the added weight of armor, the Desert Boys easily outpaced their opponents.

One boy without shoes was knocked to the ground, but before the guard he was fighting could deliver his next blow, another boy slid through the guard's legs and blocked it, giving his friend time to get back on his feet. Behind them, boys were climbing onto the buildings and vaulting off—landing behind two soldiers to retrieve lost weapons and gain the advantage.

Another boy cried out as a blade cut into his arm, and I thought maybe it was a sign we could turn the tide back in our favor. But more boys materialized out of the crowd, some to carry away the injured boy and others to take up the fight where he'd left off. They had the timing and precision of thieves in the way they'd slide in and out.

I pulled my gaze back to Cion. We circled each other. "You're a plague," I spat, "stealing water from these people." I aimed my sword at his midsection. He deflected the blow, refusing to make any attack of his own.

"I doubt you know anything about the plague," he said. He hopped onto the edge of the stone well to avoid my blow aimed at his knees. "You were locked away in the palace while it destroyed everyone out here. Maybe"—he flicked his sword so quickly toward me it was a blur in the sunlight—"you should have used that time to practice harder." His sword connected with mine, ripping it away from my hand.

It spiraled toward Sievers, who was fighting off a Desert Boy with curly hair.

Instinctively, I took a step back to avoid the sword now pointed at my chest, but I refused to drop my gaze. I stared dead into the dark eyes of the legendary leader of the Desert Boys.

He smirked. "Too bad I can't fight in the arena," he said, lowering his sword and smugly crossing his arms across his chest. "Otherwise, you'd be engaged to me now, and I'd give Achra a leader who actually cares about its people." He still stood on the edge of the well, leaning against its support beam.

I lunged for him. He expected the move, leaping off the well as I sped toward where his knees had been. I'd been hoping to knock him into the water, where he'd be trapped. But the instant his feet left the stone wall, I realized my mistake.

I ricocheted off the far side of the well, unable to get a hand on the edge. Cool air rushed around me until I splashed into the water below. When I surfaced, I punched my fists into the water and screamed.

My dress clung to my legs, making it hard to kick, but I'd

spent time in the oasis waters learning to swim because my father had wanted me to be a master of all aspects of the desert. And if I stretched out my arms to either side, I could touch the walls and keep myself afloat. Moss squished between my fingers, and droplet ants crawled over my hand, their transparent abdomens heavy with water to take back to their colony.

A head popped into the circle of light at the top of the well, and a rope twirled down. "Try not to contaminate all the water with your royal stench while you're down there," Cion called. "People still need that to drink."

"If you're so concerned about what they drink," I screamed, my voice echoing hollowly up the walls, "then stop stealing it all for yourself!"

I grabbed the rope and began to climb. The rough threads of the rope dug into my skin. My skirt tangled around my legs, and I gave up using my feet and pulled myself up purely with my arms.

By the time I'd ascended high enough to grip the edge of the well, my palms were bleeding, and the Desert Boys were gone. The only signs they'd been there were a few overturned carts and the groaning guards scattered across the square.

Sievers rushed over as soon as he saw me clinging to the edge of the well. He hoisted me over the edge, and I landed in a heap. Sand clung to my wet skin, chafing against me, but it was nothing compared to the intense heat filling my stomach and surging through my body. No one should have been able to wrestle my sword from me.

Flashbacks to the day Rodric wounded me raced through my mind. I could already feel the hatred rising in my body.

"Are you all right?" Sievers asked. He had a cut running down his cheek.

I ignored him, searching for some hint of where the Desert Boys had gone. Slowly, people were repopulating the square. I shook Sievers away and raced toward a woman with a basket hoisted on her shoulders. "Did you see where they went?"

She shook her head, refusing to look at me.

I asked the woman next to her, and the man next to her. They all refused to answer, instead looking down into the sand.

"Didn't anyone see where they went?" I raged, returning to the center of the square. "Are you all so afraid of them that you'd rather have your daily water rations taken down to nothing?" I spun in circles searching for answers. I exhaled thick bursts of hot air through my flared nostrils. I must have looked like some sort of desert monster. A mixture of blood and sand covered my sopping dress. My hair hung in limp tendrils. I ran my fingers through it. The sun had dried it slightly, but clumps of sand had taken up residence.

I shook my head.

Sievers put his hand on my shoulder. "You'll find no answers here," he said.

I let him lead me back to the palace, but I stared down every person we passed, daring them to challenge me or say anything about my appearance, to give me an excuse to release the anger throbbing in my heart.

In fact, I was so focused on looking for someone to fight that I nearly clobbered Latia when she ran into me.

"Latia?"

She cast her eyes around the scene, obviously disturbed by what she saw. The note she'd been drawing earlier trembled in her hands, and her face was pale when she met my gaze. "I heard the soldiers call out that you'd been injured by the crowd. I came to help." She lifted her hand up toward my scalp.

“I’m fine.” I shook her away and kept walking, fuming all the way back to the palace.

Though when the shadow of the palace fell over my body, a chill crawled across my skin. My heart was no longer throbbing with anger but with emptiness and regret.

And fear.

The only thing worse than letting the Desert Boys get away was having to face my father afterward.

CHAPTER 4

The palace courtyards were as different from the city as a desert night was from a desert day. A sea of green replaced the sandy stretch that led up to the gates. A row of cacti grew along the base of both sides of the palace walls. Chunks of sanded brick littered the base of the inner side of the wall.

I was told the walls had been beautiful once—carved by hand to mimic the scrolling vines and sagging flowers of the razmin plant that once grew alongside the lagoon. They'd even used dyes to bring the flowers and vines to life. But now the wall looked like it had been drilled into by countless colonies of assassin wasps.

Past the walls, palm trees curled around the natural lagoon the city had been built around, and ornate gardens sculpted out of shrubs with roots long enough to reach the water dotted the area leading to the doors.

Tiled terraces surrounded the lagoon, bright red-and-blue patterns zigzagging across the floor. Each tile had been handcrafted by the best artisans in Achra. But now so many of the tiles lay broken or were missing entirely. Even the snakes carved in loops around the columns across the back of the palace had pieces missing and holes worn through where sandstorms had hit them. The few artisans who'd survived the worst of the drought either didn't have enough water to craft more or didn't have enough skill to replicate what the master crafters had done.

Though the drought had started before I was born, I'd always been told stories of how the artisans were the hardest hit at first. They had no extra water to make their tiles and dyes and earthenware. And many of their skills had died with them, leaving Achra to decay as it continued its fight to not succumb to this new, harsher desert we weren't used to.

Ever resourceful, though, the Achrans had adapted by crafting new tiles by grinding up assassin wasps in place of water. But this made the tiles lumpier and more prone to breaking. Not to mention they didn't take color as well. And I wondered if the old ways would be lost for good before I could rid the city of the Desert Boys and find a way to get more water.

But I couldn't dwell on the past. I had to look toward the future first. Toward my final opponent. Right after my father learned what happened at the well.

Leaving my guards at the door, I slipped in through the kitchens. Warm fires greeted me. It was too much heat for the afternoon, but it would be welcome when the sun set in a few hours. Raucous laughter filtered out from the doors to the main hall.

I snuck up a back staircase and into my room. Latia's small footfalls echoed my own.

I needed a moment before I faced the wrath of my father in front of everyone. I flopped down on the bed, sighing.

New gauzy spider silk curtains that hadn't yet been weighed down by sand fluttered inward from my balcony, touching the ends of my gold-encrusted bed. Even my sheets were sewn with gold silk thread imported from the eastern kingdoms.

The numerous caravans that once passed through Achra, bringing rich goods like these, had all but stopped when the drought and sandstorms came. Only my father's royal caravans were given enough water to cross the desert to bring in new supplies. And even then, some of them never made it back because of the sandstorms that had increased each year since the drought started.

A knock at the door roused me. I sat up as Latia shuffled over and opened it.

"The king has requested a private audience with the princess. He's waiting at the tiger cages."

I didn't hear the rest of what was said.

I froze. Alone? Not in front of the great hall?

I swallowed. Between the incident in the arena and what happened at the well, I didn't know what he had in store.

My arms moved numbly as I pulled off my dress and slid into the new one, hurrying so as to not keep my father waiting.

Latia silently moved forward and yanked any tangles in my hair as she worked quickly to twist my hair into a tight bun.

"Do you want me to go with you?" she asked, eyes downcast.

"No," I snapped, too dazed to give her credit for her loyalty. It would only be worse with her there.

I made my way through the palace and down into the windowless depths beneath the sands. The tombs, as I'd called them as a child. But it was the only place cool enough in the palace to house the beasts.

I was secretly glad they were kept so far from everything else. I could still recall the events of the annual Tiger Feast a few months before, commemorating the arrival of the tigers. As always, my father had sat in the main hall with the tigers chained at his feet as he recounted how he'd found two tigers lost in the desert a few days after taking the throne. He said the tigers contained the spirit of the desert because their orange-and-black pattern mimicked the golden waves of sand and the darker valleys that hid between the peaks. When the beasts had bowed before him, he brought them back to the palace with the knowledge the desert had gifted these creatures to him, confirming he was not only meant to lead, but that he would be fiercer than any creature—a true king of the desert.

Just as my father finished the story, describing how he'd strengthened the tigers he'd found, servants approached to taunt the tigers with bits of meat to show the crowd their raw power—how my father had taken them from docile beasts to trained monsters. But one of the servants got too close. Claws raked across his thigh. He went down, and there was nothing anyone could do to save him before the tiger pulled him closer and sunk its teeth into the man's neck with a sickening crunch, staining its fur a shade of red that didn't exist even when the setting sun hit the sand waves.

I had swallowed down a cry as my father laughed, spreading his arms wide and crying out for everyone to witness the power he controlled.

I hadn't seen the tigers since that day. But I could still hear the scream of the servant as it gurgled to a stop.

That sound rushed through my ears as my footsteps clicked in hollow echoes, taking me closer and closer to the beasts and my waiting father. The weight of the ceiling pressed down around me. Dim hallways flickered with the weak light cast from torches situated at even intervals. But they were too far apart. Stretches of darkness waited between them. As a child, I'd always thought tigers were hiding in those shadows.

I paused at the door that led to the cage.

The last time I'd been down here was just after my mother had been killed nearly ten years ago. I closed my eyes, but I couldn't keep the memory from surfacing.

I'd trembled back then as I'd walked behind my father's large form. I wanted to reach for his hand, but I held back.

Claw marks ran down the long chamber housing the tigers. Each beast had a chain around its neck and was kept just far enough from the other that it couldn't swipe it with its claws. That didn't stop them from trying.

The moist room had reeked of feces and wet hair. I could barely stand it.

When the tigers saw my father and my small form walk in all those years ago, they threw themselves at the bars separating their chamber from the narrow walkway in front. Claws screeched down metal. Whiskers were thrown back to release hisses toward us. Sharp teeth longer than my bony fingers gleamed.

Their orange hue was muted with only the light of two torches illuminating them, but it made their eyes come alive. Deep oranges and reds burned when they stalked back and forth just behind the bars. But instead of a reflection of the flames, it appeared their pupils contained fire coming from inside—a rage that burned for anyone who dared keep them caged.

The shadows they cast seemed to grow higher and higher along the wall behind them until I thought they would slip through the bars and drag me closer to them.

I'd plastered myself against the wall. To get my mind off the tigers, to remind myself that my father did control them, I ran my finger along the small keyhole in the wall, to which my father had the only key. Not only did it open the cage, it activated a mechanism that pulled back the chains secured around the tigers' necks, allowing the handlers to go in and collect them for the arena.

My father stood right in front of the bars. A hair closer and the tigers would be able to tear a slit in his gut. He had stood there so often, he knew exactly how near he could get.

"We caught another of the Desert Boys," he had said with his back to me. But I knew he was smiling. "Pick one."

I hadn't understood what he was talking about. But then he gestured to the two tigers.

He'd always taken joy in selecting the tiger that would be present in the arena when a trial was needed, as if he alone controlled the outcome of what would happen based on his selection.

When I didn't respond, he turned toward me. "Are you afraid of them?" There was disappointment in his voice. I could tell he'd hoped this would be something we'd share. Something we would do together.

He snapped his fingers and a servant entered through a side door, carrying a platter of raw rat meat. My father picked up the biggest slice and dangled it in front of the cage. He had walked it back and forth, watching the tigers claw at every available surface to get to it. But I couldn't tell if the tigers wanted to get to the meat or him more.

Eventually he pointed to each tiger. "I want both taken to the arena today." My father handed over the key from around his neck.

I knew what was coming next, and yet I couldn't move. I couldn't flee.

The servant gently moved my shoulder aside and slid the key into the lock. The chains clunked backward, forcing the tigers to go with them. Then he handed the key back to my father.

The servant disappeared into the other room for a moment and reappeared with two men in metal armor thicker than that of any soldier. They had two long poles with ropes on the end. They entered the cage and moved toward the first tiger my father had pointed at. One man would loop his rope around the tiger's neck and pull so tightly the tiger could barely breathe. Then the other man would remove the chain and loop his own rope around the tiger's neck so that both men could work to control the beast—choking it anytime it got out of hand.

"Why two?" I'd asked to drown out the roars of the tiger as it fought to escape its restraints. I stared up at my father as a torch cast his long shadow across the room.

He crouched in front of me. "The Desert Boys killed your mother. We can't let them get away. This is the first one we've caught since her death. We must teach our enemies a lesson." He patted my head.

I'd looked away, sick to my stomach from the smell and his words.

I had wanted to escape, to get away from the stench. But there was no way I was going the way they'd just taken the tiger. There was a small door set into the back wall of the tiger's cage. I had no idea where it led, but I definitely wasn't going that way. Without waiting to see the look on my father's face, I'd fled back the way I'd come.

I took a breath as the memory faded. I steadied myself in front of the door I'd run out of all those years ago. This time I wouldn't run away. I'd have to face whatever came.

I squared my shoulders and pushed into the room.

My father was standing in the same spot he'd been when

I'd come there as a child, a finger's width from where the tigers' claws could reach.

"You dishonored me today." He didn't turn to look at me as I entered. He had his hands clasped behind his back.

"My apologies." I lowered my head even though he wouldn't see. I'd learned a long time ago that the only apology he accepted was one of complete and utter kowtowing.

"It's not only the fight you should apologize for. I've gotten word the Desert Boys attacked, threw you into a well, and escaped."

"They didn't throw me into a well," I countered, but he cut me off before I could go on.

"You didn't end up in a well?" my father asked, turning to look at me and eyeing my still-damp hair.

"I did, but—"

"No. There are no excuses." The vein in his temple throbbed as he stared me down. "How do you expect people to believe you qualified to rule when you cannot best a street urchin? He depleted a good portion of the well. We must show the people we are capable of protecting them, providing for them. If they do not look to us, they will look to someone else. Don't let them look away."

That was another favorite saying of my father's when he was training me. He wanted my skills to be so great that no one would be able to look away when I fought. But it always felt like more than that, like it was also his way of training me to be queen, of passing his knowledge down to me so I knew how to rule.

"I understand," I said, clenching my fists.

The closest tiger pulled at its chains. The other clawed the bars.

"I will do better. I will make you proud."

"Will you?" His eyes drilled into me.

I moved closer to him, closer to the tigers. "I will win the last fight and prove I am strong enough to be your heir. The desert will choose me."

"Are you so certain it will?"

I stepped back, mouth agape.

"If your rule is weak," he continued, "that will negate mine. All history will remember is your weakness."

I'd always known my strength reflected his, but I'd done everything he'd ever asked to prove I was worthy. I'd practiced every day since my mother died. I'd pricked myself with cacti spines to keep myself awake countless nights so that the Desert Boys wouldn't catch me sleeping when they attacked again. I'd trained until my feet were blistered from the sand and my scalp burned in the noonday sun.

"If you do not have the strength to lead these people, I must provide them with someone who will."

"What do you mean?" I said, my voice catching in my throat.

He shook his head. "I see now that Rodric has been right all along."

"Rodric?"

"He's said that while you are strong, you could be even more so if you were married to someone yet stronger, someone the desert hasn't crushed."

My stomach clenched together. The last person I wanted picking a suitor for me was Rodric.

"I will win the next fight for you, Father."

My father took a step away from the cage and moved toward the door. "Only if the desert wills it. Come. It's time to find out who your last suitor will be."

His words burned through me as I followed him down the hallways and toward the great hall. I had never doubted that he believed I would win. Until now.

He'd invested so much time training me when I was little. This was everything we'd worked toward. Everything we wanted. We were supposed to avenge my mother together.

I'd always had visions of us striding out into the desert together after I was done training, after I'd won my place as the next queen—both of us chosen by the desert and ready to rid it of the plague of Desert Boys. I'd secretly thought the desert hadn't allowed us to catch the Desert Boys yet because we were meant to do it together.

But as we moved down the hallway, him striding so far ahead of me, it didn't feel like we were in this together anymore. It felt like there was a gap between us—a set of bars thicker than those on the tiger cages keeping us apart.

The only way to close that gap was to win my last fight, to show my father the desert chose me. It would put everything right. It had to. I fortified myself with that thought as we reached the large white sheets that hung across the entryway to the great hall.

He strode into the room while I waited behind the curtain, the same curtain that would reveal my new opponent later that night.

The crowd quieted.

My father's voice rang out. "Our champion has arrived."

The benches lining the tables moved backward in a loud squeak as the men and women rose and lifted their drinks into the air to salute me.

The curtains parted, and I stepped into the room. The grandeur of the space always took me by surprise. Tall columns rose up to the arched ceiling, carved with the same snakes that twisted their way around the columns outside. But unlike the outer pillars, these snakes hadn't been pounded by the endless sheets of sand. Black- and gold-painted scales winked in the light. Eyes as green as any rumbler cactus stared out above a forked tongue.

Between the columns, sand dancers performed to the even beat of drums, swirling around and around, their feet weaving endless patterns in the sand they danced on. The celebration dance. I looked away. Their presence always reminded me of my mother's absence, of how there was nothing to celebrate yet.

My father's eyes held no warmth as I entered. It was a far cry from my first fight, when he'd walked down the aisle with me—showing me off to everyone when I'd won. He'd draped his arm over my shoulder and smiled widely, beaming down at me. I'd felt like I was already queen.

But now he stood stoically. I thought he'd at least smile, at least pretend to be pleased despite what happened.

I managed to throw my shoulders back and keep my head high, but his earlier words still had me on edge. He hadn't punished me outright, as I had expected; what he'd done was far worse. He'd left me to my own imagination—to wonder who my next opponent would be if he really didn't think I was the desert's choice. Every step closer to him suddenly felt like I was walking through Scorpion Hill, waiting for an attack to come.

All the extra bodies packed along the tables formed an aisle leading to the dais where my father waited. The bracelets worn by the married noblewomen clinked together as they cheered my entrance.

I walked down the aisle, stopping at every person who lined the way. All lowered their cup as I approached, and I took one sip from each. It was an old tradition that began when Tamlin made it across the desert and needed water so he could regain enough of his voice to speak with the then king. Nobles had offered him a sip of water from their glass as he made his way down the main hall toward the king's dais.

It had become a ritual used to reward champions and heroes.

Only what was in the cups now wasn't water. It was a spicy mead that burned my throat. I pressed my mouth against each rim, letting the liquid barely touch my lips before I moved on.

By the time I reached the dais, my head pounded and my leg throbbed, and they weren't even courteous enough to do so in unison. I bowed to my father and took my seat next to him.

His throne, shaped like a giant scorpion, loomed large over me as he took his seat. He rested his hands on the scorpion's claws while the creature's tail curved behind his back, leaving the stinger to rest above his head as if the desert itself was pointing to him, anointing him its king. The throne had been made for Tamlin and was just another reminder of what I'd yet to accomplish.

Servants carrying platters arrived the moment my father touched his chair. Two servants carried in a platter bearing heaps of three-headed lizards. My father scooped several onto his plate. Even though you could only eat the head with the purple tongue, my father insisted they be served whole. Although I didn't blame him. More than one unruly noble had died from being served a head with a purple tongue cleverly tacked in where the green or red tongue had once been.

Steam seeped out as my father opened each mouth, searching for the purple tongue. When he found it, he ripped it out and slurped it down. They always tasted like the razmin flowers smelled, and usually I loved eating them.

But in light of the day's events, everything turned my stomach.

Course after course was brought out. White-tongue teaser snakes, whose own purple tongues mimicked those of the three-headed lizard to lure in prey, entwined on skewers. Dead scorpions posed with their tails aloft rested on platter after platter. Lily pad lizards, still bulbous from floating in the lagoon, steamed inside razmin leaves.

I forced myself to eat a bite of snake as I waited for my father to announce my next opponent. My mother had always served me white-tongue teaser snake when I was sick as a child. She'd said it would settle my stomach. But the snake only ended up reminding me of those stupid rumors about Cion and did nothing for the knot growing in my stomach. Still, I forced myself to swallow.

Several scales that hadn't gotten scraped off before cooking clung to my father's lips and shimmered in the firelight as he chomped off the midsection of a snake. He flicked the scales off his lips, and one landed on my lap. I didn't dare move to brush it away.

Eventually, the sand dancers stopped and the traditional Achran dancers took their place. Men and women in garments the color of sand stood in a circle around one dancer—the sun dancer—dressed in a short yellow garment. A servant with a torch came forward and the sun dancer extended her hands, coated in a thick green substance. The servant lit both her hands and the tops of her feet.

As soon as the servant exited, the outer ring of dancers moved in unison around the sun dancer. They circled her with arms linked over each other's shoulders—signifying Achrans' unity in fighting the constant battle the sun waged against us. Then they started kicking sand, trying to be the one who put out the flames the sun dancer held.

Nobles around us were taking bets on either how many loops the dancers would make before putting out the fire or who would be the lucky dancer to put out the last flame and claim victory over the sun.

Only after a short dancer extinguished the last flame and the applause died down did my father rise from his chair.

The room went silent.

"Close the curtain," he called.

The white sheets swung downward and swished together, blocking the entryway. My father loved this part because the anticipation was like waiting to see what was behind a chosen door in the arena. And I used to love it too.

"My daughter has faced eleven men who would claim my crown for their own," he said. "She is ready to face her last opponent. Should this suitor be strong enough to be our next leader, he will beat her in single combat if the desert wills it."

The audience pounded their cups on the table in response.

The clanking made my head throb worse, but that was nothing compared to the pressure pushing tighter against my chest.

My father threw up his arms. The curtain parted.

The figure behind it stepped forward into the light.

It was Rodric.

CHAPTER 5

I put one hand over my mouth to stop myself from vomiting. I steadied myself against the table and looked again to be sure. Rodric stood there, staring straight at me.

My father looked at me sideways. "Much like Tamlin, Rodric was sent to us from the desert. He has mastered its ways, and you must master him if you wish to have my throne."

Breaths caught in my chest. Each of my father's words were like grains of sand stinging my skin during a sandstorm. Rodric wouldn't rule. He would annihilate. Anyone who opposed him would be thrown from the palace towers or have their tongues ripped out for criticizing him.

Yet this was the man my father thought the desert had chosen to be our leader and the man I was to marry. If I lost.

The knot growing in my stomach tightened. I would lose.

A thought struck me. "He's not nobility," I blurted, turning toward my father. Tamlin hadn't been nobility either, but the people had been so grateful for his saving them, they'd claimed he was the desert's choice to fight in the arena trials. And so he'd been allowed. All my other suitors had some ties to royal blood. Rodric had simply appeared out of the desert boasting of his skill with a sword. Just like Tamlin.

My father turned away to address the crowd, as well as me. "Rodric may not be royalty, but it is only fair we honor the desert's will and pit its champion against our own. Just as Tamlin was given the same chance."

My stomach dropped. I had promised my mother I would lead her people. I couldn't let this happen. I couldn't let Rodric waltz in here and take everything. The people had loved Tamlin. No one loved Rodric.

Except my father.

I'd known they'd been spending more time together, and my father had thought Rodric's skill so great he'd allowed him to take over training me these last few months. I didn't think it had gone this far. I didn't think Rodric had twisted his mind so much that my father actually thought Rodric was the next Tamlin.

But I could see it now. The gleam in my father's eyes when he turned to look at Rodric. And I wondered if he thought he was seeing a new way to keep his legacy intact, one that would link his name with the greatest king we'd ever had. Or maybe he was seeing the brother I always should have had.

A thought tore through me. My father didn't care who won. If I did, I'd prove his strength. If I didn't, picking Rodric despite his lack of nobility would be seen as his way of backing the desert's choice, of ensuring the strength of the throne.

No one else would speak up about the lack of nobility. Not against Rodric. The soldiers who crossed him had an odd way of disappearing. Sometimes their bodies were found in the desert by the caravans coming into the city. Sometimes they were discovered in their beds covered with scorpion bites. Sometimes they were never found at all.

Rodric saw anyone who questioned him as questioning the will of the desert itself since he was a product of the desert—no, a master of it. He saw ruling with an iron fist as the only way to rule. I hadn't really cared before, but now I might find myself under that fist.

I'd spent years training, years trying to live up to my father's legacy, to gain the strength to take the throne and protect my people like my mother had always wanted me to do. And now I would be stopped at the bitter end by Rodric?

He sauntered forward and bowed before my father. When he righted himself, his eyes were on me. "I've trained you well," he said. "Now it's time to find out how well."

I balled my hands into fists. I wanted to wipe the smile from his face, to wipe away every memory of him, because he'd done this. While I'd been so busy training, he'd been poisoning my own father against me. And I'd played right into his script by getting injured today.

"I'll arrange for another trainer to come in," my father said, as if that were the reason I was fuming.

I didn't need another trainer. I needed a miracle.

Rodric smirked. "In a month, this will be our wedding feast," he said, throwing his arms wide.

It irked me that he was so confident. I should have known he was simply trying to get into my head, to wreck my confidence, but he didn't need to. His presence was enough to send every thought of victory fleeing from my body.

"I'm tired after my fight," I said, pushing away from the table. "I'm going to my room." I needed to get away from all the prying eyes. I needed time to think, to figure out how to get my father back on my side.

Rodric bowed as I exited the hall, but I felt his eyes following me the entire way. By the time I left the main hall, I was shaking.

Even though sunset was an hour or two away, Latia already

had a thick nightgown pulled out when I arrived in my room. "I can't believe you're going to face Rodric," she exclaimed. "He'll make an excellent leader. He's as strong as your father, I imagine. No one will dare cross him. Not since the desert sent him to us." She hugged the nightgown to her chest. "That's if he wins, of course," Latia added when she saw my face.

"Get out," I seethed, sending her fleeing from the room with the nightgown still clutched to her chest.

I paced the length of the room. I threw open my wardrobe and tore all the gowns out one by one. The shimmering fabrics caressed my skin as I flung them away. They felt like ghosts against my skin, the same kind of ghost I would become if I married Rodric. He would take the throne, and I'd be left with nothing. I wouldn't even be able to go after the Desert Boys. No, he'd want that glory for himself.

This had probably been his plan all along. Train me well enough to fight everyone else—everyone but him—while he maneuvered his way into my father's good graces. My hands instinctively went to the scars concealed beneath the cuff on my neck.

How could I possibly win my father back after this? My only option was to be the champion in the arena. But that seemed impossible.

I stared down at the pile of wilted gowns. I kicked one away and strode out to the balcony.

I leaned over the railing, hoping to catch the first breeze of night and ease the heat coursing through me, but there was no relief from the sun's gaze. Not even guards patrolled the walls, keeping instead to the shade by the gate.

Below me, voices floated up. At first, I paid them no mind,

too absorbed in my own problems to care about anyone else's. But then my name was mentioned.

"Kateri fights better than most of the soldiers, though she won't beat me," Rodric said. "I only hope she doesn't cause a scene."

"She will come around to marrying you," another voice replied. Probably one of his soldiers. "She will abide by the rules of the arena."

"I still plan on keeping extra guards on her until our fight." Rodric's comment froze me in place. "I want everyone to see her cower before me, to recognize that the desert is choosing me. But she already knows she can't beat me, which is why I question if she'll even try to flee."

Their voices grew louder, their footsteps shuffling across the balcony directly below mine.

"If she did," the second voice said, "there's nowhere she could run. Even if she were lucky enough not to get hit by a sandstorm, only the caravans know the safe way through the desert, and all the drivers are loyal to you. She couldn't carry enough water on her own to make the journey."

"She wouldn't survive a day in that desert, let alone a sandstorm." Rodric laughed. "She'll bend under my rule like everyone else. And after I'm king, if she gets in the way of my plans, she'll meet the same fate as the queen."

My stomach plummeted downward. I gripped onto the balcony railing to prevent myself from plummeting too.

"Or I should gift her to Cion," Rodric continued. "The only thing she'd hate more than me killing her would be to die at a Desert Boy's hand."

I couldn't hear what else they said. The pounding of my heart drowned out the world. I slid down against the railing and clung to it, afraid the balcony might drop from beneath me as the rest of the world had done.

Several fire-legged flies buzzed around my head. I didn't even bother shooing them away.

I pulled my knees close to my chest and ran my fingers through my hair. I forced myself to breathe, to think.

I needed a plan. That's always how I prepared for a fight. It started with studying my opponent and finding his weaknesses. But Rodric was an excellent swordsman. He acted in anger more often than not, but that wasn't a true weakness since he had brute strength to back up his actions. Not to mention the guards. None of them would train me. They'd see it as a betrayal of Rodric.

There was no way I'd ask my father to train me again. Not now. And there wouldn't be time to bring another trainer in on the caravans.

That left me back where I started, with no plan and no allies. This wasn't how I'd pictured going into my last fight.

But it wouldn't be a fight. It would be a massacre, and whatever Rodric did to me in the arena would be a dream compared to what he'd do after we married. The thought made the scars on my neck prickle.

What could I do?

Escape. The word whispered through my thoughts.

I turned to look out over the rolling desert.

Could I? But where could I go? I'd be found in the town, I couldn't take one of the caravans, and I'd die in the desert on my own with all the sandstorms and no water.

Or would I?

I pulled myself up the railing, not taking my eyes from the shifting sands that zigzagged all the way to the horizon.

Hadn't Tamlin run across it without water and lived to tell the tale? Hadn't he avoided all its traps? Hadn't I always thought that I was Tamlin in a way?

I'd always put honor and strength above everything. Would I prove I wasn't my father's daughter if I ran away? Wasn't I failing him and demonstrating I wasn't strong enough to rule?

Or had I already shown I wasn't the desert's choice? Isn't that why he'd thrown his lot in with Rodric?

He didn't think I was worthy. He didn't think I could win.

I'm not sure which hurt worse.

A part of me screamed I should stay and fight Rodric. There was still a chance I could prove my father wrong, that I could show him I was worthy, that I could protect and lead these people like my mother wanted—like I thought my father had wanted. But the other part of me shouted to get away. By staying to fight, I was giving Rodric the easy option while sentencing myself to death. I couldn't deny him the throne, but I could make sure he didn't get me in the process. Then, I wouldn't have to stay and watch as he slowly drained the life out of these people while I was helpless to stop it.

The town spread out below me. Beyond it, the desert waited. I turned away and tossed aside my curtains.

I moved toward my bed and slid my hands between the frame and the mattress, pulling out book after faded book.

My mother had been the only royal to use the library when I was younger. She used to take me there and read me stories of far-off places. I think she enjoyed it more than I did. Probably because she counted her learning to read once she was queen as one of the greatest accomplishments of her life.

My father thought books took too much time away from

training. That's why he destroyed the library a few years after my mother's death. But not before I'd smuggled out the books I knew would be useful to tracking down her killers. The ones that described lizards in detail or charted the stars in the sky for navigation. I even had one written by Tamlin himself.

I'd spent endless nights poring over the books looking for details that hinted at a location where the Desert Boys could hide or that talked about creatures I'd need to avoid. Most volumes were too vague or only mentioned the creatures you could find within the city walls.

The only one who'd written anything useful was Tamlin.

In the one book he had written, Tamlin had drawn a map through the desert. The only problem was that the few men brave enough to use it never made it out of the desert alive, and the one caravan my father had sent that way had also been lost.

I flipped through the pages until I landed on the crudely drawn map. A line snaked across the page toward the city of Hartirm on the other side. I traced the route with my finger. There were no other landmarks on the map, no explanations for why the line dipped here or turned there, nothing of note at all but that line weaving its way across the page.

It was better than nothing. I took a deep breath and ripped it out.

Next, I raided the only clothing I'd left untouched in my wardrobe—my gladiator gear. I pulled out a fresh tunic and new sandals, then slid the leather overlay over my head, settling the pleats into place over the tunic. I took out a black cloak and wrapped it around my shoulders. I tied an empty water skin to my belt and belted my sword around my waist before sliding two daggers into the high straps of the new sandals.

Hopefully the weapons would serve me better in the desert than they would have against Rodric.

I tucked the map into my belt.

I returned to the balcony and surveyed my kingdom for the last time. I would miss sitting there watching the sands perform their golden dance, a reminder of the sand dancing lessons my mother had given me as a child, and what I believed was her way of letting me know she was still watching over me, reminding me I was the desert's choice and worthy to be queen.

I shoved the thought away that the desert had instead sent Rodric to us. That I had never been strong enough to beat him because I was never meant to take the throne.

Instead I focused on the fact I'd already beaten eleven suitors. I was strong enough to rule. I'd practiced every day since my mother died to be powerful enough, to be what she hoped.

I still remembered the last conversation I had with her. She'd been in the early stages of labor. At the time, she'd been certain she was going to have another girl. My mother sent her servants away and hoisted me onto the small portion of her lap not covered by her swollen belly. Sweat dotted her body.

"Kateri," she said, stroking my hair, "soon you will have a sister. And if that's the case, you'll have solidified your place as our next queen."

The curtains across the room had hazed in and out with a breeze that didn't reach us. The stagnant air festered with the smell of slimy salves the servants had left behind.

"Someday this will be yours." She'd taken her crown from the table next to her bed and placed it on my head. It slid down my forehead, covering one of my eyes. She smiled and pushed it back up, balancing it on my brow. "It might seem heavy now, but it will only be heavier then. Always remember what it means to wear this."

I straightened the crown on my head. "Do I look like you?"

"Of course you do. You look like both your father and me." She pulled me closer, stroking my hair. "You also have the strength of your father and my heart. Your father will expect you to become hard. He'll want you to channel his strength, especially when you fight in the arena for the crown."

I nodded. Even then, I understood what would be expected of me if my mother had another girl.

"I don't want . . ." She trailed off as her face scrunched inward, and she clasped her belly. She inhaled sharply, but after a few moments released her breath. Her face relaxed. She took a moment to focus her breathing before she continued. "I don't want you to forget that sometimes being the strongest isn't about having the most physical strength. Control isn't strength. True strength is about being kind. It's forgiving wrongs with words and not with swords. It's about caring for our people, standing for those who cannot. You are their voice. Never forget that."

I nodded again.

She cupped my chin. Her green eyes were weary, and yet there was still a fierceness to them that wouldn't let me look away.

"You will be a great leader." Another spasm of pain racked through her body. "Promise me you'll look after our people."

"I promise," I replied.

A small amount of tension left her face. "Now go." She helped me slide off her lap and removed the crown from my head. My father didn't like me wearing it—he said I hadn't earned it yet.

"I love you more than all the sands in the desert," she said, using the phrase she always did when she tucked me in at night.

I blew her a kiss, spinning my hand around as though the kiss were caught in a sandstorm so it would get to her faster.

I had padded barefoot out of the room, only looking back once at the door. I knew the pain still raced through her, but she smiled through it. With her strength combined with my father's inside me, I'd thought I'd be unstoppable.

Yet here I was, ready to run away, ready to forsake my promise to my mother after fighting so many years against the Desert Boys to keep our people safe. Would she really rather I stay and fight only to later die at Rodric's hands? If I had any hope of winning against Rodric, I'd stay. But I didn't.

I leaned against the balcony railing. Across from me, a cactus flyer hopped across the palace wall. The bird had broken off the spine of a cactus and was using it to poke into holes looking for grieving spiders, tarantula termites, or any other creature that had taken refuge from the day's heat in the holes. Again and again it hopped forward, stabbing its spike—one more reminder of what Rodric would do to me if I stayed.

I looked away toward the desert sands stretching far past the city. If I waited long enough, would my mother send a gust of sand scattering across the hills, beckoning me, letting me know it was okay to go?

The desert was still and stifling.

I shook my head. She'd want me to stay and protect the people as long as I could. To find a way to restore the kingdom using the strength she'd given me.

Isn't that what she'd done? She tried to do what little good she could for the people instead of running away when my father picked her as his bride.

I raised my head from the railing and watched the wind

blow small trickles across the tops of the dunes in all directions, as though they too were confused about where they belonged.

I knew then I would fight. I would train as hard as I could on my own. I would honor the promise to my mother.

But as I stared out at the sands, a realization struck. I couldn't beat Rodric, but I knew someone who could. Someone who could train me. Someone who was rumored to be the best swordsman in the desert.

I shook my head. The heat must have gone to my mind. I couldn't ask a Desert Boy to help me.

I wouldn't.

They'd murdered my mother and the baby boy my mother had barely had time to deliver. Asking them for help would be too close to forgiveness, and they would never get that from me.

I turned my back on the desert, leaning against the railing. What if I went there to kill Cion? My father and Rodric would have to see I was a force to be reckoned with. My father would realize I was capable of ruling. I'd become the source of my own legends, the one who took down a legend. My father would see me as the desert's choice. He'd have to.

The only flaw in my plan was that I couldn't beat Cion any more than I could Rodric. The scene at the well had proved that. I sighed.

It all came down to what I hated more, the Desert Boys or the idea of marrying Rodric. They both seemed bent on destroying the people and letting them die of thirst. At least with the Desert Boys, I wouldn't have to marry one of them, and there was still a chance I could help the people. And after I beat Rodric, I could figure out what to do with the Desert Boys.

I groaned. I couldn't believe I was actually considering this.

Not only did this go against everything I'd ever held dear, but it was practically suicidal. Cion would no sooner let me face him with a sword than he'd make his bed on top of a yellow-spotted sand snake's hole. Rodric's own words bounced back at me. The only thing worse than him killing me would be if the Desert Boys did it.

But what choice did I have? If I was going to stay, I needed help. No one here would train me. Cion was my only shot at keeping my promise to my mother, and my love for her outweighed my hate for him. I'd take the lead from her. I would forgive with words and not swords. I could never forgive the Desert Boys for her death, but I could at least approach them without hostility. I could bargain with them somehow. Give them access to one of the wells in exchange for Cion training me.

If I was going to leave, it had to be before Rodric stationed more guards around me. It had to be now. I couldn't risk going through the palace. People would question why I'd put on my gladiator gear.

Before I could rethink what I planned to do, I moved to the side of the balcony and scanned for handholds. The palace was built out of clay bricks baked in the desert heat. Like everything else in the city, sand had found its way into the small cracks and crevices. Bits had begun to crumble enough for small holes to appear down the wall. I climbed over the railing and anchored my foot on the first ridge I found.

Then I waited. My path would take me down to the balcony Rodric had been talking on earlier, but it was the fastest route. From there, I could hop from one balcony to another until I reached the corner of the palace where there was the most decay.

When no sound echoed upward, I slid down the wall and

landed on the balcony. For once I was thankful for the layer of sand that covered everything. It muffled my landing.

I crouched low against the wall away from the railing in case any guards looked upward.

It wasn't that I couldn't leave through the palace gate. It's just that I had no reason to. At least no reason that wouldn't tip off Rodric when he was given the nightly report of any notables who'd gone in or out. I didn't plan on being on that list. I'd climb over the wall, using the decayed pattern as my handholds if I had to.

I listened at the open archway that led inward from the balcony. I didn't hear anyone inside, so I dashed past the opening, hopped onto the railing, and vaulted to the next balcony. I somersaulted across it as I came down. I shook sand out of my hair and kept going. My leg stung, but I ignored it.

I crouched low on the wall lining the balcony and looked down. I was only two balconies away from the corner of the palace, but if I missed my landing the overall drop was high enough that it would kill me. Steeling myself, I jumped to the next balcony, sending up a spray of sand where I landed. I rose to my feet, and then froze.

A voice echoed behind me. "Kateri? What are you doing over there?" Rodric said.

I didn't hesitate, and I didn't look back. I leapt to the next balcony and frantically scanned for cracks in the clay blocks.

Rodric's weight thudded onto the balcony separating us. "I knew you'd run away scared."

I scrambled to find a hole in the wall big enough for my hands. Finding the biggest crack I could, I shoved my hands into it and slipped over the edge of the railing. My fingers burned from clasping bricks that had absorbed sunlight all day long, and I forced myself to hang on as my feet kicked against the wall.

I finally found a small indent my toes could slide into. I steadied myself and examined the wall for the next handhold. I'd just transitioned my hands lower when a fist sank into the wall where my head had been.

Chunks of clay spilled down. Through the mess, I could make out Rodric grabbing for me. His hand found my bun, and he ripped upward as I pulled downward. I nearly lost my grip, but I managed to jerk free, my hair spilling loose around me.

I quickly dropped down, forcing my hands to find places to grasp. I was so lost in the movement of finding a secure hold and transferring my weight to it that I didn't realize Rodric had disappeared from view.

It wasn't until I touched the ground and dashed toward the wall that I realized where he'd gone. He sped down the steps of the palace facing me, a stream of guards at his heels.

I backpedaled, heading straight for the palace gate.

Over my shoulder, I heard Rodric shout for the gate to be closed. I didn't bother wasting any breath to contradict his orders. These men answered to him.

Thankfully, the guards seemed confused by all the sudden commotion. They scrambled to close the gate as I approached.

It sank lower and lower.

Rodric's footfalls sounded loudly in my ears. He always was faster than me. I forced my legs to pump harder. It suddenly felt like the air was full of sand.

The gate was two feet from the ground when I dove forward and rolled under. Rodric crashed into it behind me.

"Up," he shouted. "Raise it up." He pulled on it, rattling it, but even his brute strength couldn't rip it from its moorings.

I heaved and scrambled to my feet. That gate wouldn't hold him back for long.

"I'll find you!" he shouted, spraying spit through the bars. "This kingdom will be mine."

I fled toward the desert.

CHAPTER

6

My empty water skin flopped against my legs as a reminder I wouldn't survive the dangers of the desert long if I didn't have any water. I had no idea how much time it would take to find the Desert Boys.

I veered off toward the western marketplace, hoping to go unnoticed in the evening crowd as I stopped at the well. I ignored the fact I didn't have a ration coin. I'd figure something out.

I pulled the hood up on my cloak and slunk onward. I twisted through streets lined with squat houses. Beneath a layer of sand, a few patterned tiles still clung to some of the houses. The small channels that ran in front of each house and down the sides of every street, which used to carry fresh water from the lagoon throughout the city, were clogged with sand. The clay bricks that had walled them in were visible as little more than rocks in the sand.

It was still early enough that many of the houses had their wooden window covers propped open by sticks to let in what little breeze there was.

Mothers shouted at their children to knead the dough for that evening's bread and husbands yelled for their wives. In one house, a woman not much older than me alternated between staring out the window and at the small gold bracelet dangling off her left wrist.

She must be newly engaged. Peasants typically only wore

the engagement bracelet and wedding bracelet. These days, they didn't have the money to spend every year on a new one to add to their collection. Metal was better used repairing holes in walls or leaks in buckets.

That's probably why Latia was always staring at my mother's bangles in my dressing room and why she and her soldier hadn't gotten engaged yet. If golden bracelets weren't passed down through the generations, getting one was very expensive.

I kept my head low, realizing too late I hadn't taken off the metal cuff around my neck. I pulled my cloak tighter to conceal it. I stepped over the bits of brick that had eroded from the houses and followed the crowd forward.

The well was located in the open square at the heart of the market. A maze of streets and vendors lined the way. The heavy scent of ground cactus root made my mouth water as men and women cooked in large dishes on the edges of the market.

A few camels were tied off in clumps at various locations around the street. One vendor had water beetles crawling over one another as they fought to the top of the pile. Their little blue wings clicked against each other as they became more agitated. Of course, the vendor hawked their agitation as a desire to head straight for water. I didn't believe his lies for a second. If water beetles actually led us to water, we wouldn't be in this mess.

More likely, the beetles were motivated by the smell of the lizards cooking in the stall next to them—the vendor was inadvertently spreading the scent by waving small bits of cloth over the lizards to keep the fire-legged flies away.

I hadn't seen lizards with bumpy backs like that described in the books I'd read, which made me question how accurate those accounts truly were. But I didn't have time to dwell on that now.

I kept my eyes peeled for any ration coins that may have gotten dropped along the way.

I squeezed past a crowd of small children playing a game of sandstorm, where one child stood in the middle of the group and tried to bump into the other children, knocking them down without using their arms. The last one standing won.

Past the children, a crowd gathered around an older woman in baggy pants and a multicolored vest. She bellowed her name was Hannavas and that she had trained lizards to do amazing things. By the looks of her clothing, she used to be part of the traveling Aicilan menagerie known for training animals to put on shows.

But usually they performed with much bigger creatures like fluffy ellehcar, horned eiznekcam, or roaming nitsirk. Though bigger creatures required more water. Water we didn't have. I wondered as I moved past if her group had gotten stuck here during the initial drought so many years ago and if all her exotic creatures had died of thirst, leaving her with nothing but desert creatures to train.

I continued past the stalls selling jars of dyed sand for sand ceremonies. Fiery reds and vibrant greens stared back at me. Each color had some meaning, some gift it would bestow on a new baby or newlywed couple.

I passed by the Sand Sayers. One woman swirled her fingers through the layer of sand on the table before her as she crouched on her stool.

"Care for a reading?" she called to me, raising one finger to beckon me to the empty stool across from her.

I shook my head and continued. Even if I believed in her powers to tell the future by guiding my hands through the sand

and interpreting the picture I made, I didn't know if I'd like what I was told.

I stopped when I spotted a cart holding bolts of cloth and other wares, peddled by a small child on top. It was the boy from the arena. He was dressed in the same tattered pants and fraying sleeveless shirt he'd worn in the arena.

My hands instinctively went to my sword, but I stopped myself from pulling it from its sheath. I took a deep breath, forcing myself to focus on the task at hand.

How long would it take Rodric to catch up to me? I still needed water, but most of the goods on the boy's cart had already been sold. If I waited, I could follow him back to his hideout.

In case I didn't have time, I moved toward the well, casting quick glances in the boy's direction to be sure he wasn't going to leave anytime soon. I wasn't paying attention to where I was going and ran into the back of a large man holding two water skins. He turned and gave me a disgruntled look. I backed away, or at least I tried to, but a crowd had gathered at my back.

"What do you mean the king has reduced water rations to one bucket a day?" someone shouted at a soldier close to the well. "How does he expect us to survive?"

"He doesn't," the man I'd bumped into shouted. Sunlight glinted off the metal molded over his ears. He must've been one of the Lorians passing through on a caravan who got caught here when the drought started—much like the lizard trainer I'd passed. Lorians were famous for their ability to carry large weights using their ears. I'd never spent enough time in the marketplace to see them weaving through, but others had told me of seeing a jar of beetles and lizards hanging from one ear and a cooking bowl full of hot coals on the other. This left the Lorians' hands free to cook the beetles and lizards, change money, and roll up their delicacies in spiced shed snake skins.

He was probably angrier than the average Achran at the drought because he'd been forced to make a new life here after the lack of water made travel back to Loria impossible. I wished I could've moved away from him, but there was nowhere to go.

Next to us, a woman collapsed from the heat. Or maybe it was from dehydration.

A frail man next to the woman attempted to catch her as the crowd swallowed them both.

The smell of unwashed bodies was overwhelming. And I'd never realized how long the lines were at the wells.

The Lorian man charged forward, using his bulk to force others out of the way so he could move to the front. "I've been waiting for hours to get my two buckets, and none of you are going to stop me." He tossed his ration coin at the guard's feet and moved toward the well.

The ration coin winked in the late afternoon sun, all but forgotten as the guard stared the man down while he filled up his first skin.

I made my way through the crowd in the man's wake, ready to go for the coin when there was an opening.

As soon as the man produced a second skin, the soldier pulled out his sword. "I don't care how long you've been waiting. One bucket from now on. If you don't like it, take it up with the Desert Boys who drained the eastern well earlier today."

"The Desert Boys are the only reason we survive," the man said, and dipped his skin into the bucket he'd pulled up from the well.

I didn't have time to figure out what he meant because the

guard stepped forward and readied his sword. The man had his back to the soldier and wouldn't even see the blow that would strike him down.

I noticed the guard had left the ration coin unattended on the ground behind him.

I went for it.

Before my fingers grazed the ground, hands grabbed me. I was wrenched upright and roughly shoved forward. I crashed into the Lorian filling up his skin. We tumbled into the dirt. The skin slipped from the man's hands, and water spilled out onto the sand.

"No!" he cried, clawing at the damp ground. He turned on me in a rage but stalled when he saw the sword pointed at us.

Using his blade, the soldier motioned for us to rise.

Thankfully, it was a soldier I didn't know, so he didn't recognize me. Rodric kept the newest soldiers stationed at the wells. They had to earn the right to work at the palace.

The Lorian man and I untangled ourselves and stood with our backs against the well. The man kept sending me hate-filled glances as though he really thought he would've gotten away with two skins of water.

The guard's gaze moved between the man and me. "Stealing a ration coin's the same as stealing water. You should both be taken to the arena. But . . ." His eyes settled on me, and his lips turned upward. "I think instead I'll hand you over to Captain Rodric. He's always had an eye for a pretty face, and I'll get a promotion. And you"—he looked at the man—"you, I'll save the king the trouble of dealing with a fool like you."

His sword arced toward the man. My blade was out in a flash, honed to expect such attacks without a moment's notice.

Metal met metal in the air. He had muscle behind him, but I had years of training.

I spun around and used my momentum to rip his sword from his hand. When he went to reach for it, I kicked his chest, sending him reeling.

Several more guards appeared in front of me.

I'd half hoped the man I'd saved would jump into the fray, but he stood there, stunned.

I didn't have time for this. I stripped one of the guards of his sword and spun to meet another. My blade bit into his thigh, and he went down. Two more guards tried to stand in my way. I leapt up and ricocheted off the well, jumping over their swipes. I kicked one in the head, sending him and his helmet back into the cheering crowd.

The other soldier kept his distance. He nervously darted forward to deliver a blow. I parried it and kicked his shoulder. He took one look at me and the swelling crowd before running off.

My victory was short-lived. From my perch on the well, I spotted Rodric and a contingent of guards pour into one corner of the square. His eyes met mine over the crowd.

I wouldn't even have time to dig the ration coin from wherever it became buried during the fight and try my luck at another well.

"Everyone can have as much water as they want," I shouted before leaping down and pushing through the crowd in the direction opposite from the one Rodric had arrived. He would never get through this mob, but I also couldn't easily get out.

I elbowed my way through the crowd as quickly as I could, though it was several minutes before I found myself in an empty alleyway leading away from the square. In the chaos, I'd also lost sight of the boy, and I still hadn't gotten any water. I'd have to hope I could find water somewhere in the desert.

Three guards appeared behind me.

I darted down an alley and merged onto a larger street. I ran along it, searching for any direction that looked like it led to the desert.

I skidded to a stop as I ran past one alcove. In it, two guards had the Desert Boy I was after backed up against the wall. The boy had a knife out, ready to attack.

"Think we'll get as good a reward for bringing this one back in as we would for the princess?" one guard asked the other.

They both had their swords raised.

The other three guards were catching up behind me. I only had a split second to decide.

Letting out a cry, I forced myself down the alcove. I sliced my sword along one guard's arm before he even knew what happened. The other guard barely got his sword around before I cut him across his leg, sending him sinking to the ground.

I was just about to tell the kid to run for it when shadows fell across the mouth of the alcove. I placed my hand behind me, hoping the kid was smart enough to stay plastered where he was.

I scanned for a way out.

Two windows were built into the side of the house forming the alcove. The upper one was open, but the window below had its wooden shutter closed tight like a flap. I'd never pry it open before the guards reached us.

The guards who'd been chasing me advanced, pushing me back toward the boy.

"Rodric wants to talk to you," one said. They all had their swords drawn and pointed at me.

I pointed my own sword in response. That slowed their approach.

"Just come with us willingly," the first one said. "No one needs to get hurt."

"Let us pass, or I'll have no choice." I tightened my grip on my hilt. My palms were sweating.

"Go get Rodric. Let him know we've got her cornered," one of them said. The third guard nodded and dashed off. The other two spread out to clog the only exit.

My heartbeat sped up, blood pumping faster as I prepared to fight.

My odds were better with two, and since I wasn't sticking around until Rodric appeared, I attacked. I brought my sword up and swung at the first guard. He fumbled with his sword but raised it in time to block the blow.

I spun and sliced at the second guard in the same motion. My blade clawed against his breastplate but didn't break through. The second guard smashed his sword hilt into my back. I staggered forward. I knew another blow was coming, so I rebounded off the wall and caught the other soldier with a kick to the stomach as I turned. I smashed my heel into his groin for good measure, and he dropped to the ground.

The other guard had turned toward the boy. He swiped his blade at the kid, who leapt backward.

I sent the back of my weapon crashing into the guard's helmet. He fell instantly.

The boy turned toward me, and I tried to duck my head, hoping he wouldn't recognize me. He'd never help me if he did.

His eyes widened, and I thought he'd realized who I was, but he was looking past me. "Rodric," he whispered.

I turned just as Rodric planted himself in the mouth of the alcove.

"Can you climb?" the boy whispered. He nodded to the window shutter. "Pull yourself up. The roofs are safer than the streets when guards are after you."

"What about you?" I asked. There's no way Rodric would let him off this time. Both doors would hold tigers.

"Don't worry about me. Go," he said.

I took off for the window, then hoisted myself and began to climb.

"Get back here," Rodric raged. He stepped forward, but the kid moved into his path.

"I didn't think I'd see your ugly face again, Rodric," the boy said. He puffed out his chest and threw his arms wide in a show of bravado. He was just far enough away that Rodric couldn't strike him with his sword.

"If it isn't little Dimic," Rodric sneered. "Haven't crawled back to your hidey-hole yet? How's your brother, the one I didn't kill?"

"Still plotting his revenge," Dimic said.

"Good thing your family's used to disappointment," he replied. He advanced forward and rammed his sword in Dimic's direction.

Dimic shuffled backward.

I reached the window ledge on the second floor and drew myself up. Curtains fluttered around me, blocking my view of the scene below. I leapt higher and caught the roof of the building, pulling myself up onto it.

Below, Rodric pushed Dimic back into the dead end of the alcove with a smile on his face more curved than a scorpion's tail.

"Dimic," I shouted. I held my arm down to him, urging him to find a way up.

The next thing I knew, Dimic had thrown himself against the wall of the alcove, but instead of smashing against it, he'd kicked up and off it to the adjacent wall. He sprang once more, grabbing ahold of the roof.

He scrambled up and across the roof quickly, forcing me to run to keep up.

"Wait," I cried. "Come back."

"You're on your own now," Dimic yelled over his shoulder.

I threw up my hands in frustration. "I saved your life."

"And I saved yours. We're square." He didn't stop running. Instead, he vaulted onto the next roof over.

I struggled to keep pace with him as we ran across crumbling ledges and over small wooden planks.

Rodric tried to follow us on the streets below. One spear spiraled past my head, after which I heard Rodric roar he needed me alive. That should have been comforting but wasn't.

Dimic leapt from one roof to another, easily outpacing Rodric. I put all my energy into copying his moves, landing where he landed. I was concentrating so hard I almost missed when he stopped on a roof at the edge of town.

He turned to see if I was still following. When he saw I was, he dropped off the roof and ran out into the desert sands.

Panting, I skidded to a stop at the edge.

The eroded wall of the city was the only thing that lay between the desert and me. Fallen parapet bricks littered both sides of the barrier and lay across the top. Where soldiers once patrolled, small plants tried to grow in the uneven shadows and now-open cracks.

I turned back toward the city to look over the landscape. The dried-out, cracked roofs gave way to darker ones that hadn't been hit quite as hard by the sandstorms. A little farther out, some buildings had posts with canopies hoisted between them for shade. Rising above them all was the palace. Its walls blended into the sea of sand around it.

It was too late to go back. The only way was forward. I dropped off the roof and followed Dimic into the desert.

CHAPTER 7

Dimic cut a quick pace. Already, he was two dunes ahead of me. I'd spot him cresting a peak just as I did another. I made sure to step where his foot had plunged into the sand. I was so worried about losing him I couldn't waste time to look where I was stepping, and I didn't need a yellow-spotted sand snake taking me out before I could face either Cion or Rodric.

Sweat soaked through my clothes by the time I made it over the fourth sand dune. I didn't dare take off my cloak. It protected my identity as much as my skin, though it did little to protect my stinging eyes.

I could only hope Dimic had the same trouble seeing as I was. He hadn't looked back once, and I could only hope he was concentrating too much on his feet to locate me behind him. That way, I could follow him straight to his hideout and plan from there.

Though the kid was like the wind. He flew over the sands, whereas my feet got caught in the plunging surface more than once. But every time I fell face-first into the dust, I pulled myself up, telling myself that if a child could keep going, so could I.

With every dune I climbed, the setting sun would torment me on the way up, disappear once I reached a valley, and then stalk me again as I climbed the next ridge. Eventually, the sun descended behind a dune and didn't reappear. The sky became a spread of dripping pinks and oranges that faded into the yellow of the sand.

The coolness of night setting in did nothing to revive me. And the ache in my throat only reminded me how long I'd gone without water.

My skin burned where fire-legged flies landed. I shooed them away and told myself to keep watching Dimic ahead of me. My survival depended on keeping up with him. Though I had no idea what exactly I was going to say when I did confront the Desert Boys. Maybe something along the lines of needing their help to defeat Rodric. They certainly would be on board based on what I'd witnessed in the alcove.

I was playing out the conversation in my mind when I realized Dimic no longer appeared ahead of me.

I ground to a stop.

I crept up the next dune cautiously, my sword out and ready. But when I peered into the next valley, Dimic wasn't waiting to ambush me. His footsteps led halfway up the next dune and simply stopped.

I half rolled, half walked down the dune to the spot. There was nothing there. There was no one there. I slammed my hands into the sand, but I knew he didn't have time to bury himself.

I spun in circles. I climbed up the next dune. Nothing. No footprints. I waded back down into the valley.

Could the Desert Boys really dissolve into sand? I shook my head clear. That wasn't possible. He was here somewhere. He had to be.

"Dimic," I cried, my hoarse voice crashing out over the waves of sand.

Silence answered me.

"Please," I cried. "I need your help to defeat Rodric."

I stalked the edges of the valley waiting. Hoping.

Still nothing.

Exhausted, I collapsed on my knees. I'd lost him. Even worse, I'd been so intent on following him that I hadn't even thought to take out Tamlin's map and track the location.

I'd been stupid to believe he'd lead me to his hideout. He'd led me as far out as he could just to leave me to die.

I never should've trusted the stupid little street urchin.

The only map I had now was my scattered footprints leading back to the city, and thanks to the wind even those were disappearing every moment I sat here. Not to mention my path had grown harder and harder to see as the last bits of sunlight fled.

I slammed my fists into the ground.

"I saved your life," I cried. But I knew it was useless.

I hauled myself to my feet and stared listlessly at the sand, trying to decide what direction to take, what to do.

Then, the earth around me shifted.

Hot bursts of sand sprayed up in all directions. I flung my hand over my eyes as they cascaded over me. I shook it off as quickly as I could. When I could finally see again, I was circled by boys of all ages and sizes. Most of the boys looked younger than me. One had a scar running from his scalp all the way down his face. Another was missing both his thumbs—a price sometimes paid for stealing water.

They all had lips chapped from thirst and rib bones poking through their shirts.

Only one was older.

"Cion . . ." I started to say, but he launched at me with such ferocity, I barely got my sword up in time.

He swung again, barely missing cutting into my scalp. I ducked under the blow and turned to face him. I blocked the sword streaking toward me, but I didn't see the kick that landed me on my back.

I hadn't even sucked in a breath before metal slid across either side of the metal cuff protecting my throat. Cion stood over me, the blades of his forked sword pinning me to the ground.

"Good job, Dimic," Cion said.

"Told you I'd caught her," Dimic boasted from somewhere off to my left. "And we weren't even followed. Does this make up for being taken to the arena?"

Something dark passed over Cion's face, and he ignored the question. He kicked the sword from my hand. I sucked in air as pain radiated through my fingers.

"You can't be sure you weren't followed." Cion ground the forks of his blade a little closer against my cuff, forcing me to dig deeper into the blazing sand to breathe. "How many men did you lead here, Princess?"

"I didn't lead anyone here. I'm as much a fugitive as you are, and I need your help."

"We're not falling for your lies."

"She was being chased by the guards and Rodric," Dimic offered. "And she saved Lister at the well."

"Just more of their royal tricks," Cion said. He leered over me, the loose strands of his hair almost reaching my face. "What was your plan? Make us think you were on the run? From whom? And"—he kicked the empty water flask at my waist—"leaving without water? If you were going to trick us, you should've at least made it convincing."

"Rodric is my next opponent in the arena. I can't beat him.

He's too good, but . . ." I prayed Cion responded to flattery, because I didn't want either end of his blade to get any closer to my neck. "But you're the best fighter in the desert. You could train me." I forced myself to meet his gaze.

Cion scoffed, an unreadable look passing across his face. "You want me to train you so you can keep your place in the palace? Why would I want to do that? I'd be much happier watching you and Rodric fight it out." The desert breeze dragged his hair across his forehead.

"Do you really want Rodric on the throne?" I replied, unable to hide the rage searing around inside me. "Do you think any of your boys will receive just trials under his reign?"

"No," Cion said. He flipped a few strands out of his eyes. "But I don't want you ruling either." He moved his sword a little, and the blades grated against the cuff.

I swallowed.

"In exchange," I said, "I could give you access to one of the wells."

"No doubt one of the empty ones," he said. "I'm tired of empty wells and empty promises."

Things weren't going the way I'd thought. I knew there'd be some opposition, but I'd assumed they'd want to bring Rodric down. And now that I had sword blades trapping me in the sand, any chance of escape was receding.

My instinct was to place Cion off balance. But I wasn't in a great position to get enough strength behind the blow. Maybe go for the knee? But what would that accomplish? If I wanted his help, I couldn't attack.

"I'm not like Rodric," I said instead. "I care about the people."

"You care?" Cion looked around to see if anyone at all seemed to believe me. Several of the Desert Boys scoffed. "Where were you when Rodric enacted stricter punishments for anyone caught stealing water each time the water levels dropped? Where were you when more sickness could be found in the city than sand? Where were you when the poor and elderly needed help rebuilding their walls after the sandstorms finally blew them in? Where was your 'care' when we were cast out because of your father's two-child rule? Where were you when we became orphans and had no other choice but to steal to survive?"

"You're a skilled fighter," I said through gritted teeth. "You could have become a palace guard."

Cion shook his head. "I would never work for that man. Not even with the extra water rations they get. And if I did, who would raise the other orphans? Who would teach them to survive? Who would supply them with the extra water they need?"

Listening to Cion defend his actions spread a fire through my body. Nobody had much water, and his kind and their greed was only making it worse for everyone else. "If you didn't steal water, there'd be enough for everyone. My father wouldn't have to keep cutting rations."

Cion's fingers tightened around the hilt of his sword. I watched as his muscles snapped to attention under his skin.

I tensed, expecting a blow. His arm twitched, but no attack came.

Instead, faster than I could react, Cion crouched over me, grabbed my arm, and clapped a shackle over it. He tried to force me to roll over by twisting my arm back.

Panic welled up within me.

I contorted and fought against his grip, which loosened the sand holding the sword pinning me down. Cion's hand darted out to catch it before the hilt could crash into his temple, giving me the chance to rip my hand free. I didn't know where my sword had landed, so I swung the only weapon I had, the yet-unfettered end of the shackle. It crashed into Cion's head, sending him and the sword sprawling into the dune. I shifted my weight quickly and knelt atop him. I tore his sword away and pointed it at his neck just as he opened his eyes and looked at me. Surprise flashed across his face while blood trickled out from a cut at his scalp.

I sat there heaving for a moment, my body tensed to strike.

His eyes, dark and unreadable, never left my face.

Slowly, I eased off. I knew if he got that sword away from me, I was finished. It was sheer luck that the sand had shifted earlier, providing me an opening to knock him down in the first place.

The circle of boys around me had tightened at my outburst, but none dared get too close.

I dropped his blade and backed away. "I told you I need your help."

He sat up slowly, watching me like a vulture watches its prey. His attention never left me as he brushed sand off as he stood, then shook his hair out of his eyes and grabbed his sword. His eyes searched mine, no doubt trying to figure out whatever secrets I might hold.

"If you did lead men out here," he said, "they won't survive a desert night or a sandstorm."

"I didn't lead anyone out here." I crossed my arms as much to look nonthreatening as to hide how much my hands itched to hold my sword again, to have some barrier between us. I tried not to show that I was watching him while also flitting glances at the boys around us. There were probably at least six I couldn't see directly behind me. It made my skin crawl.

Cion glared at me several long, hard moments. Everyone was so quiet, you could've heard a snake coming from ten dunes away.

Finally, Cion shuffled a few steps back and grabbed my sword from where it had landed. He used the tip to motion me forward. "Inside."

I looked where he indicated, and all I saw was sand. Then one of the Desert Boys rushed forward and lifted a wooden sheet from the ground. He struggled under the weight of the sand pouring off it. Light emanated from the hole he revealed.

No wonder we could never find them.

"Go," Cion said.

I ducked inside. The Desert Boys had built their hideout into what had once been a rock formation, maybe even a cave, before sand had covered it over. Different archways led into other lit areas.

"Move." Cion again tapped the end of my sword into my back once he ducked in behind me.

We ventured through one archway into what could have passed for a sort of hallway, with alcoves jutting off on either side. In one, stacks of goods were piled up to the ceiling. Earthen jars flanked empty cages. Bolts of cloth snuggled against piles of rope. In another alcove, pillows were thrown over the thick rugs that lined the floor.

I tried to memorize the layout in case I needed to escape.

None of the other Desert Boys followed us as Cion forced me down a tunnel so narrow I had to duck. I had no idea where he was leading me or why. My heart thudded in my chest with every step forward. Where could he possibly be taking me? Was he going to help? Did he want me dead? Then why not kill me outside? If he didn't want to kill me outright, it meant he wanted me to suffer. A pit of snakes? Scorpions? My mind raced at the possibilities as the tunnel opened into a large cavern.

Falling sand piled into pyramids wherever it snuck through cracks on the surface. On the ground, large stalagmites rose like fangs.

The first thing I noticed were several crumpled human shapes lying against the wall. The second thing I noticed was that there was no way out.

CHAPTER 8

Since there was no other exit, he'd brought me here to die, to cast me off with the other bodies lying along the wall.

My stomach roiled at the sight of them.

But then one of the bodies unfolded itself and brushed away the sand. Partially covered by a tattered blanket was a woman whose face was weathered beyond her years. Sand lined the wrinkles of her face, despite her probably not being more than a few years older than my mother would've been.

She began shuffling toward us, favoring a foot I realized was turned to one side. I skittered in the opposite direction as she approached, but she only gave me a passing glance.

"Cion," she said, "did you bring us more water? Tania's so thirsty. Her belly grows bigger every day with child."

"I'm sorry, Bala," Cion said, using the term often reserved for grandmothers, aunts, and others worthy of respect. "An unexpected complication arose, and I called the boys off. We'll get more soon."

Bala nodded solemnly. "At times it seems as though it is the desert's will she not survive. The sands know nobody wants another one of Rodric's illegitimate children running around, but I'll do what I can for her."

I coughed to cover up the gasp that escaped my lips.

Cion shot me a silencing look. "Don't worry," he said to Bala. "We'll get you and Tania on the next caravan out."

She wrapped her hand around Cion's. Her small fingers barely surrounded three of his. Once she released his hand, she turned toward me with a tired smile. "Are you going on the caravan too?" Her eyes went to my stomach. I couldn't help from crossing my arms over it. The shackle pressed awkwardly against me.

I shot a glance at Cion. His face was unreadable.

"She's staying here," Cion replied. "I'm showing her around."

I had no idea what he meant by that, but the small smile widened across the woman's face in response. Her eyes darted back and forth between Cion and me. "There's no safer place than with Cion. I'm sure he'll watch over you very carefully."

I choked on sand I must have inhaled. "I don't need anyone to take care of me."

The woman clasped her hands over her stomach. "In this desert, we all have to take care of each other." She smiled at Cion and patted his cheek before moving back into the darkness of the cavern. She didn't seem like a prisoner, though it was clear she wasn't part of the Desert Boys' activities either.

I turned on Cion. "What is this place?"

He threw his arms wide. "This is where we keep all that excess water we steal." He leaned back against one of the stalagmites. "You said if we didn't steal all that water, there'd be enough for everyone. Do they look like they have enough?"

Clearly he was lying. There was no water anywhere I could see.

Confusion must've played across my face because Cion mumbled, "Of course you wouldn't understand." He lowered his face to meet mine. "We steal the water for people like them. So they can cross the desert and escape this place. Whatever extra we have, we distribute to those who need it most in Achra."

"If you didn't steal all the water," I retorted, "we could ease the restrictions."

Cion exhaled loudly. "There's already plenty of water for everyone. The four wells are all fed by the same underground river that runs directly under the palace, where the water levels are controlled by none other than *your* father."

"That's preposterous." There were no water controls in the palace. I would have seen them. And even my father would never be so cruel as to keep water from his own people. "The only controller of the water levels is the desert itself." I bit my tongue before I threw out that many people—my father included—blamed the continuing drought on the Desert Boys and the desert's attempts to rid them from its dunes.

"Think about it," Cion challenged. "The only reason everyone doesn't flee this forsaken sand pit and its increasing sandstorms is because they can never store enough water for the crossing. Your father knows that. He knows no one would stay, so he controls everyone by controlling the wells."

"He wouldn't do that." My father had always talked about how great Achra had been before the drought. He and I both wanted to make it that way again. If there really was enough water, he would've released it to the people so Achra could rise once again, so we could lead it back into prosperity.

"Wouldn't he?" He pushed off the stalagmite and moved toward me.

I skittered backward, keeping the same distance between us. I tried not to notice how silently he moved.

"The same man who puts tigers behind both doors at his 'just' trials wouldn't go so far as to control the water levels to keep everyone dependent on him?"

I shook my head.

"He wouldn't lower them further after one of our raids to make it look like we'd taken more than we did so he could set even stricter ration laws, all in an attempt to turn the people against us?" His soft voice mixed with the falling sand.

"You don't know what you're talking about." I shot back. I'd lived in the palace my whole life and never seen anything that would control the wells.

"Back when the drought started—before you and I were even born—the original Desert Boys were locals and caravan leaders who didn't have access to water. As a result, they knew the desert and its dangers better than anyone, and they used that knowledge to go out searching for water. All they ever found was the nearly dried-up underground river that leads directly toward the city."

Obviously, something had to feed the wells. It didn't all come from the small oasis within the palace walls. But his words didn't prove anything—especially as he was saying the river was as dry as the wells.

"The entrance to the cave that houses the river has been buried over the years by the blowing sands," he continued. "The one time I set out to find it, I nearly died on the three-day journey, but when I dug down into the cave, you know what I saw? More water than I could imagine. That river isn't dry anymore. It's flowing with as much force as a sandstorm."

"If you know there's a river," I said, "why not just bypass the wells and take water from it?" It would be the simpler solution.

"Even if you had enough water for the trip and to sustain you while you dig, the hole fills in every time the wind blows. We're afraid if we dig the wrong way, the channel will cave in and cut off the water." He sounded so sure of himself, like he'd gone over it again and again in his mind. And maybe he had, but that still didn't mean he was right about everything.

"Just because you've seen this river doesn't mean my father controls it."

"We have sources throughout Achra," he said. "They've heard your father and Rodric whispering, wondering how little water the people could survive on, how long until they revealed our location."

"Of course my father and Rodric wonder about those things. That doesn't prove they control anything." My father and I always used to talk about our people, the water levels, the caravans—everything I needed to know to be queen. But that was before Rodric showed up.

"My source told me they'd overheard Rodric say he was going to drop the water levels after one of our raids. We know those controls exist."

I scoffed. If I didn't know about these supposed water controls, I didn't see why Rodric would.

Except that he and my father were as thick as thieves.

I shook the thought away. It still didn't make sense. The lagoon didn't have any water controls, and I couldn't think of anywhere else in the palace that would either.

I gave Cion credit for wanting to help the people, but more than likely, this water control idea was something dreamed up by Rodric as a way to tempt the Desert Boys to try another attack on the palace—and this source was probably in on it too.

"Who told you these things?" I questioned.

"Not even Rodric could torture that out of me."

I rolled my eyes. He was impossible to get information from.

Could it be one of the guards? A cook? There were hundreds of possibilities.

"My friend will find where your father controls the wells. Then we'll go in and change the levels in our favor."

I sighed. I still didn't believe those controls existed. This was Cion, the snake of the desert. He'd say—and apparently believe—anything to get more water. And there was clearly nothing I could do to convince him those controls didn't exist. But as long as he believed in the water system, I had an advantage.

"Would you train me if I agreed to never restrict the water levels again?" I eyed him.

"Now it's my turn to ask why I should believe you," Cion stated.

"I could've killed you out there and didn't." I dangled the shackle as a reminder.

"Maybe you wanted to learn the way into our hideout."

"I'm not stupid enough to come here by myself and think I could take all of you on." Well, I had considered that plan, but he didn't need to know. "I told you before. The only person I want to take down is Rodric, and I'd imagine the only person you hate more than me is the person capturing you, torturing you, and throwing your kind into the arena—Rodric. We have a common enemy. That's your reason to trust me."

"I still don't trust you any more than I trust Rodric."

I balled my hands into fists. Couldn't he see that we both wanted the same thing?

"Rodric will kill you and your boys one by one."

"And you won't?" he retorted.

"I've fought against you for so long because I thought you were a plague draining the life from the people. My people. But

I see now that you had your own reasons for stealing water." Assuming he was telling the truth, he believed he was doing what he could to help others. But his raids continually forced my father to drop the water rations. Not to mention he was the leader of a group that had killed my mother. But we still had the same goal. "Train me, and we can both help the people. That's what you want, isn't it?"

Before Cion could reply, a low moan echoed through the cavern. I turned toward the sound expecting to find Bala or Tania, but instead I saw Hardesh.

I froze, my mouth going slack.

He had bandages wrapped around his face where I'd bashed his nose.

"We found him in the desert," Cion said, following my gaze. "He'd been bitten by a yellow-spotted sand snake. We got to him just in time."

I couldn't force myself to move to Hardesh's side. I doubted he'd want to see me, but I couldn't tear my eyes away either. He hunched in the corner with his arms wrapped around his drawn-in knees. There was a brokenness to his demeanor, so unlike the man I'd faced in the arena. It was as though all the bones had been removed from his body, and he'd collapsed in on himself. Even his hair looked grayer than I remembered. Could he truly have suffered so much in a matter of hours?

I'd never really thought about what happened to my suitors after I'd beaten them. I knew they were exiled, and somewhere deep down I knew the desert would kill them. Finally having to face it made it real. And I could see what made me a monster in the eyes of the Desert Boys.

"Did you save all of my opponents?"

Cion didn't answer, and I didn't have to look back to know he was shaking his head.

I couldn't bear to look at Hardesh any longer. I ground my toes into the sand.

"How can you claim you're going to help the people when you do this?" He waved his hand in Hardesh's direction.

I stared down. "I did what I had to, to prove the desert knew I was its next leader."

"You did what your father and Rodric would do."

"I didn't have a choice."

"Didn't you?"

Something in Cion's tone forced me to look at him.

"Couldn't you have refused to fight? Couldn't you have stopped Rodric from killing and torturing nearly every Desert Boy he could find?"

I swallowed down the words asking why the Desert Boys had killed my mother and brother—because I was doing this for her, and arguing about the past would get us nowhere. "If you want Rodric dead, I'm your best chance. I'm here offering you a deal, a way to change things. I doubt Rodric will ever make you such an offer."

"There is a reason wise men say you should stay in the same desert your whole life. Because you know its dangers. You know what to expect. I don't know what to expect from you. How do I know I'm not placing someone worse than Rodric on the throne?"

I took a deep breath. I needed to give him something more—something real—if I ever wanted him to believe what I said. I told him the only thing I could. "I don't expect you to understand, but I made a promise to my mother before she died that I'd protect her people. It's why I came here to look for a way to fight a man I know I can't beat."

We stood face to face, only a foot apart. As we studied each other, I wanted him to look into my eyes and see the sincerity there.

He looked at me for a few more moments. Then he reached down and scooped up a handful of sand. He weighed it in his palm. "Have you heard of a desert's promise?"

I shook my head.

He held my gaze. "It's said if anyone breaks a desert's promise, the desert will know, and it will suffocate the life out of them any way it can."

I watched the steady trail of sand escaping back toward the ground.

I bent over and picked up my own fistful.

"I'll train you to beat Rodric in exchange for you never restricting the wells' water levels again," he said. "But you first have to pass the Desert Boys' initiation test to prove you're capable of becoming one of us, of thinking and acting as we would."

He held out his hand. "Do we have a deal?"

I didn't like the sound of this initiation test, but I didn't feel I had much of a choice. Besides, if all the other boys had passed, there was no reason I couldn't.

I shoved my fistful of sand into his. "Deal."

The sand trickled out between our fingers as I tried not to think about the knot forming in my stomach.

He smirked and pulled his hand away, letting the remaining sand fall to the ground. "Good. Follow me."

CHAPTER 9

Once we left the light of the cavern behind, Cion stopped me. He undid the shackle on my wrist before pulling out a strip of cloth. "You can't know the way until you've passed initiation," he said.

I eyed him. This sounded like a trick, a way to make sure my defenses were down.

He sighed at my hesitation. "If you can't even trust me long enough to put on the blindfold, you should leave and try your chances in the desert."

Everything in me shouted this was a trap, that there was some deceit coming that I simply hadn't figured out yet. But what option did I have? I'd chosen not to run away, and now I'd thrown in my lot with his.

Reluctantly, I turned around. Though I jumped and reached for my empty sword hilt when his hand touched my shoulder.

"Relax." He swiftly tied the fabric across my eyes. Then a weight landed around my stomach. My sword. He'd put it back into its sheath. It was the smallest comfort as I adjusted to a world without sight.

He grabbed both shoulders and turned me around. "Walk forward." He guided me through a series of twists and turns, telling me to duck at times or turn sideways to fit through a small crevice.

I honed in on every sound, anything that might be footfalls

or signal an attack was coming. What on earth had I gotten myself into? My heart rate sped up. The severity, the finality, of what I was doing sank in as I let the desert's most well-known snake lead me blindly forward.

Then, suddenly, his hands disappeared from my shoulders. I heard a large rock slide into place.

"Cion?"

No answer.

When I ripped off the blindfold, I was surrounded by complete darkness. Raising my arms out in front of me, I turned and ran in the direction we'd come until I hit hard rock. I flung my hands around, looking for an opening.

There was nothing. Not a single detectable crack. I kept my hand on the wall and walked, certain I'd find an opening. I didn't. Instead, I ended up walking in a circle.

I pounded my fist on the rock. Certain I'd missed something, I moved farther back into the room trying to feel for a breeze, anything that would signal there was a way out.

"Cion," I called again. The word echoed lifelessly back.

My heart rate increased with each passing moment. I was trapped. No, worse. I was a prisoner. Darkness pressed in around me like a heavy cloak. It weighed against my chest, making it harder and harder to breathe.

Had this been his plan all along? Was he selling me back to Rodric? I wondered what price I'd fetch. Unfettered access to a well for a day?

I kicked the sand at my feet. It trickled unsatisfyingly against the wall. This is what I got for trying to be like my mother, using my words, when I should've been like my father.

"You'll pay for this, Cion," I cried. I paced back and forth.

I pulled out my sword and skittered in circles, sending sand in wide arcs. "Come in here, and let's see who's the best once and for all."

"Sit." Cion's voice sounded through the room from somewhere above me.

"And make myself an easier target?" I called out to the darkness. "I don't think so."

"Sit." His voice echoed more forcefully this time.

I prowled the length of the small circle a few more times. Staring up into the darkness, trying to find where he was hiding, where the attack would come from.

Now I knew how the tigers felt in their cages.

"Sit," he said one last time, "or you will fail initiation."

I gripped and regripped the hilt of my sword. My instincts had been off since I'd left the shade of the city behind. I couldn't tell what was a trick and what wasn't.

I breathed heavily in and out of my nose. My throat scratched with thirst, and the more I paced, the more I'd wear myself out. I'd need my strength for whatever test or attack was coming.

I shoved my sword back into its scabbard and plopped down on the floor. Sand squished underneath me. I threw my arms up as much in frustration as to show I'd complied. I felt like a child waiting for instructions.

"Since Cintric founded the Desert Boys, we have dedicated our lives to helping our fellow members and those who need our protection most. We shed our lives, our wants, our pasts, and are made new in the desert."

Sand pelted me from all angles. I protectively held up an arm. I sputtered and spit out some sand. As much as I wanted to leap away, I remained seated.

"The desert has claimed you as one of its own."

Another blast of sand covered me.

"We claim you for our own."

I didn't flinch as another bout rained down around me.

This was like a version of the sand ceremonies we used for special occasions in the city. When a child was born, parents poured sand over the child's head, not only to signify it was what we would all return to one day, but because it was also said that the amount the child cried during the sanding signified how hard their life would be. For marriages, couples tossed sand onto the head of their betrothed. The number of grains that hit their head and stayed through all the wedding festivities signified how many years of happiness they'd have together.

This sand was nothing like the fine, colored sand I'd seen for sale in the marketplace. This was coarse and unrefined, like the desert itself. It scraped against my skin as it trickled over my body.

"Arise, child of the desert," Cion said. "You've been reborn." As he said it, lights flared up all around. Every boy I'd seen earlier was situated on a circular ledge that ran above the room. They each held a torch, and over their heads, names were carved in the rock.

"To claim your place among us," Cion continued, "you must prove you are capable. You must find your way out of the pit and carve your name here among ours."

I spun around, thinking there must be a handhold somewhere, because the ledge was taller than the arena wall. There was no way I could jump that high.

"You may use anything you see to help you," Cion said. "But fail to get out of the pit, and you have failed."

I moved toward the wall, inspecting it. The stone was as smooth as before. I tried jumping anyway. I stopped a good three feet from the top.

I could feel all the boys silently watching me. Most of them were short and underfed. If they could do it, there had to be a way out. I had to be missing something obvious. I'd beaten eleven suitors using my wits and skill. This was nothing compared to that.

The crackling torches echoed my shuffling around the circle. I went back to inspecting the wall. The only break was the doorway we must've come in through. I figured that wasn't an option. I still tried pushing against the rock that blocked it. It didn't budge. I searched for some sort of switch that would open the door.

Nothing.

I moved more frantically around the circle. What was I missing? I tried digging through the sand looking for some hidden treasure that might help me. Only when my knees ached from sand grains digging into them did I finally stop.

I inspected the blindfold I'd ripped off. Could I fashion it into some sort of rope? I shook my head. It was far too short.

I tried jumping and kicking off the wall like I'd seen Dimic do in the marketplace, but the circle was too wide. I didn't even come close to the other wall.

I expected the boys to laugh at my failed attempts, but they didn't. They stayed as still as the stone around us, watching, waiting as torchlight burrowed into the hollowness of their cheeks.

Next, I tried piling up sand, but even after working for several minutes, the pile was barely a foot tall. And when I tried to use it to jump off, I nearly broke my ankle landing on it. I ungracefully rolled down into the sand.

I shoved my hands through my hair as I sat up. “What am I missing?” I called.

They all stood silent.

I rammed my sword into the largest crack I could find. I didn’t even leave a scratch in the rock.

Still, I tried over and over again, slamming my blade against the fissure in hopes I could create a handhold. Soon, I realized that couldn’t be the way. Otherwise, there’d be handholds all over the wall from other boys. But still I tried. I tried until sweat plastered my hair to my forehead and my hands nearly bled from all the sand that ground against my palms with every strike.

I threw my sword down in frustration and stalked around the perimeter again. I shoved my dripping hair from my eyes.

Finally, when I was too tired to keep trudging in circles, I sat down with my back against the wall, directly across from Cion.

“Is this some trick?” I called up to him. “Are you just toying with me?”

He stared, unblinking. Only the flame next to his head wavered.

I leaned my head back against the cool rock wall and went over Cion’s words again. He said I could use anything I could see to help me. But there was nothing in the pit. No rocks I could pile up. No rope. No handholds.

There were only the silent boys and their ever-watchful eyes.

I studied their faces. They were all too thin, but they each had a light in their eyes. Something that spoke to the fact they had more strength than I would ever know. These boys had been tested by the desert and lived to tell the tale.

That made them dangerous.

But I refused to admit that made them better than me. I just had to figure out what they had seen that got them out of the pit. What was there in this room that could help me?

And then it hit me. Anything I could see.

It was so devastatingly simple. So like what Cion had said moments before. I needed to think like them, act like they would.

I ignored my aching muscles as I rose to my feet and grabbed my sword from where I'd thrown it.

I moved until I stood below Cion.

"Help me," I said. I stretched my arm up.

Cion stared down at me, and for a fleeting moment I thought I was wrong, that he was going to leave me in the pit. But he gave his torch to the boy next to him, knelt down, and pulled me up.

Sharp rocks ground into my knees as I clamored to my feet.

I couldn't help the smirk that spread across my face. I'd beaten his little game.

But the smile disappeared in a flash when Cion pulled a dagger from behind his back. I scrambled backward. I eyed the boys around me, watching for more weapons to appear as I went for my sword hilt. Before I could pull it out, Cion flipped the dagger into the air and caught it, holding the hilt out toward me.

My hand froze. My heart drummed in my chest.

"The only way to survive as one of us is to help each other," Cion said. "You have passed the test. Carve your name and take your place among us." He stretched the handle closer to me.

I edged forward and grabbed the dagger. The blade had more nicks in it than there were desert boys, and rust clung where the metal of the blade met the hilt. Cion gestured to the wall next to us.

Every ounce of training I'd ever had screamed not to turn my back on them. Nevertheless, I took the dagger and jaggedly carved my name into the rock, not far from Cion's. It looked like another name had been there, but it was scratched out.

I handed Cion the dagger when I was done. He stuck it into his belt and then pressed his palm against my name. Then he bent down and took a handful of sand, which he dribbled over my head.

"Welcome, Kateri," he said. "May the desert give you its strength." His face was soft in the torchlight surrounding us. He moved back to stand by his name.

Another boy approached. He stood silently in front of me. I resisted the urge to go for my sword. My eyes darted between him and Cion. Slowly, the boy bent down and repeated what Cion had done.

One by one, the boys mimicked him, touching my name, pouring a handful of sand over my head, and then repeating Cion's words. Some of the shorter boys sort of tossed the sand toward my chin.

Some approached warily, like they expected me to lunge for them like a tiger in the arena. I couldn't blame them. I was watching them too, wondering if they were old enough to be part of the raid that killed my mother and brother. None of them were.

Dimic approached almost sheepishly. He scooped up two handfuls of sand. Before he tossed them, he leaned close. "Since Cion didn't kill you, I'm glad you passed that test. I never would've lived it down for bringing you here if you hadn't."

He pelted me right in the face with sand. Then with a wink, he went back to his place. Boy after boy took his place.

As much as I wanted the silly ritual to be over, I figured I could use all the help I could get. I closed my eyes and let the sand fall down my skin, willing the desert to give me the strength it had given these boys.

Once the last boy had gone, Cion cried, "Kateri, our newest Desert Boy."

A great cry went up that echoed through the room.

My eyes snapped open. This wasn't what we'd agreed on. I didn't want that title anywhere near my name. I could work with them, but I didn't want to be a part of the group that killed my mother.

The boys began extinguishing their torches and filing out through an opening I hadn't noticed from my position in the pit. Cion was the last one to go by.

I grabbed his arm. "You said I had to pass initiation, not become one of you."

"That's what the initiation is," he replied. "It's you becoming one of us. I thought you understood that."

I shook my head. "I don't want to be one of you. I just need to beat Rodric."

"Being one of us is how you beat Rodric. You need to stop thinking like him and think like us. That's the first lesson you need to learn, and if you can't, then leave." He put out his torch and ducked through the opening in the wall.

I wasn't sure if he expected me to follow or not, so I stood there in the darkness. I curled my fingers into fists and took a deep breath.

If pretending to be a Desert Boy was what it took to beat Rodric, then fine. I could play along. I kept telling myself it would be worth it as I cried out with as much humility as I could muster, "Wait."

I stepped into the hallway. Small torches cast flickering pools of light across the sandy corridor. Cion turned, his face caught in shadows.

"I . . . I want to be a Desert Boy," I said. The words tasted foul in my mouth.

"Changed your mind so quickly?" Cion sauntered back toward me. The shadows of the tunnel made it impossible to read his face.

"I'm here to learn," I said.

"Then learn this." He flicked hair out of his face so he could look me in the eyes. "When one of us suffers, we all suffer. When one of us drinks too much water, the rest of us ache. When one of us gets hurt in a fight, we have one less person to watch our back. I put you through initiation because I need you to know that you will suffer right along with us and to remind you that it's you who needs us. If you lose, we'll survive and keep fighting as we always have. Never forget that."

He waited to make sure his words had sunk in before continuing down the corridor. It surprised me how easily he'd turned his back to me. I didn't know if that meant he actually trusted me or if he just thought he was quick enough to hear an attack coming. I didn't want to find out, so I silently followed after him.

He led me to a small offshoot off the main tunnel where a blanket lay folded in the corner with a layer of sand atop it. "Get some rest," he said. "Compared to my training, training with Rodric will seem like lounging around one of those fountains you keep at the palace." He moved to leave but turned back. "Know that if you betray us, you're going to wish you were fighting Rodric and not me."

With those words, he left me in the dark.

I thought he'd set up guards outside the alcove, but no one approached. He probably figured I'd never be able to find my way in the unlit tunnels, and he was right. I'd always thought I had a good sense of direction, but when your only landscape is the palace and city, there wasn't much to navigate. Not to mention you had the sun as your constant companion by whose path you could trace your own.

I was too tired to explore or fight or run off or do any number of other things Cion probably suspected I might try. I was even too tired to care if Cion murdered me in my sleep.

Although, as I laid down for the night, I slid my sword out of its scabbard and kept it in my hand just in case.

I pulled the blanket up around me. It scratched against my skin and was barely enough to keep away the night cold. I lay awake despite my exhaustion. Somewhere, sand whispered into the room, measuring away the hours. Counting down the minutes until I would have to face Rodric.

CHAPTER 10

Light spilled into the alcove what felt like mere moments after I'd shut my eyes.

I reached for my sword, which had tumbled away during the night. I blinked, trying to make out the figure.

Cion stood at the mouth of the cave with a torch in his hands. "Let's go."

I sat up and worked to focus my sleep-addled mind. My whole body ached. I just wanted to collapse back into the sand and pull the blanket over my head, but I didn't.

I double-checked that my daggers were still strapped against my calves, and I slid my sword into its scabbard. "Where are we going?" I asked as I braided my hair in a poor copy of the style Latia usually gave me for training.

"The shifting hills."

It wasn't a location I knew, but I was beginning to realize there was a lot I didn't know about the desert that had surrounded me my whole life.

Cion offered me a small cup of water and tossed me a spiked kana fruit as he led me out of the alcove. The water trickled down my throat, cooling as it went. It had never tasted so good.

And where did he even get spiked kana fruit? I took small bites off the soft red spines and tried not to show how hungry I was. Juice burst into my mouth with the first bite. I'd never recognized how much I relied on Latia for my meals.

I bet she was scared without me there. What would become of her? Maybe she'd go to work in the kitchens. I hoped Rodric hadn't kicked her out or, worse, accused her of helping me. The bits of spiked kana settled uneasily in my stomach.

I added her name to the list of those I was here to protect, to fight for, as I followed Cion.

He led me out a different way than I'd come in the night before. We climbed through a small opening in the rocks and emerged above ground. I was surprised to see it was still dark outside.

"It's a long hike to the shifting hills," he said. "It's best done when the sun is down."

He started off across the endless dunes. I hesitated for a moment, surveying the landscape. There was still no discernible landmark, no way to be sure we were headed to the shifting hills and not back to the city. But at this point, I had no other option than to follow.

Sighing, I trudged after him. I could easily pull my sword if he tried anything.

The night chill clung to me, making me shiver and producing goose bumps down my body.

"You'll warm soon enough," Cion said, falling into step beside me.

I moved a few inches away. Anytime Rodric came that close, it was usually because he had some unpleasant surprise waiting. I didn't trust Cion enough not to do the same or worse.

If Cion noticed my subtle movement away, he didn't let on. He strode confidently over the hills such that even Tamlin would have been forced to admit the desert belonged to Cion. Where I had to trudge through the sand, it seemed to part for him.

I shook my head. There was no way that rumor was actually true. He was just more used to it than I was.

Still, I couldn't help but eye him. Wind caught the ends of his loose, long hair. Dirt stained his skin. The last signs of youth had left his face and had been replaced by a hard jawline. His dark eyes hid what he was thinking. The corners of his mouth tugged upward, suggesting he laughed easily. I doubted I'd ever find out.

"Watch out for that yellow-spotted sand snake hole," Cion said as he pointed to what looked like regular sand to me.

"That's a yellow-spotted sand snake hole?" I asked, stopping to look.

"You can tell by the small depression in the sand," he replied. "And if you want to get bitten, keep standing there."

I jumped away from the hole, realizing for the first time how quickly I could've been killed out here on my own. My books and training had not prepared me for this. The drought had kept us all within the city walls—within close distance of the wells—for far too long. We'd lost our knowledge of the desert and its dangers.

"Keep an eye out for spiral cacti too," he added, and kept walking.

I wanted to ask what a spiral cactus was, but I didn't want to sound stupid.

But I couldn't think of a single topic as we walked that would keep the conversation going, that would make us feel more like allies. Every subject we had in common would either be painful for me or painful for him.

Eventually I settled on the only safe topic I could think of. Training. "I thought we were going to train," I said, "not go see the desert sights."

"First we will condition. Your best bet is to tire Rodric out. He's stronger with a blade, but you'll be faster."

I couldn't argue with his logic, so either he was a good liar or he was actually going to train me.

"Who taught you?" I asked.

"Cintric. He was a wandering nomad. He knew every hideout, every danger, every route through the desert."

"That's how you get your caravans through?"

He turned toward me, an eyebrow raised. "If you're trying to figure out our routes, I'll never tell you."

"I wasn't," I backtracked. "I've just always been curious how you found a route that is as safe as the royal caravan route."

Cion looked away. "I never said our route was safe. But the people trying to get out of here are willing to face just about anything to get their freedom."

His words struck me to my core. I'd never thought about the people who were forced to risk everything to escape Achra. Maybe it was because until Rodric had been announced as my last opponent, I'd never thought of leaving.

I'd been so focused on training to not only win the throne but to be strong enough to defeat the Desert Boys—to prove to the people they were to blame for everything and not me—that I hadn't paid enough attention to the people suffering right before me.

I'd known they didn't have water, but I hadn't realized the wells were so crowded that sometimes people waited so long that the number of buckets they were allowed dropped while they were in line. Or that the guards were not only killing people who'd demanded the original amount of water they'd been promised, they were also collecting women for Rodric.

I'd thought eradicating the Desert Boys would be upholding my promise to my mother. But there was so much more I should have been doing. So much more I hadn't seen while locked away training in the palace.

I didn't know how long this all had been going on, but I had my suspicions that things had only gotten worse under Rodric, that he was bending the entire city to his will just like he was doing to my father.

And I had to find a way to put a stop to it.

"Unless you know that feeling—of being willing to face anything to win your freedom," Cion continued, "you'll never beat Rodric, because you'll never have the intensity that will push you to keep going, knowing it's your only chance."

"I'll do anything to beat Rodric," I said. Even more so now. Because even if my father didn't know how bad things had gotten around the wells, Rodric did. And he was the one standing between me and my mother's crown—my mother's legacy. And nothing would stop me from that, from finally leading these people how she would've wanted me to.

"We'll see."

We fell into silence again. Wind picked up around us, filling the void.

Something flapped against my wrist as it brushed past my belt. It was the map I'd torn from Tamlin's book. Part of me shouted to keep it hidden, but the other part whispered that this could be the first peace offering between Cion and me, the first sign that we could eventually learn to trust each other.

I cleared my throat and held the crumbled paper out to Cion. "Maybe this would help your caravans."

Cion took the paper, smoothing it out so he could study it.

"It's a map of the desert drawn by Tamlin himself," I supplied. I pointed toward the wandering line. "That's the route he used."

He eyed me. "Is this how you were planning on finding us?"

I couldn't admit that's how I'd been planning to run away, so I merely nodded.

"Many men and women have lost their lives following replicas of this map." He folded it and handed it back to me. "As you'll see in the shifting hills, nothing in this desert stays the same for long. It's a living, breathing creature that alters and moves. Maps are no good out here."

"Oh," I said, sliding the map back into my belt.

Couldn't I see the wind reshaping and blowing the dunes even from my window? It didn't occur to me that the whole desert didn't stay the same.

"But thank you," Cion said.

And even though we fell back into silence, the iciness of it had been broken.

We continued hiking up the dune in front of us, but just as we crested the top, Cion vaulted toward me. "Get down."

We rolled down the side of the dune, spraying sand around us.

Cion landed on top of me, his hand clamped on my mouth. He held one finger to his lips, urging me to be silent.

"If she's out here, she's probably dead," a voice said from somewhere not too far away. "And if she's dead, the vultures and blood beetles have already picked her apart. We're not going to find anything."

"Soldiers," Cion mouthed at me.

I swallowed, though my mouth had gone suddenly dry. I didn't know how many were looking for me.

Sand ground into my exposed skin, but I didn't dare move.

"At least we'd get promoted if we found her," another voice said. "Rodric might even give us extra water rations."

The first voice laughed. "That's the only reason I agreed to come out here."

As they moved farther away, I couldn't help but be struck by how much these soldiers must really need the extra water if they were willing to come out here to look for me.

Cion waited until we couldn't hear anything else before slowly easing off me and pulling me to my feet. He smelled like warm smoke. Maybe from all the torches he carried around.

"I haven't seen guards in the desert in a long time and never this far out before," he said. "Normally, they won't chase us past the city gates."

"Why didn't you kill them?"

"We don't kill just because we can," he said.

"What about at the wells?" I countered.

"We only fight when we have to, when it's a matter of survival. The water we get isn't just for us. It's for the survival of all the people who desperately need it."

I eyed him. There was so much about the Desert Boys I didn't understand, or that I was starting to admit I'd possibly been wrong about.

As the sun rose higher, we trudged onward, pausing to look for soldiers.

My stomach rumbled. One spiked kana fruit as a meal wasn't enough, especially after barely eating anything since my fight in the arena.

I studied Cion's movements again to distract from the hunger pains ripping through my stomach. He swayed with the sand the way other people swayed while riding a camel. It was a natural movement that anticipated the ebb and flow of the ground beneath his feet. He barely left a trail where he walked, like he was a snake skimming the surface. He was taller than I was by about a hand's height, and his long legs allowed him to take one step for every two of mine.

I must have been staring too hard because I tripped in the sand. Cion's arm shot out to steady me.

"We're here," he said. He pulled me to the top of a sand dune.

At first, it didn't look any different from any other part of the desert we'd passed. Then, every hill in front of us shifted as a blast of wind tore through the area. Sand rolled and tossed. Buried cacti were exposed before being thrown back into a cyclone of sand. The hills would stabilize for a moment before once again spilling across each other and rearranging themselves as another gust of wind smashed into them.

Cion was right. The desert was a living, breathing creature. And it was vicious.

"Are you crazy?" I shouted at Cion over the rush of the wind. "We'll be killed if we go down there. That's worse than a sandstorm."

"You'll be killed if you go in the arena and face Rodric without proper training."

"That's not training." The sand dunes heaved upward and rained back down. That was suicidal.

"It teaches you to watch for unforeseen opponents, to expect an attack from every direction. Watch," Cion said. He took out a mask with two eyeholes and tied it across his ears so that his eyes were mostly covered and a flap fell around his nose.

Then he pulled out his sword and rushed into the fray.

"Stop." I reached out to hold him back. If he wanted to die, he could do so on his own time, because there was no way I'd find my way back without him. He brushed past my arm into the spray.

Walls of sand pounded against his body. He pushed through them. The sand shifted again, dragging him forward. A cactus appeared through the draining sand. Cion sliced through the top of the plant before its spikes could impale him.

He'd mastered how to flow with the sand. His instincts were mesmerizing to watch. His sword swung forward before I even noticed the hint of a cactus peeking out.

Eventually, he somersaulted and used the waves to push him back to where I stood. He climbed up the dune and ripped his mask off.

The sky had only just begun to lighten but sweat dotted his brow. "If you can master that," he said, smiling, "you can master anything."

I forced my mouth closed, unaware it had dropped open. "I can't do that," I said.

"Learn to use the sand and wind to your advantage."

"That's easy for you to say," I scoffed. "You spend every day walking these dunes. You're used to how the sand flows."

"Don't think of it as sand. Think of it as your opponent. You can't predict where an attack will come from. These hills will hone your reflexes faster than any sword training exercise." His dark eyes turned toward me. They had small flecks of gold hidden beneath the swaths of brown, almost as though sand had embedded itself there. Or as if he were slowly becoming one with the desert.

I pulled my gaze back toward the hills and squared my shoulders. This was a test. He was seeing how much I could handle.

Up until Rodric had entered my life, I liked challenges—liked showing my father what I could do. But Rodric's idea of a challenge was to see how long I could hold my breath in one of the fountains or to see how many times he could kick me while I fought to get sand out of my eyes.

I hadn't decided if Cion was doing the same thing, but I sensed he hadn't brought me out here for humiliation. No, Cion didn't seem like the type to waste time or energy on something so frivolous. He genuinely wanted to know if I had the reflexes of a fighter. There was only so much you could teach someone. And my fight with Rodric was in one month. That wasn't much time to train.

Cion held out his mask to me.

It smelled like sweat and leather. It squashed my nose flat, but the flap hanging down would hopefully keep out enough sand that I could breathe. I gripped my sword in my hand and stared out over the tossing hills for a moment.

"Wait until you see an opening," Cion said.

I nodded. I licked my parched lips, but my tongue was too dry to do anything.

I plunged downward after a wall of sand had tossed its mane to the side. Tendrils of sand poured down on me, trying to drag me down into the swirling mass.

Puddles of sand swallowed my legs instantly. I fought to free them but only sank lower. A wave of sand cascaded over me. I tumbled with it, losing sight of the sky. Sand pushed upward and downward before pulling me to the side. A cactus brushed along my back. I couldn't cry out because grains would have poured into my mouth and choked me as the mask flipped to the side.

The hills stabilized for a moment. I clawed in what I hoped

was an upward direction. I broke through the sand and pulled myself out just as the ground shifted again. I tried moving with the tide, running in the direction it pulled. But everything tossed into the air, including me. I fought to keep my grip on my sword.

Dunes swirled around me so thickly they obscured the sunlight piercing the desert. I landed on a mass of sand and was immediately swallowed. A whirlwind sucked me downward, the weight of it crushing against my body. My heart pounded so loudly it seemed to echo through the sand, giving it life as it slowly drowned me.

I tumbled over and over again. I jerked right and then rolled left. I collided with something solid and glanced off. The waves continued to toss. Another burst coated me in intense heat. Sunlight disappeared.

My lungs tightened as more sand crashed on top of me. I was slowly being buried layer by layer until I'd eventually be pushed down to the center of the earth.

I clawed at the sand, but my arms were packed against me. The sheets pressed down on my chest, threatening to collapse it. I tried to breathe. Sand rushed in to fill the space when I exhaled, pressing harder and harder until I thought it would break through my skin and fill me up.

The honey glaze before my eyes disappeared. Darkness overtook me.

I hit something hard as the sands shifted again.

CHAPTER 11

I thought I'd hit a cactus, but I was wrong. Cion's arms wrapped around me.

"Roll," he shouted. He heaved his body sideways, and I had no choice but to move with him. I gulped in a mixture of sand and air that did little to relieve the aching in my chest.

Sand bucked all around us. A wave rushed toward us, curling in on itself.

"Hang on." Cion gripped my shoulders and somersaulted us in the wave's direction. We barely stayed ahead of it. The upsurge was almost ready to collapse when Cion yanked me to my feet and pulled me up a slope toward a stable dune.

I dropped to my knees and ripped off my mask. Coughing, I expelled the rest of the sand from my throat. Grains rattled around my lungs with every breath, but each rush of air calmed my nerves.

Cion shook sand out of his hair and looked unfazed. He stood watching the rippling sand like I might watch the sunset from my balcony window. "Not bad," he said.

I tightened my grip on my sword, amazed I'd managed to keep ahold of it. "Not bad?" I repeated, forcing myself to stand. "You think intimidating me and showing me how much better you are is a good way to teach me?" I wobbled on my feet as wind tugged at us. "You're no better than Rodric."

I kicked sand away as I swayed down the hill. I didn't care which direction I went. It seemed no matter what I decided, something was waiting to kill me. At least if the desert took my life, it would deprive everyone else of the satisfaction.

Cion skid until he was next to me, sending a small avalanche down the dune. "I didn't bring you to show you what you couldn't do," he said. "I brought you to show you what you could do. Do you think I bring all the boys here to train? Most of them wouldn't last half as long as you did out there."

For reasons I couldn't explain, I blushed. I rubbed my cheeks, pretending to wipe away sand.

"You have good instincts, good natural movement," he continued. "I've seen you fight in the arena before. That's half the reason I agreed to train you—though Rodric taught you to fight like he does. You're built differently, and you can use that to your advantage. But you'll need to be faster, quicker. These hills can help you."

I stared over his head to where bursts of sand puffed into the air at odd intervals.

I'd always believed that only a true master of the desert could sit on the throne, and I'd thought I was one because I was strong. Because I took after my father, after Tamlin. But there was so much that we didn't know about the desert. In order to be truly strong, I'd need to master all parts of it. Just like Tamlin had done.

Cion was the only one who could help me do it.

"Fine," I said.

"Good. Do it again."

I tightened my grasp on my sword and nodded.

Cion seemed pleased I didn't object. He motioned for me to

join him on top of the hill. Once there, he pointed to our feet. "Watch the sand," he said. "See how your steps cause ripples to spread down the dune. It's only a few grains before a big wave. The hill does the same thing. Don't watch the big wave coming at you. By then, it's too late to react. Look for the small trail just before the wave. That will show where the wave is coming from." He plunged his foot in and out of the sand to show me the effect.

"That would have been helpful to know last time," I mumbled.

Cion ignored my comment. "It's the same with each opponent. If you can recognize where they're aiming, not only can you block them, you can form an attack of your own." He gestured for me to head back down into the tossing sand.

I straightened the mask on my face and plodded down the hill. I waited at the edge, watching the formations. There was no pattern to the movements. Sometimes the waves would crash together and spread outward like wings before dropping back into the sand. Other times, they'd simply toss upward and shake until they settled down into place.

I watched the hills, and then I began to see it. A small trickling of sand preceded each wave. I studied the movement over and over again before I threw myself back into the chaos.

Sand spiraled around me. It grabbed at my feet and pulled. I fought upward with every step. But every time I looked down at my feet, I lost sight of the trail indicating a wave was coming. Sand pelted me in the back, sending me staggering forward. I barely kept my footing, running to stay ahead of the tosses.

Each gust of wind brought with it more and more sand. It piled around my ankles. I tripped. A layer sprayed across my back. I rolled before any more could bury me, and then I half stumbled, half crawled until I was out of the surf. I collapsed near Cion's feet.

Grains stung my eyes and burned my throat. I wanted nothing more than to lie down and catch my breath. But I forced myself up. I shook off the sand and strode back toward the twisting pit.

This was my destiny, to be master of the desert. Rodric wasn't the next Tamlin. I was.

I watched for the trail indicating a wave and threw myself forward. I stopped watching my feet and kept my eyes on the waves. Still, sand juggled and tossed under me as I fought to maintain my balance. Every time I fell, I rolled and launched myself up before the swirling sand could suck me down.

I sped to the right on one wave before spotting another forming in front of me. I spun so I could ride that one. Ripples appeared before me; I realized just in time it indicated a cactus. I brought my sword up and cut off a portion of one of its arms.

As more cacti appeared in the surf, I worked my way toward them, imagining Rodric's face on each one. I sliced off tops and severed spines with each pass. I became lost in the dance of the waves. I'd partner with one before spinning to follow the path of the next one. Hot breath pulsed against my mask as I exhaled.

Even when I did stumble and sand clogged my lungs and filled my ears, I didn't go crawling back to Cion. I kept going, kept fighting.

I allowed the waves to finish what the initiation ceremony started, to wash away all traces of the palace. I let it claim me, make me part of itself like it had Tamlin. I belonged to the desert now.

I didn't know how long I stayed in the waves, but by the time I emerged, Cion lounged on the side of one of the dunes the wind left untouched, his hands clasped behind his head. The sun was nearly to its peak.

Sweat glistened across my face and arms as I took off the mask and tossed it to him. My legs were too shaky to hold me. I collapsed next to him.

He caught the mask and sat up. "If I didn't know any better," he said, "I would think you were raised out there in those hills."

I tried to smile, but I couldn't. I'd been raised far from the coarse sand that ground into your skin with every rush of wind. I'd grown up behind sturdy walls that kept the sand out.

I couldn't imagine what Cion's upbringing had been like. Achrans were known for being able to adapt to anything. But you couldn't truly adapt to a lack of water—always wondering if there'd be enough or when you'd run out. How many people had he watched die of thirst because of this drought? A thirst I was now experiencing for the first time.

My father had always said we didn't have to conserve water, that in order to rule we needed to be hydrated so we could think, plan, protect. He said a few buckets wasn't going to make much difference. But after seeing what I had at the well and being out here, we should've been rationing along with everyone else. And I planned to bring that up to him, to open his eyes to what we'd both been too focused to see, once I won my crown.

Once, a few years ago, I'd tried to see how long I could go without water, to somehow do my part to help conserve our resources. I'd lasted less than a day before breaking down and chugging nearly the entire pitcher of water in my room. But I hadn't been afraid then because the water had always been in view, clear and sparkling and waiting.

Out here, it was different. There was no water in sight, and the sun leered down at us, laughing at our foolishness for being out in its heat.

And my body felt it. My muscles pulled tighter against my bones, groaning with every small movement. My brain seemed to be banging up against my skull as though it were still being tossed around in the shifting hills, causing a massive headache. Even the skin on my fingers ached.

What I wouldn't give for some of Latia's coconut lotion. No wonder she was always discreetly rubbing the excess on her skin. I couldn't imagine what my skin would feel like if I'd lived out here as long as Cion. I pulled at the gold cuff around my neck, trying to dig the sand out of it.

"You want me to help you take that off?" Cion asked.

I dropped my hand away from the cuff. "The sand's not that bad."

"You'll get a rash if you let it fester in there."

The particles were already beginning to itch where they mixed with my sweat, but I didn't want him to see the cuts on my neck. "It's fine."

"I'm not going to steal it, if that's what you're worried about," he said.

I shook my head.

He shrugged. "It's your neck." He hoisted himself to his feet and brushed sand from his pants. "We should get back before the sun gets any higher."

I nodded and followed him over the dune, my legs still shaking and threatening to collapse under me. I did my best to hide it, to prove to Cion I wasn't weak.

"Watch out for that spiral cactus," Cion said.

I focused on the path in front of me. A small cactus grew in an upward spiral, reaching to my knees. It wasn't too different from some of the cacti the palace gardeners grew in big clay jars around the fountains and near the lagoon. Except it had much longer spikes.

And it seemed to be growing by the minute, twisting out of the sand.

"I used to tell the rest of the boys one would grow up around them if they didn't practice every day," he said. His tone was light, conversational. Unexpected.

He didn't seem to distrust me at all or worry I'd turn on him. Maybe he thought his skills were so good that he didn't have to worry.

He was probably right.

In a way, that helped me to relax, knowing he had the greater skill and hadn't used it against me. It made me want to trust him.

"How big do the spiral cacti grow?" I asked.

"The biggest I've ever seen was probably about this tall." He held his hand as high over his head as he could. "They topple over and get buried pretty quickly. But the spikes will go straight through a sandal if you're not careful."

"Thanks for the warning," I said. "Anything else I should be on the lookout for?"

He slowed his pace, allowing me to walk next to him. This time, I didn't move as far away.

"The usual. Sandstorms." He stared off toward the horizon. "There will probably be another one of those in a day or two."

I tried to see what he was noticing in the distance, but I couldn't figure out what made him so certain. "How do you know?"

"You can feel it in the air, in the heaviness of the sand on your feet, like even it's hunkering down, preparing for what's to come."

His knowledge amazed me, but I guess out here, you had to know when one was coming if you wanted to survive, unlike in the city where you had walls to block the worst of it.

"There are also fire-legged flies, blood beetles, and scorpions." He paused to see my reaction.

But I didn't flinch. I'd been expecting those. Fire-legged flies were a nuisance no matter where you lived, although the spider silk curtains we had up at the palace had meant I'd dealt with them far less often. The blood beetles, on the other hand, hadn't become a problem until the artists no longer had water to make dyes with. They stopped hunting the beetles, and the population had flourished since the drought started. But I'd only seen a few close to the palace.

Once while training, I'd given one of my instructors a cut on his ankle. The blood had run down his sandal into the sand. It didn't take long for a blood beetle to catch its scent and burrow upward, ready to eat its way into whatever creature was reckless enough to get injured.

And with scorpions, I'd known their danger secondhand. I'd once asked Latia about her parents; she'd grown stiff and said they both died from scorpion stings. She told me they'd been apothecaries and had kept numerous scorpions on hand because some claimed the heat of the poison would bring down a fever if it was rubbed over the body.

In fact, most scorpions I'd encountered had been raised for food, already dead and on display in the market or on my own plate, stingers long since removed. I'd only seen a live scorpion once or twice in my entire life. "Don't the scorpions keep mostly to Scorpion Hill?" I asked. Not that I had any idea where in the desert that was.

"Why? Do you want to go?" He eyed me.

It's not that I hadn't thought about it, but I had bigger things to deal with. I shook my head.

He nodded. "I just wanted to make sure you weren't going to run off and test that insane theory about royals being immune to scorpion stings."

"I have no plans to go there."

"Good," he said, "because the only way to . . ." He cleared his throat like he thought he was scaring me. "We won't be going anywhere near there. Besides, scorpions are easy to see against the sand. The real dangers you have to look out for are creatures like the yellow-spotted sand snakes, lizards with black markings, and double-taloned vultures, especially if you've fallen down a hill and appear to be dead."

"Seriously?" I asked. I'd never seen a double-taloned vulture up close, but occasionally I'd seen their dark silhouettes floating across the sky far out over the desert. I'd always wondered what was out there for them to eat. Now the thought made my stomach crawl.

"I sprained an ankle in a yellow-spotted sand snake hole my second week out here," Cion said. "I rolled down the hill and lay there trying to decide what to do. I was too ashamed to go back and tell the other boys what had happened. But after the vultures started circling, I figured I'd rather be embarrassed than be eaten by them, so I hobbled back to the hideout."

I scoffed. "You mean the great Cion wasn't born with perfect balance along with a sword in his hand?"

He shook his head. “I had to earn it. This desert tests everyone. Don’t think because you’ll only be here a short time that it won’t test you too.”

It was strange how quickly I’d forgotten I did have to go back.

I focused on my feet as we walked. “Is it truly so hard to survive out here?”

“We manage. We mainly subsist on the goods the caravans bring in. The men and women we’ve helped in the past send us supplies when we drop off more refugees. Otherwise, we eat the lizards with green spots and the insides of cacti. It’s not easy, but for most of us, it’s the only life we know.”

“You do what you must to survive,” I supplied. Even if it meant going to your enemy to team up against an even greater evil.

I felt his gaze on me. “Exactly.”

Unspoken words hung in the air between us. A moment ago we’d been having a normal conversation. I’d even call it pleasant. And I’d forgotten he was my enemy, part of the group that had killed my mother and brother.

But if I voiced the real issue between us, there was no going back. And I needed Cion. I needed his skills.

I cleared my throat and looked out toward the horizon. “Is that why you became a Desert Boy? To survive?”

“I was a Desert Boy long before I was ever labeled one. I stole buckets of water for my brother when he was sick. But I didn’t move out here”—he gestured to the sands around him—“until I was twelve. That’s when Dimic was born.”

“Dimic’s your brother?”

He nodded. “By the time he was born, our father was gone, and I could hear my mother weeping every night. She knew if there was a raid and Dimic was discovered, the guards would kill them for breaking the two-children law. I disappeared into the desert so Dimic had a chance at life."

His selflessness surprised me. In a world where people fought for their place in the well line, he'd given up his spot for his brother.

"And that's where you learned to fight?" I asked.

He nodded. "I channeled my anger over what my family went through into training. I thought if I could become good enough, I could defend my family against the guards. It wouldn't matter if there were three kids or not. But by the time I was skilled enough to come back to the city, my mother was dead of the plague, and I discovered a new family in the Desert Boys. Cintric, my teacher, was getting older. He left on one of the caravans, placing me in charge. By that point my brothers were living with me, and I realized I couldn't defend every family against the guards. But I could supply them with the water they needed."

"Where's your other brother?" I asked.

Cion shook his head. "He died out here."

"I'm sorry."

He nodded at the words and fell silent.

I didn't know what else to say, so I looked at my feet as we trudged onward.

It was hard to fathom the life Cion had lived. Stealing water to survive. Abandoning home so his brother could live. Surviving out here while his own brother didn't.

Maybe we weren't as different as I'd thought. We'd both made choices, concessions to survive. He'd taken to the desert sands while I'd given myself over to training. Both of us fighting to find our place in the world.

Those choices had pitted us against one another. Until now.

Because now we'd made new choices. We'd chosen to put the past behind us. And while there was still that edge of tension, of fighting to understand each other, I also felt an underlying understanding growing between us.

And I was starting to understand him. All those times I'd thought he was a monster, maybe he was acting to protect those he loved, to save them from dehydration and death. I couldn't blame him for hating me, for hating that by luck of birth I had all the shade, food, and water I could want—at least until I left the palace.

We were both in the fight together now. And with Cion on my side, I had hope for the first time that I could beat Rodric.

Only time would tell.

CHAPTER 12

We didn't encounter any guards on our way back to the hideout, but that was probably because the sun was well past its peak, and they knew enough not to be out in the desert during the hottest hours.

Cion gestured for me to go through the opening he'd revealed in the side of a dune.

I lingered inside the refreshing darkness. It took my eyes several minutes to adjust.

I didn't feel quite like a prisoner, and yet I didn't know where I should go either. I dug my sandal into the ground while I waited for him to show me where I should head or what I should do.

He climbed inside and secured the opening. He paused at a barrel and dipped a small cup in, careful to let any drops drip back into the barrel before offering it to me. I drank eagerly.

Cool water careened down my throat. I could've drunk the entire barrel and not been satisfied. After I finished, I handed the cup back to Cion, who took only a few small sips.

"Are you hungry?" he asked.

I nodded.

"Good. I asked the boys to prepare dinner early."

I followed him as he led to a common room. Colored tapestries had been nailed into the walls to guard against the jagged rocks while pillows were thrown over a patterned rug. Several lanterns gave the room an easy glow and a feeling of warmth.

The number of boys seemed to have multiplied. They lay across each other as I imagined the scorpions at Scorpion Hill did. Some of them could've been girls with closely cropped hair, but it was impossible to tell under all the dirt and grime. They all looked worn out.

I realized for the first time that not all of them were Achrans. One boy had the three blue triangles painted on the backs of both hands that Neribians inked on with cerelic dye at birth. It was supposed to remind them that no matter where they roamed, their home was in those mountain peaks represented on their hands, and that every time they extended their hand, whether in greeting or violence, they were representatives of all Neribians.

Another child had the typical stretchy Mesian threads tied around their ankles, probably put there by their parents. It was said when both anklets finally wore away and fell off, the child was considered old enough to be an adult in their culture.

I swallowed at the thought of how worn those anklets looked in comparison to the small frame of the child who stood before me. The desert had made these children grow up much faster than any child should have to.

I could only imagine their parents had gotten trapped here by the drought. Or maybe they'd had relatives who had escaped to the thriving Achran oasis during the Romaldihide raids on Mesia several generations ago.

Whatever the reason, they were stuck here now, covered in sand and strapped by thirst as much as any Achran. And I didn't want to think about what had to have happened to their parents for these kids to end up out here.

Everyone stopped what they were doing when they noticed our presence.

The only open space was at the back of the room, near a green cushion. For lack of a better destination, I headed toward it. Dark eyes watched me as I passed.

There was barely room to walk between the bodies, and a few of them curled away from me like I used to do from the tigers. I stepped over Dimic and another boy, who had pebbles laid out to play some game I'd never seen before, and waited for Cion to weave his way through.

When he made it through the maze, he lounged on the pillow. I sat next to him with my knees curled up to my chest.

No one spoke.

The boy next to me had eyes as big as moonstones, but his skin had an ashen tone and his lips were peeling. He held his breath when I settled into place.

I looked away.

I'd never spent much time around children; after my mother died I'd spent every moment training. But nothing my father had taught me showed me how to interact with these boys.

Several boys arrived carrying sticks holding lizards with green dots down their backs.

"One for everyone," Cion said.

A cheer went up.

I looked to Cion, confused.

"Normally we share them," he said.

"What's the occasion?"

"You," he said. He took a skewer that was passed to him and handed it to me.

The lizard had its tongue hanging out the side of its mouth. Its eyes were glassy, and its tiny claws were curled inward. I'd heard once that you should never eat a lizard whose claws weren't curled in like that. If they were extended, it meant it had died where it stood and poison had time to seep out of its green spots into the rest of the meat.

I'd never actually eaten a green-spotted lizard for that reason. I gingerly held the stick between my fingers, careful not to touch the green spots.

"You won't die if you touch them now," Cion said when he saw my hesitation.

He grabbed another skewer, and I noticed he was the last to receive his, which was a far cry from the palace where my father always was served first. Cion pulled out a knife and sawed vertically down the back of the lizard, slicing off its spots, before handing me the knife and motioning for me to do the same.

I ended up hacking off most of the meat because I was so worried about not cutting deep enough. Once all the boys had sawed off the spots, they held their sticks tightly and looked to Cion.

Cion rose to his feet. "We owe this feast to Princess Kateri," he said. "The desert can tear us apart or force us together. And it has delivered us a powerful ally, one who will help us bring down Rodric."

I couldn't help but scan the eager faces of the boys—the same ones I'd planned on using and then turning on after I won my throne. I looked away. How could I have thought that? They were nothing more than children without water. Children doing what they had to do to survive.

Cion continued. "You've each been given your own lizard in her honor tonight because I want you to be strong. Our fight is almost over." He held up his skewer and then bit the lizard's head clear off.

The other boys didn't hesitate to dig in after that.

Cion flopped back down.

"What's wrong?" he asked when he saw I hadn't taken a bite.

"You're sure it's safe to eat?"

He studied where I'd cut off the spots. "Looks fine to me." He bit a leg off of his own. "Mmmm, tastes like rat."

My jaw dropped open. "Rat?"

"I'm kidding," he said. "This is more like smoked scorpion."

"Oh," I said. I should've realized this was a delicacy to them. And that he probably had been forced to eat rat before.

"We always try to have a feast where everyone gets their own lizard after we initiate a new member," he said. "Only we weren't exactly planning on you dropping in, so we didn't have enough on hand. The boys went out today to find more."

I scanned the room. That's why they all looked exhausted. They'd spent the day looking for a feast. For me.

And I hadn't even wanted to eat the lizard.

I bit into the meat. It was hot and melted almost instantly in my mouth. It wasn't so bad. The skin had a bit of a grainy texture to it, and it did taste a little like scorpion, but it wasn't as bad as eating dried raw worms. Those exploded into small segments that felt like they crawled down your throat.

He shook his head. "They really don't joke up there in the palace, do they?"

"If we had time for jokes, we weren't training hard enough," I said. "I haven't really laughed since my mother died." And it was true. All joy had gone out of the world along with the light in her eyes.

"Don't you think she'd want you to laugh?" Cion said. He took another bite of his lizard. He'd almost finished all of it.

"I'm sure she would," I said, "but I'm sure you've noticed

that there's not much to laugh at these days." I swallowed down another hunk of flesh.

"Then you've come to the right place," Cion said. "The Desert Boys know how to have fun better than anyone else. And you could do with a little loosening up."

"I don't need to loosen up." I shoved a dangling piece of meat into my mouth. "I need to focus."

"Focus can be woven into training in a way that is fun." He licked the juice from the lizard that ran down the heel of his hand. "Dimic, bring that game over here."

Dimic did as he was instructed. He balanced a long wooden board on one hand while refusing to let go of his half-eaten lizard in the other.

He picked his way through the tangle of boys and put the game down in front of us.

The pebbles clinked together and slid into one another.

"Are you going to play?" Dimic asked, eyes jumping between us. Even in the heat of the day, his hair still stuck out on all sides.

Cion shook his head. He pulled a crumpled piece of parchment from his pocket and glanced at it before shoving it back in. "I've got someplace to be," he said. "So you're going to play her."

Dimic's smile stretched nearly across his face.

"No betting," Cion intoned.

Dimic's smile faltered. "Oh, come on. That neck cuff's probably worth more money than I've ever seen."

Cion looked down at him.

"Fine," Dimic grumbled, and began setting up the board.

I didn't like that he was leaving me here alone with the boys. Some of the looks they'd given me weren't exactly kind. I didn't see what choice I had though.

"I'll leave you to it," Cion said. He rose to leave, but he stopped to whisper in Dimic's ear. Dimic nodded solemnly and watched his brother disappear through one of the flaps that led outside.

Something about the exchange had been so secretive, so unlike the rest of what I'd observed so far. These boys seemed so open, sharing everything they had. It made me wonder all the more about what Cion was up to.

Before I could ask, Dimic's smile had returned, and he rubbed his palms together. "The name of the game is Skips."

He explained that each person took a turn flicking one of their pebbles at the rows of their opponent's pebbles, trying to knock as many as they could into the little gulley carved into the board behind the rows. This went on for several rounds, each person trying to get the most points. One point for every pebble you knocked into the gulley and ten points if you knocked them all in without any of your aimed pebbles going in as well. And you lost one point for each of your own pebbles that went into the gulley. A round was over once one player's pebbles had all been knocked into the gulley, and whoever accomplished that first got five extra points.

It wasn't too complicated, but I still felt unsure.

"You can go first," Dimic said after he'd set up the pebbles in two triangular outlines on each side of the board—one made of white pebbles and the other of darker gray ones. He handed me several round white pebbles a little wider than my thumbnail.

"I think you only want me to go first so I can't copy how you do it," I replied.

He snorted. "I'm going to win anyway," he said, "so it's not like it matters."

I rolled my eyes and then selected one pebble. I aimed toward the other end of the board, but the pebble I shot went way past the board and hit Dimic straight in the chest. It bounced harmlessly off and landed in his lap.

Dimic tossed it back to me. "You did hear the part about aiming for the board, right?" After barely glancing at the board, he flicked a dark pebble with his thumb. It crashed into the pebbles on my end and sent three of them scurrying into the gulley.

"How'd you do that?" I asked, mouth agape. He made it look so easy. I should've been able to do it, and I couldn't understand how I'd missed so badly.

Dimic proudly crossed his arms across his chest. "Focus and practice."

"You barely looked at the board."

He shrugged.

I hated to admit he really was good, and I wasn't looking forward to losing. "What does this have to do with training?"

Dimic uncrossed his arms. "It's about realizing our actions also have consequences. Look." He pointed to where his dark pebble had landed on the board in front of two white ones. "This rock is effectively sheltering the ones behind it, meaning it'll be harder to get them in later, especially without knocking mine in. It's all about thinking ahead and not blindly making moves."

He leaned in closer so the other boys couldn't hear. "Cion mostly uses it to teach the younger boys how you shouldn't go into a fight without a plan." Dimic nodded as though he'd told me a great secret then leaned away.

"Ahh," I said.

I weighed a white pebble in my hand and then took my time aiming at Dimic's darker ones.

Just as I flicked my finger forward, Dimic cried out, "Miss, miss, miss."

I was so startled I jerked to the side. My white pebble skidded off the board and onto the carpet.

"Dimic," I scolded.

He shrugged. "Cion always does that to the new kids. It teaches them to be aware of their surroundings and not just what they're focusing on."

Of course Cion did that.

"Besides," Dimic added, "I've always wanted to try it."

I rolled my eyes.

Dimic beat me three games straight. Either my pebbles ended up knocking in one or two or I shot wide.

When I'd finally had enough, I said, "All right, you win. I give up."

Dimic smiled. Somehow his hair had gotten even wilder while we were playing. He looked more like a kid now. Much more than he had the first time I'd seen him.

"Dimic," I said as he collected the pebbles in little pouches, "about the arena . . ." But before I could continue, Dimic cut in.

"Don't worry about it," he replied. "At least now I have the distinction of being one of the few Desert Boys ever to make it out of the arena alive." His eyes lit up as he said it and a wide grin spread across his face.

His resilience shocked me. Nothing seemed to break his spirit. I didn't know how he lived that way in such a harsh environment. Then again, maybe it was the only way to live in this environment—to count the blessings you have. Otherwise, the sadness and despair would crush you.

Dimic finished scooping the pebbles into their two bags. One he tied to his waist. The other he held out to me. "Can you carry this while I get the board?"

I reached for the bag, but Dimic tossed it to his other hand before I could grab it. "Too slow," he intoned.

Sighing, I reached for his other hand.

This time, he tossed it over my head. One of the boys caught it, and then all the boys were on their feet shouting for him to throw it their way.

I turned back to Dimic.

He shrugged again. "Cion thought you could benefit from a game of Hands of Thieves,"

I threw up my arms. "And what do I need to know about this game?"

"It teaches you to hone your reflexes and keep different opponents in sight."

I put my hands on my hips. "I meant, what are the rules?"

He smiled. "It only ends when you get the bag from us."

Without a word, I turned back into the fray. The boys took particular delight in showing off their skills. Some would toss it behind their backs to another kid when I lunged for it. Others shot it through their legs.

"Too slow, Princess," one supplied as I dove into the carpet, narrowly missing the bag as it soared away.

"Try harder," another quipped. They were enjoying beating me a little too much.

I was sweating by the time I caught the bag from a small kid who hadn't thrown it quite high enough.

But I'd seen the benefits of the game. Sometimes the boys

would toss it. Sometimes they would all gather into a huddle around me so I couldn't tell who passed it. I'd scramble to find it as they all pretended to throw it to someone else.

It really did keep me on my toes. No wonder Cion was as good as he was.

But I wasn't there yet. I tossed the bag back to the kid I'd stolen it from.

"Again," I said.

By the time Cion returned, I was under a pile of boys, fighting to maintain my grip on the bag I'd rightfully grabbed after a boy named Yeri tossed it behind his back as he'd done every other time. I'd been ready and snagged it midair.

Of course, Yeri claimed no one could catch one of his pitches, causing him to fight for it back.

Although it wasn't a fight in the true sense of the word. There was a lot more yanking, shoving, and name calling than actual brawling.

But above it all was laughing as the other boys joined in.

"Enough, enough," Cion called over the melee. He yanked boys off by their shirt collars.

"I see you're all getting along well," he said with a grin as he helped me up.

"Did you expect anything less?"

He looked around the room. "Well, I half expected at least one of them to pull a knife on you."

"Glad I didn't know that before you left," I said.

"I told them they could trust you," he replied. "I told them you promised not to restrict the water levels anymore."

I swallowed. I'd forgotten about the water levels. A pang of guilt raced through me. These boys were helping me, and I'd promised them nothing in return because those controls couldn't exist.

"Right," I said, unable to meet his eyes. I could always give them access to a well or something similar. Plus, I'd work to make things better around the wells too.

"Seems like I didn't need to worry about them though," Cion said. "It appears you won them over." He nodded to where Yeri was waiting for me.

"I want a rematch," he said.

I grinned and tossed him the bag of pebbles. "You're on."

"Not tonight," Cion said. "You should get to bed. The sun's almost down, and training starts early in the desert."

Yeri's face dropped.

"Tomorrow," I said.

Yeri's eyes sparked, and a grin slowly spread across his lips. "You better hope Cion trains you really good if you want to beat me."

"All right," Cion said, trying to hold back a laugh. "Time for bed."

He walked me back to my small alcove, which somehow did feel much more like mine even after only one night.

"Good night, Kateri," he said. He offered me a small smile as he turned to leave.

I watched until his shadow disappeared down the long tunnel.

But the image of his smile stayed with me because it, along with those of the boys down the hall, were the first ones since my mother's death that held warmth. They weren't like the sneer Rodric wore or the sly expression that slid across my father's lips when he knew the tiger was going to be released.

These boys shared a sense of togetherness that made their cave seem more like a home than the palace ever had. I'd just gotten my first glimpse of what a true family with siblings was like. And I liked it.

I fell asleep that night with a smile on my own face.

CHAPTER 13

When I awoke, I had no idea what time it was. The caves had a way of concealing the hour so that you never knew what was going on above ground.

But while I was awake, my muscles weren't. They pulled taut with every tiny movement I made. A pang of hunger raced through my stomach. I curled inward until the pain stopped.

When I swallowed, my tongue stuck in my throat.

Ignoring the flashes of pain in my legs, I rolled myself up and went in search of water and food.

I ducked out of my alcove and nearly ran into Cion.

"I was just coming to wake you," he said. "The sun's already well up."

"Are we not training today then?" I prayed the answer was yes.

"Not outside," he said. "There's a sandstorm raging. That's why I didn't wake you earlier. We can practice in the cavern instead." He gestured down the tunnel, but my eyes were too busy following the spiked kana fruit in his hand.

"Hungry?" he asked when he saw me looking.

I nodded.

He tossed me the fruit. "You'll get used to that."

I devoured it, not even able to slow myself enough to savor it, as I followed him to the large cavern where I'd first seen Hardesh.

Pairs of boys were practicing with wooden swords. The clacks of each hit echoed through the room.

"Higher, Adem," Cion called to one boy who had his sword so low I wasn't sure how he was managing to block anything.

Maybe that explained why when he called out his thanks to Cion, both his front teeth were missing.

"Do you teach all of them?" I asked.

"I train a few. They in turn train a few, who then teach others. Anyone who knows even one skill well can teach someone else. We use every resource we have."

A cry went up, and Cion ran toward where a boy had collapsed.

"Bring water," Cion called.

Dimic ran to fetch a bucket. Cion gently cradled the boy, and when Dimic returned he ladled water down his throat, careful not to spill a drop. The boy's eyes slowly fluttered open.

"Rest today," Cion said. "Take an extra water ration tonight."

The boy shook his head. "No, Cion. I'm stronger than that."

"No one is strong enough to go without water, and the people are counting on us to bring water to them. We can't do that if we're not strong enough."

The boy lowered his gaze and nodded.

"Everyone, take a break," Cion called as he rose to his feet.

Hardesh was sitting against the wall not far from the boy who'd passed out. A visibly pregnant woman I recalled was named Tania sat next to him, trying to coax him to eat some bread.

His eyes, which didn't seem to focus on anything, went wide when he saw me. His arm rose and shook, pointing at me as though I were a phantom that the others might not see. Several of the veins in his arm still carried the yellow coloring typical of yellow-spotted sand snake bites.

"Calm down," Tania soothed, sending me a scolding look. She wasn't much older than I was, but she was beautiful, with large, dark eyes that went along with her shining hair. She took Hardesh's hand and made soothing noises.

"She's come for me," he said. He tried to scramble to his feet. Tania easily held him down.

"It's okay." I held up my hands in what I hoped was a non-threatening gesture. "I'm not going to hurt you." When he didn't go into hysterics again, I went on. "I'm sorry about what happened in the arena."

He trembled and tucked himself against Tania.

"He hasn't been right since the snake bit him," she said. She stroked Hardesh's hair. "He's lucky he survived at all. Most don't. It's a testament to his strength." She actually smiled at me, and I wondered if she had any idea who I was. "Soon he'll start having more good days than bad. And right now, that's all we can ask for." She had one hand around Hardesh and one around her stomach.

I couldn't stand to look at Hardesh, to see how quickly the desert had knocked him down. How quickly I'd written him off.

Cion picked up a practice sword and tossed it to me, shaking me from my thoughts.

We moved away from Tania and Hardesh and took up battle positions.

"I'm used to fighting with a shield," I said.

He nodded toward the daggers strapped in my laces. "You'd be better with one of those in your other hand. A shield will only protect you from one or two of Rodric's blows. He'll target it, and once he's ripped it away from you, you'll be left exposed. That's why I was able to get your sword away from you so quickly when we met at the well. You were off balance without it. Besides, its bulk makes it harder for you to maneuver. Your strength is your nimbleness. You need to be able to move, not to stand there and take blows."

He tossed me a small wooden dagger. It was smaller and lighter than the ones strapped to my calves. I felt exposed without my shield.

"From now on, think about your sword as both shield and sword. You've got the muscle to stand up to the force of Rodric's attacks. Your dagger should go in for the killing blow. Like this."

He grabbed a practice sword and charged toward me. I met his blow, but I didn't see the wooden dagger he produced from behind his back until it was already ramming into my ribs.

"Ooof," I cried out and stumbled backward.

"Effective, right?" Cion said.

The pain in my ribs proved his point.

"How much training have you done with your daggers?" he asked as I straightened.

"I use them only if I lose my shield or sword. They buy me time until I can get back whatever I lost."

Cion appeared to mull this over. "As far as I know, Rodric doesn't carry a dagger on him. He thinks his sword is enough. It takes patience to learn two weapons, patience he doesn't have, which is why he probably never taught you to use them properly. That'll be another advantage you'll have over him. He won't be expecting to face you with two weapons in your hands."

As much as I missed having my shield to grip onto, Cion was right. I was going to need new skills, new surprises, if I was to win the throne.

"Here," Cion said, "stand like this." He moved behind me and tapped my right thigh until I brought it forward. Then his arms were on my shoulders, angling my right side forward as well. It felt all wrong. I was used to leading with my left side, letting my shield take a blow while I wielded my sword with my right.

There was no way I could learn an entirely new stance in less than a month.

I whipped my head around to see if there was another way. His face was so close to mine. His eyes lingered, the golden flecks gleaming even in the low light.

For a moment I forgot what I was going to say.

"Something wrong?" he asked, his eyebrows shooting up in puzzlement.

"I'm . . . I'm used to standing the other way," I stammered. I dropped my gaze.

"I know. And so is Rodric. Remember what I said about your sword functioning as your shield now too? You have to lead with that side. Try attacking me with your dagger," Cion said, moving in front of me.

I tightened my grip on the dagger and mimicked the move Cion had demonstrated. He ducked out of the way easily.

Then he swung back around. I barely blocked his attack. He was faster than anyone I'd ever seen. By the time I remembered to bring up my dagger, he was already spiraling away, knocking my feet out from under me as he went.

I landed with a thud on my back. A haze of sand puffed up around me. Cion waved it away and offered me an arm.

"Try again."

I accepted his hand and repositioned myself like he'd taught me.

It took me three or four tries before I even grazed his side with my dagger.

"Not bad for the famed Achran Flower," Cion said, and I couldn't help the blush that crept across my cheeks.

We spent the next hour practicing a variety of moves meant to test my skill with a dagger. Toward the end, Cion knocked my sword away. He tossed another wooden dagger toward me, and we resumed the fight. If fighting with one dagger had been hard, fighting with two was worse.

After stripping me of both daggers for the fifth time, we took a break. I collapsed next to Tania while Cion went to fetch us both a sip of water.

"You fight well," she said. Hardesh had fallen asleep with his head on her shoulder. "I hope you will have the strength to do what so many others have failed to."

I was pretty sure she was talking about Rodric, but it sounded like more. Like she was talking about everything. Rodric. The people. The water restrictions.

"That's why I sought out Cion," I said, unable to stop the image of Cion's star-riddled eyes from popping into my mind.

"Is it?" she said, her eyebrows rising in question. "Are you sure it wasn't to protect yourself?"

My eyes jumped to hers. She hid a quiet strength behind her tiny frame.

"I'm here to protect everyone from Rodric taking over Achra. I thought you of all people would understand why no one wants that to happen." I couldn't keep my eyes from going to her swelling belly.

"I do," she said, crossing her arms over her stomach. "Just remember that Cion has as much at stake here as you. He's putting his hope in you, and hope is a resource more valuable than water."

"I won't let them down."

She eyed me. "Remember that when you're playing tiger queen back in your palace."

When Cion appeared with a ladle of water, I gulped it down quickly, eager to get back to training. But Tania's words clung to me like sweat. Would I let them down? The water controls didn't exist. I couldn't change that. All I could do was deal with Rodric and better ration water after I was named queen—and rule as best I could.

Still, I cast a glance over my shoulder at Tania as I joined Cion again. Her eyes were on me.

I turned away and focused on the task Cion had just given me. He wanted to give my muscles a break, so we were practicing how to evade an attack when you had no weapon. He taught me how to roll across the sand like he did and how to skim my hands along the surface, looking for any hidden rocks I could use for weapons as I went.

We'd just finished an exercise on keeping your eyes on your opponent while searching for a viable weapon when one of the hidden entrances to the cavern was thrown open.

A small boy was blown in by a wave of sand. Cion rushed over to drag him away from the door and pulled it closed.

The boy coughed and collapsed in a pile. It was Yeri.

Cion turned him on his back. "What were you doing out there in that?" He motioned to the storm raging outside.

Sand clung to Yeri's exposed skin, making him appear paler.

"I was visiting my mom," he said. "I was going to wait for the storm to end, but I had to get the news to you. I ran across the desert to tell you."

"What news?"

"The king's cut water rations down to half a bucket a day." Yeri sucked in deep breaths and scrunched his face in pain. "That's barely enough to make one loaf of bread for a family. As soon as the storm's over, there will be rioting at the wells."

Other Desert Boys had stopped their training and gathered around.

"Half a bucket a day?" I said, although no one was paying attention to me. I shook my head, trying to gather my thoughts. The Desert Boys hadn't gone to the wells today, and they'd barely taken any water during the raid two days ago. There was no reason to cut rations. Unless the drought was getting worse.

Or unless my father was using the Desert Boys as an excuse to ration water, to make them dependent on him like Cion had said. And if that was true, maybe it wasn't far off to believe there might actually be water controls somewhere to make sure people stayed under his power.

I shook my head. That couldn't be true. Rations had been reduced to one bucket a day when I'd gone to the well to get water. And I'd caused a riot. A riot where I told everyone to take as much water as they wanted. They must've reduced our supply drastically before Rodric got things under control. That must be why my father had reduced rations.

But that meant it was my fault.

The spiked kana fruit I'd eaten weighed heavily in my stomach, and the gold cuff cut into my neck as I took a deep breath.

Or maybe this was another of Rodric's tricks. But why would my father go along with this? Why would he make the people suffer with so little water?

A thought tore through me. Because he didn't care if they suffered. I hadn't cared when rations had been dropped in the past to try and tempt a raid. Because I hadn't been the one without water. It had merely been a tactic. We'd been using our people as pawns. Like in Skips, we'd been reckless, sacrificing a few of our own pieces if it meant winning later.

But the games had to stop. Too many lives were at stake.

Another boy with a nose too big for his face pushed toward Cion and spoke, pulling me from my thoughts. "My family wasn't able to get any water yesterday because of the line. They won't survive on half a bucket. My sister's sick with fever."

"Did you see how many guards were at any of the wells?" Cion said to Yeri.

"Around twenty at the one I was at before the sandstorm hit. There might be more after the drop in rations though."

Cion sighed and rubbed his temples. "We were going to do another raid before the next caravan anyway, and we still need to deliver the water we weren't able to last time."

"But the king's going to be there," Yeri stammered.

Now it was my turn to push through the circle of boys. "The king?" He never went amongst the people. That's what Rodric was for. If my father was coming, something had to be very, very wrong.

Despite the sweat dotting my skin, goose bumps shot across my arms as my body went cold.

"He's going to make some sort of announcement from each well this afternoon."

Cion's eyes searched out mine. I had no idea what my father was up to. All I knew was that it wasn't going to be good for us—especially if Rodric was the one advising him now. If he'd already cut water rations, I didn't know what else he was planning. Was the drought truly worsening? Did it have to do with me running away? Was he simply going to hand the throne to Rodric?

"Good work, Yeri," Cion said. He moved to help him sit up, but Yeri cried out.

Cion bent low over Yeri. He pushed back Yeri's hair and scraped sand from his forehead. A pale yellow taint had taken hold underneath Yeri's skin. It slowly spread down his face.

"Bring the spiral cactus juice," Cion cried. Feet took off, pounding into the sand. "Why didn't you tell us?" Cion said, his fingers digging into Yeri's shoulders.

"I'm sorry, Cion," Yeri said. His chest shook with each word. "I was running so fast and sand was blowing everywhere. I didn't see the hole until it was too late. I was hoping maybe I'd just stepped on a spiral cactus."

Cion dropped his head against Yeri's chest. "It's okay." He pulled himself up and looked Yeri in the eye. "You're going to be okay."

"Here." Another boy shoved a clay jar toward Cion. He tipped a green liquid into Yeri's mouth.

Yeri choked and gagged.

Dimic stood next to me. He bit his lower lip so hard I thought it would bleed.

"Is that what you gave Hardesh?" I asked him.

He nodded.

"So it'll cure Yeri?" We were supposed to play another game of Hands of Thieves. He was going to be all right. He had to be.

When Dimic looked up at me, tears clung to the corners of his eyes. "Hardesh is bigger. It takes the poison longer to kill him. It's why us smaller boys have to be so careful. There's not always time."

My eyes swung to Yeri. His chest barely rose and fell. His lips had gone yellow. The veins in his arm had already turned from yellow to black. "What are you saying?"

Dimic didn't answer. He didn't need to.

With one rattling inhale, Yeri stopped breathing.

I waited for Cion to do something, to give him more of the liquid, to save him somehow. He simply held Yeri close to his chest, staying in that position for a long time. No one else moved.

Finally, Tania appeared with a blanket. "Let me." She put her arm on Cion's shoulder, pulling him away.

Gently, she wrapped Yeri's small frame in the blanket.

Cion exhaled loudly and tilted his head back to stare at the cave ceiling. "Bring the wood," he said quietly.

A few boys disappeared and reappeared moments later with stacks of wood. They arranged it in a row in the middle of a ring of rocks.

Cion picked up Yeri's body and laid it on the wood. All the Desert Boys moved forward in unison, as though they'd practiced the movement, circling the ring of rocks.

Cion picked up a handful of sand. "May the sand you walked on in life cradle you in death." He scattered the handful across the top of the blanket.

The lanky boy next to him picked up another handful. "May the warmth of the sand never depart your soul." Sand skittered across Yeri's body.

Boy after boy around the circle sent Yeri off with one handful of sand and one last wish for happiness. They stopped midway around the circle. It took me a moment to figure out why. They were all looking at me.

I was standing back from the circle. Cion gestured to Yeri, inviting me to say something.

I started to shake my head. I wasn't part of this. I didn't want to intrude on their grief. But I stopped myself. Maybe if I hadn't started the riot at the well . . . If I'd never run away . . . I owed Yeri something.

I moved forward. The boys closest to me scooted aside to make room for me in the circle. I scooped up a palmful of sand and weighed it in my hand.

"May your spirit be freer than the sands of the desert." I sprinkled the sand over Yeri's still form. It wasn't as personal a message as some of the other boys', but it reminded me of my mother and her sand dancing, about how the sand could go anywhere it pleased. It was as much as I could offer him now. But it didn't stop me from wondering what I could've done to prevent this from happening.

Once everyone had said their blessing, Cion took one of the torches from the wall and lit the logs beneath Yeri's body. "May your spirit burn brighter than the sun."

I blinked as smoke twirled around us. I hadn't realized they were going to burn the body now, so soon. They'd waited three days to burn my mother, but out in the heat of the desert, bodies rotted faster. A quick funeral was kinder, it seemed.

A few boys cried. The rest took it in stride, as if this were a regular occurrence. Maybe it was.

Only once the fire had consumed the blanket and figure inside did Cion open one of the panels leading to outside, letting the smoke out. A snarl of sand roared in on us. It twisted around me, stinging my hands, my face, my legs. The boys didn't flinch. Their eyes stayed glued to the flames that the rush of sand was slowly extinguishing, leaving behind nothing but charred ashes.

Cion shut the panel. The last bit rained down as the swirling sand cut off.

"Yeri brought us this information, and we will use it," Cion said. "Get ready for a raid."

The boys who'd been stoic a moment before leapt into action now that they had their orders. No one stopped to question Cion or to wonder if they were walking right into a trap. I pushed through the throng of boys lacing up sandals and shoving daggers into belts.

"It's too risky to go into the city," I told Cion. "It could be one of Rodric's ploys."

He moved to shove past me. "Yeri died bringing us this news. I won't let it go to waste."

"You can't be serious about going out in that storm." He had to see that more boys would die. "And do you really think it's a good idea to raid after they've just lost a friend?" I gestured to the boys around me.

Cion clenched his jaw. "These boys see more death in a month then you've probably seen in your whole life." His voice took on a darker undertone. "Haven't you ever wondered why most of the Desert Boys are so young? Most don't make it. For them, death is a way of life. Losing Yeri makes them want to fight more, not less."

I swallowed. It was clear he was trying to conceal his pain in anger, and it was clouding his judgment. "The wells will be clogged with people. It'll be impassible."

"The people will let us through and keep the guards away."

"The guards—"

"We can handle the guards." He stared me down. "Now, have you run out of excuses why we shouldn't take more of your precious water?"

"I . . . I . . ." I didn't know what to say. That wasn't it at all. I didn't want to watch more Desert Boys die. Watching Yeri die had woken something up within me, something I didn't want to name. It came to me anyway: Guilt. And shame.

I'd once again had it thrown in my face that I hadn't been taking care of my mother's people. I'd been ignoring them, looking past their dirty faces and thinning frames to blame the Desert Boys instead of doing anything to truly help them. I'd seen their thin bodies and chapped lips, but they had been as normal as the sand stretching around us. But Yeri dying wasn't normal. It took his small form rasping for breath to remind me what I should've been fighting for all along.

I had failed my mother so profoundly that it felt like the sandstorm raging outside had found its way under my skin and was tearing me apart.

Cion turned away from me toward the boys. "Everyone, grab a bucket. As soon as the storm diminishes, we'll need to steal as much as we can."

The boys accepted Cion's words and flew into a flurry of movement once more.

I stood alone with my thoughts. Was it better to raid the wells? Is that what would help my people most? If the townspeople supported them, there had to be something to it.

It was high time I found out for sure and actually started taking care of my people.

"Where are the buckets?" I asked.

Cion turned back toward me. "You're not coming."

"You can't face twenty guards and carry away water with only a few boys."

"We know what we're doing, and there are more of us than you think," Cion said while shoving a knife into his belt, next to his sword.

"You made me a Desert Boy," I countered. "I'm one of you. You know I can fight."

"But can you fight your own kind?" Cion said.

"What's that supposed to mean?"

"You'll be fighting your own guards. Can you can draw your blade against them, to kill them if necessary? Can you put the life of a Desert Boy above the life of one of your guards?"

I opened my mouth to speak but hesitated. Could I draw my blade against Sievers? I'd fought the other guards at the well, but I hadn't given them grievous injuries. They were just following commands, as misguided as those commands were.

When I didn't respond, Cion answered for me. "I didn't think so."

"The guards are simply following orders." I realized now how many must follow those orders for the extra water rations. They were choosing to follow Rodric because it's what it took to keep their families alive.

"Rodric's orders. It's either the guards or the families dying of thirst," he said. "You can't save both."

But maybe I could. I had to.

"Let me be a distraction," I said suddenly. "My presence will throw off the guards. I'm sure at least a few of them would follow me once I revealed who I am. I could lead them away from the well while you go in and steal the water."

Cion paused. He was studying me, weighing it all in his mind.

"All right," he finally said. "You can come."

CHAPTER 14

As the storm died down, we made our way to the city. Cion said they didn't usually travel in large packs like this. It would make it too easy for the guards to catch them going in and out of the main gate.

Normally, he'd send the boys to slip into the city through cracks and holes in the wall over the course of a few days or hours so they'd be in place for a raid. But with the sandstorm as our cover, he was willing to chance it, especially since we were carrying buckets of water back across the desert for the townspeople still waiting on the extra rations they hadn't received after my guards and I had interrupted the last raid.

Boys struggled under the weight of the buckets they'd covered with thick cloth and spider silk netting to keep the flying sand out, yet not a single boy uttered a complaint.

Cion had made a few boys who looked particularly haggard stay behind. Their gaunt frames probably would've blown over in the storm. And with their chapped lips, I don't know how they would have resisted chugging the water. Even I eyed the buckets, longing to quench the thirst that had been gnawing at me. I felt so dried out. I was surprised the sandstorm didn't erode me away piece by piece.

We snuck into the city in small groups after Cion gave instructions on where each bucket was to go and where each boy was to be stationed for the raid.

I followed Cion as we dashed into the city with the last few gusts of sand.

The streets were deserted, each window patched with whatever was available to keep out the sand—rugs, pieces of cloth, even a perfume bottle was wedged into a crack in a wall. Achrans were once again adapting to whatever the desert threw at us.

I got lost in the streets I'd never explored. Blasts of sand hit us every time we crossed a new street. I couldn't have been more grateful when Cion handed me one of the buckets he was carrying and rapped quietly on a door weathered by the elements.

A small man opened it barely wide enough for us to slip inside. His presumably once-dark hair had whitened considerably. Wrinkles hung across his face and under his eyes, each deeper than the valleys between sand dunes. Upon seeing Cion, his wide smile displayed several missing teeth. His lips had receded with age, curling in on themselves, and it didn't seem like he could speak anymore. He ushered us in by waving his arms.

The room was smaller than my arena prep area. Across the floor lay a rug so worn I couldn't tell what the pattern had once been. Several misshapen pillows rested in the middle around a central unlit brazier, and a tapestry that perhaps should've been hanging on the wall covered the only square window in the room.

Without any breeze, everything smelled spoiled and hot.

The man bent over and brushed the sand from Cion's feet, an honor usually reserved for royalty. Many nobles had done so with me after I'd won my first match in the arena. They were all trying to show their loyalty, to show they knew I would win. Of course, they'd be just as quick to congratulate any man lucky enough to beat me in the same manner.

But this man wasn't wiping Cion's feet to curry favor. No, there was something more meaningful in the glances he cast upward.

Cion gently helped the man to his feet. "Thank you, Lison," he said. "You don't have to do that."

The old man merely smiled and patted Cion on the shoulder.

"I'll drop this in the back." Cion held up the bucket.

Lison motioned for him to go ahead.

Cion headed through a curtain hung at the back of the room. I didn't know if I should follow or not. The man looked at me with bright eyes as he sat on one of the pillows and picked up a small hammer and slats of wood no longer than my forearm, which looked rotted and ready to break under the slightest touch.

His knobby fingers shook as he ran them over the wood until he found a spot he liked. He picked up a nail and started driving it through one piece and into another. I bit my lip to keep from telling him that he was going to break the wood.

But his smooth tapping slowly drove the nail in without breaking the planks. He picked up another couple slats and added them to his project until he'd formed a small box.

Before I could figure out what he was making, Cion reappeared through the curtain and held his hand out for the bucket I was carrying.

I hastily followed him through the curtain.

Inside, an older woman with hunched shoulders turned to greet us. In her arms was a tiny bundle.

A baby.

And all behind her on the floor were misshapen wooden boxes, each one containing a small form.

There must've been at least twelve or fifteen. But it was dead silent in the room. I couldn't understand why none of the children were crying or fussing.

Coffins.

The man had been building coffins.

But no, one of the babies kicked, and another stretched its tiny fist into the air defiantly.

I let out a relieved sigh. They weren't dead, but they were weak. And there were just so many of them. I couldn't fathom what they were doing here.

"This is Lison's wife, Insa," Cion said.

Insa was a bit taller than her husband, though her hunched shoulders hid her true height. Her hair had also gone white, and she wore it tied up off her shoulders as most women did to escape the extra heat. Her weathered skin was visible in the holes in the shoulders and hem of the simple shift she wore.

Yet she wore a smile more vibrant than the sun when she turned to look at me. She gave me a small nod so as to not disturb the infant in her arms.

"She takes care of the abandoned children," Cion continued.

His words rang through me. Abandoned children?

I knew the Desert Boys were mostly abandoned children or third children their parents could no longer hide, but they could care for themselves. These were babies, children tossed away by parents who had to make the choice of which child to give water to, which one to save, when rations got cut further because of the drought. Their only crime was being born after their siblings.

"They're so quiet," I said.

"They stop crying once they realize no one will answer them," Insa supplied. "But it's better that way. The less the guards hear, the better."

I couldn't tear my eyes away from their tiny frames.

Their mouths opened and closed, looking for food, water, something to sustain them.

Two buckets. That's all we'd brought for these children. I knew we were doing another raid, but would any of that water be brought to Insa and the infants in her care?

I'd drunk more water in a day than those infants would get in a month. I'd bathed in bucketful after bucketful of water until the tub was so full water spilled over the sides and was swallowed by the earth. I'd been so wasteful.

I finally understood what Cion had meant that first day at the well, that people would've killed to drink the bloody water Sievers had used to wash my wounds. You'll drink anything when it's your only chance at survival.

The pressure of that knowledge combined with the heat of the room and lack of water over the past few days made everything start to spin. Cion caught me before I could drop my bucket of water. He gently took it and handed it to Insa.

"Maybe you should rest a moment," she said, her eyes wrinkled with concern. She shot a look toward Cion, who nodded at her as though he agreed that was best.

"Take all the time you need," she said as she disappeared through the doorway.

I wanted to cry that I didn't need to rest. But my throat was so dry and my legs didn't want to hold me up anymore.

I knelt down next to the closest makeshift crib. A baby slept peacefully, his chest slowly rising and falling.

I never saw babies around the palace. Most nobles had maids who cared for the children, keeping them out of their hair until the children were old enough to behave.

The baby's tiny hand rested atop the woven blanket. I placed my hand over it. His face scrunched together, but he didn't wake. I wondered if that's what my brother would've looked like. I couldn't stop tears from springing to my eyes.

"Are you okay?" Cion knelt down next to me.

I hastily wiped the tears away. I'd steered away from this topic on purpose. "It's nothing."

"No, something's wrong. What is it?"

I looked at him. His face held the same concern Insa's had. I wanted to ask him why the Desert Boys had killed my mother and brother, two innocents in this fight. I wanted to believe we could somehow move past it, that these past few days had changed things. But they hadn't.

I shook my head and looked away.

"Kateri," Cion said. "Please tell me."

"I . . . was just thinking about my brother." I shoved off the crib and moved toward the door. "We should go before the other boys miss us."

But Cion didn't move. He stared down at the baby in front of him.

"Your brother?"

"Forget I brought it up," I said, moving toward the doorway. But Cion's next words stopped me cold.

"What brother?"

My stomach twisted. How could he pretend not to know? Cion had said he'd joined the Desert Boys when he was older, so maybe he wasn't part of the raid on the palace. But he had to have heard about it.

I swallowed down my anger and straightened my shoulders. Defeating Rodric was more important than having it out with Cion.

Realization dawned in Cion's face. "You can't believe the tale that claims the Desert Boys killed your mother and her baby."

I slowly turned around. Sweat trickled down my back. I could feel the camaraderie melting between us as he faced me.

"Are you saying they didn't kill them?" He should've at least been able to admit it.

"It never occurred to you to question what you were told?"

I shook my head. I didn't know what he was talking about.

"You really think the Desert Boys raided the palace even though they'd never gotten inside before or since then? You think they moved past all the guards without a single one noticing? And you think the only thing they would take from the palace is the life of a woman and child?"

His words pounded through my head. They struggled to fit in with what I knew of the past—of what I knew about the Desert Boys now.

"The Desert Boys didn't kill your mother and her baby," he said. "Your father killed his newborn daughter and the wife who didn't produce any sons."

CHAPTER 15

"How can you say that?" Heat seared through my veins. I clenched my hands into fists. My fingernails felt sharper than tiger claws as they pierced into my skin. My father may have done terrible things, but he wouldn't have done that. He couldn't have. Not the man who raised me, the one who tended to my wounds.

"The same man who cuts off well access to control the people wouldn't kill his own wife to avoid making himself look weak for having another daughter?" he said.

"He didn't have a daughter. He had a son."

Cion straightened. "It was a girl."

I shook my head. "You're lying."

"My aunt was the midwife called in to assist at the birth." His eyebrow arched up.

My mind reeled, trying to make sense of his claim, weighing it against the truth I'd staked so much upon. All I could muster was, "You're trying to turn me against my father."

"Isn't that why you're here?" he said. He gestured around us. "You've already betrayed your father."

My hand twitched toward my sword as the rest of my body went stone cold. No. I hadn't betrayed him—I'd been finding a way to impress him. I was going to show him the desert chose me. I was going to loosen Rodric's hold over him and prove my worth because he and I were in this together. My father loved me. Didn't he?

But then why had he chosen Rodric?

Cion's eyes tracked the movement of my hand, but he made no move for his own sword. "My aunt had gone out to the balcony to dry some of the sheets used in childbirth. Through the curtain, she saw your father suffocate your mother before doing the same to your sister." There was no deception in his voice, only pain. His eyes drifted toward the children at his feet. "I wasn't a Desert Boy back then. I was just a child. But I saw the look on my aunt's face when she rushed down from the palace. She still clutched the bloody sheets to her chest like she was holding on to the last shreds of her sanity. She hid in our house, afraid to speak about what she'd seen. My parents had sent me to bed, but I heard every word, every description of how the king had wrapped his hands around his wife's neck and pressed his thumbs into the flesh of her throat as she lay weak and bleeding, unable to fight against him.

"I can still hear the sobs my aunt let out when she described the way your father smothered your sister. He picked her up like she was a snake that might bite him. I recall my aunt had run so quickly from the palace she'd made her bad foot worse. My aunt's wails had lasted the entire night, but I never learned if they were from the pain in her foot or from what she'd seen. Because the next morning, she was gone. The Desert Boys had come in the night and spirited her away. For weeks afterward, the captain of the guard would harass my father, thinking he knew my aunt's location. Eventually, one night, just as the Desert Boys had taken my aunt, the guards took my father. I never saw him again."

"No." My stomach tightened. I tried to swallow, but my throat was too dry. "You're lying." He had to be. My father wouldn't do that. He couldn't have done that.

"You can ask my aunt—my Bala—when we get back to the hideout. The woman you met your first day, that's her. She came back to help Tania make the crossing in case she goes into labor. She'll tell you . . ." Cion reached out to me.

I moved away. "Don't touch me," I growled.

I needed time to think. To find the lie in his words.

Tiny children slept all around us. I looked at all their miniscule forms as heat pressed in around me, making my skin sticky and unbearable. I paced the room, running my fingers through my hair. The room was too hot to think.

The children's faces blurred together as I spun past, faster and faster. Who could kill such a small, innocent, defenseless creature?

I froze. Out of Cion and my father, who was more likely to kill a child?

I looked from Cion to the babies. We were here helping them, saving them.

No. I shook my head. Cion wouldn't have cared about a royal baby. He wouldn't have wanted another ruler on the throne like my father because . . .

I didn't want to finish that thought. I clamped my eyes shut, hoping it would go away. It didn't. They didn't want another ruler on the throne like my father because he was cruel. Because maybe he had it in him to kill his own daughter to cover up a perceived weakness. Because there are no weaknesses in the monarchy. Isn't that what he'd told me over and over again as a child?

I took ragged breaths. It was such an old belief that not fathering sons made you weak. Could my father really still put faith in it? Could he really have killed my mother and his own child? I cast around for some reason, some flaw in Cion's explanation that would signal he was making this all up, but I just kept coming back to my childhood.

My father had barely tolerated me when I was little. It was only after my mother and sibling had been killed that he finally paid attention to me, turning me into a fighter. He'd thrown himself into training me. Because I was the only way to prove his reign was not weak.

I could still remember him standing before me, telling me the Desert Boys had killed my mother and brother. His hand had rested heavily on my shoulder. "You must not cry. Your strength will define you from this moment. You must not show weakness. You must be strong enough to help me find and kill the Desert Boys, and you must be strong enough to win in the arena, to secure our legacy."

I had nodded numbly. But my father's words spread through my body faster than scorpion poison. That was when I vowed I'd be so strong that no one could ever take someone from me again. In the middle of the desert, my heart had turned to ice. My father would never again have to tell me to be strong. I would be strong for my mother. I'd keep my promise to her. I'd be strong enough to fight back, to protect her people.

But if what Cion said was true, all those years I spent training to make my father proud meant nothing. I meant nothing to him. I was just his last chance at keeping his legacy alive. That's why my father hadn't killed me too. It would taint his own rule to lose both his children. Kings had been murdered far too often after failing to produce heirs or because they'd lost their heir to the desert. The traitor always justified their actions by saying if the desert had taken the king's children, it must not want their line to rule. They would've come after my father next if I'd died, claiming the desert had already cut off his line. That's the only reason he would've kept me.

No bruise or cut I'd received in the arena hurt more than this realization. And the more I thought about it, the more Cion's words took hold in my mind.

How could the Desert Boys have gotten into the palace unseen? Why weren't any guards hurt in the attack? Why would they only kill a woman and her child?

I sat down by the makeshift cribs as the certainty of it rushed through me. My stomach leapt into my throat. I fought to keep from throwing up.

I looked up at Cion.

How could I have been so blind? How could I have not seen what had been right in front of me?

I hadn't wanted to. I trusted my father. I was going to make him proud because it was up to me to replace everything we'd lost.

But only I had lost something, something my father had taken from me.

And this whole time I'd thought Rodric was poisoning my father against me. But he didn't have to. My father already had that venom inside him. He was just better at concealing it.

"I didn't know," I finally said to Cion. Tears slid down my cheeks from some reserve I didn't know I had. I tried to wipe them away before Cion saw.

His knelt down in front of me and gently clasped my chin, turning my gaze toward him. "We Desert Boys have a saying about tears," he said. "We say that crying is good, natural. It's returning the water you've taken from the earth."

I turned away. "Emotions make you weak, and the weak don't survive."

"Is that something your father taught you too?"

I nodded, not trusting my voice. Not trusting anything anymore.

Cion shook his head. "It is our emotions that give us strength. They are what drive us to make ourselves stronger."

I prayed he was right, because a storm of emotions was blowing through me. Disbelief. Anger. Hatred. They spun around and around, each fighting to overpower the other.

"Stay here," he said softly. "I'll come back for you after the raid. It'll give you time to think about things. I'll have Insa check in on you." He rose to leave.

Too numb to respond, I stared down at the tiny baby next to me. It still hadn't woken up. Maybe it never would. Maybe it would die like everyone else. Like Yeri. Like my mother. Like my sister.

Unless I helped it.

Unless I changed everything.

I may not have been able to save my mother and sister, but I could save these children. This was no longer about having made that promise to my mother. It was what I wanted, what I needed to do.

"Wait," I called out to Cion.

He turned back, one hand on the curtain to the next room.

I wiped away the last of my tears. I would shed no more for my father.

I was done being left behind and kept out of decisions by the man who killed my mother. I didn't want his strength anymore. It was time I found my own.

"I'm coming," I said. "These people need our help, and I'm not going to sit by while they slowly die of thirst."

I couldn't stand back anymore and let my father drain the life out of these people—my people—like he'd done my mother and sister. I climbed to my feet and stood before Cion, forcing him to look at me, to see the fire burning in my eyes.

Cion studied me for a moment.

I clenched my jaw and stared him down, daring him to tell me no.

Finally, he nodded. "Then let's get going. The well's this way."

CHAPTER 16

Rage still burned through me as I walked alone into the square. Bodies were smashed into every available space. Sunken eyes watched me warily as I approached, wondering if I was going to shove myself in front of them or steal the ration coins they clutched in their hands.

"Water," voices rasped, holding buckets in the air.

"Stay back," a voice called. "Form a line."

It was like everyone had scuttled out like scorpions, hoping to be the first to the well after the storm. In this crowd, it'd be nearly impossible for the Desert Boys to make a quick entrance and exit. But Cion had said the crowd would part for them, and if they didn't, the boys were good at ducking under arms and through small gaps.

I couldn't see Cion and the Desert Boys on the other side of the square waiting for my signal, but I knew they were there. The plan was to wait until after my father spoke and left the area, hopefully taking guards with him.

I still hadn't decided if I was going to let my father leave that square alive. If anyone deserved to be thrown into the arena with two tigers behind the doors, it was him. But today, I felt more powerful than those tigers and had already passed judgment on him. So I ignored the protests of the crowd as I shouldered myself closer to the front. I wanted a good view. If my father was going to torture these people, I wanted to be close enough to stop him. I wanted to be close enough to kill him.

I waited with the crush of bodies. The whole mass swayed and shifted as some tried to push to the front while others gave up and moved backward. Elbows caught me in my ribs and side. Feet stomped on my exposed toes. It was a constant battle just to stay on my feet with the sun beating down from overhead and the people crushing me from all sides.

Sweat slid down my collarbone, but I didn't take off my cloak.

Finally, a tall figure pushed through the crowd, and people parted for him and the trail of guards at his heels.

The crowd stilled. Wind passed through, dragging the edges of tunics and tendrils of loose hair to the side. Everyone's eyes stayed forward.

My heart beat twice as fast, begging me to release the energy building like a sandstorm in my chest.

I wasn't sure what I was expecting when I saw my father again, but his face hadn't melted into a grotesque imitation of the snarl Rodric often wore. He was still the man I'd grown up with. A man who did cruel things. A man who'd murdered my mother out of his own fear of weakness. A fear he'd instilled so deep in me.

You could tell by his gait he didn't consider himself like these people. He walked with his shoulders thrown back as if the pounding sun didn't beat against him. He heaved himself onto the edge of the well. It was the same well I'd fallen into not days before.

He shook back his hair. The crown atop his head gleamed as he surveyed the crowd. The key he used to draw back the tigers' chains was in full view and weighed heavily around his neck. No one here would know what the key was for. But I did, and it was a stark reminder of what the Desert Boys would face if they got caught.

Everyone went silent.

Instinctively, my hand went to my sword hilt.

My father had taken up the same exact position, a constant reminder of both his skill and power. I released my grip and clenched my hands into fists instead, refusing to mimic him, to do anything like him ever again.

"My people," he began, "as you've heard, water rations have been cut to half a bucket a day."

Shouts went up from the crowd.

He waited for them to quiet before he continued. "You have only the Desert Boys to blame for this. They nearly drained this well." He gestured to his feet. "There's barely enough left for anyone."

"Lies," someone called out from the crowd.

My father straightened. "Bring him." My father motioned to two soldiers.

The man tried to fight back. A woman clung to him, pleading with the soldiers not to take him, but they wrestled him forward and made him kneel before the king. I tried to push ahead, to get closer. But the crowd had closed ranks, as though by blending together it would be harder to pick out individuals.

My father beckoned the man to rise. "Take a look for yourself. Tell me if you see any water in here."

The man stood, casting wary glances at the crowd behind him. He took tentative steps closer to the well and peered in.

"Tell them what you see," my father said.

The man turned back to the crowd. "There's . . . there's nothing! No water as far down as the eye can see."

My father held up his arms as if that proved his point.

The crowd let out a roar. They threw their fists into the air and cried for water despite what the man said. My father ignored them, and with a flick of his wrist he sent the man back to the crowd.

It took me a moment to wonder why he hadn't killed the man outright for calling him a liar. But it was because he was playing his role of the fair king. The good king. The one they needed. Oh, he'd deal out justice, but it was in the form of the arena. So it was never him punishing the people. It was the tigers. It was their own choices.

He could play the benevolent king when he needed to, like now, when he wanted to turn everyone against the Desert Boys. Because there was no way the Desert Boys had emptied that much of the well. I'd been there not days before. The water had been so high it hadn't taken me long at all to climb out.

Even if Yeri had been at the well where I'd caused the riot, my actions could have lessened the supply, but they wouldn't have depleted this well. Nothing would've. Not that fast. Not even the drought.

The one and only time the wells had gone dry was at the very start of the drought, before I was even born. But all the records said the water levels had decreased slowly, that there had been a noticeable decline over several weeks as the wells refilled less and less each night.

The only ways the wells would drop that drastically would be if the drought had reached a terrifying new level or if Cion was right about there being water controls.

My father didn't look worried about there not being enough water. He wasn't telling people to conserve and prepare in case the wells went dry. In fact, the more I thought about it, he was never worried about us having enough water in the palace.

No, he'd once again blamed the lack of water on the Desert

Boys. Because he wanted the people to turn against them. But in order to do that, he needed to ensure the water levels would be low enough to be convincing—low enough to control these people.

Which meant Cion had to be right about the controls. About everything.

Rage blinded me as I started to elbow through the crowd. This was going to end here.

But I stopped when I heard my name.

"The Desert Boys haven't just taken our water," my father continued. "They've also taken Princess Kateri."

A gasp went up from the crowd.

"If you see her, alert the guards immediately. And know this . . ." He paused and eyed the crowd.

I was far enough back it would be hard to see me. Still, I ducked my head when my father's eyes passed over me—though I had nothing to worry about. His eyes held no recognition. I was one of them now, part of the masses, covered in dirt with lips chapped by thirst.

It was obvious now why he always insisted we wear white. He gleamed like a beacon atop the well amongst the seas of muted browns and tans around him.

Untouchable.

"If it's discovered that any of you are concealing her or helping them," he finally continued, "my captain of the guard will deal with you."

He threw back his shoulders. "Rest assured my captain of the guard and his men are doing all they can to recover her. She will be found. And if you're the one to find her and bring her to us, you will be rewarded."

With a crook of his finger, my father motioned for a soldier to come forward. The man carried a carved box roughly the length of his forearm. My father threw open the lid. Thick golden ration coins gleamed in the sunlight as the soldier held it above his head for all to see. There had to be at least a hundred coins in there. Maybe two hundred.

Murmurs traveled through the crowd. People stood on tiptoes to get a better look.

My father motioned again, and the soldier snapped the lid back into place.

"But if she is not returned, things will only get worse. So think about what is best for our people, for your families." He looked down on us all once more. Then he leapt off the well and pushed through the crowd in my direction.

People pressed tighter against one another to make a pathway. I somehow ended up on the edge of the crowd. I swallowed, all moisture gone from my throat.

My father sauntered right toward me, unaware of my presence. Unaware of the suffering around him. Of the suffering inside me. The suffering he'd been causing for years by controlling the water levels and letting us all think there was a drought when he could've ended it.

My hand went to my sword.

But just as I was about to pull it, a small hand covered mine. I looked down to see Dimic.

He shook his head. His dark eyes stared intensely at mine, refusing to look away. "If you die," Dimic said, "we all die."

I stared at him, puzzled by his words.

"You're our hope. You're the only one who can fix this, the only one who wants to help us and has the power to do it. Don't throw it all away for revenge."

Somehow I got the sense those last few words weren't his, that they'd been spoken to him sometime in the past. And not only just to him, but to countless Desert Boys just like him.

They were counting on me now.

I eyed my father and his contingent of soldiers. Could I take them all on? Or would they strike me down before I could even reach my father, before I could even make a difference?

I let go of my hilt.

Dimic nodded, assuring me I'd done the right thing. "We'll wait on your signal," he said.

"Should we even raid? How do we know there's any water left?"

Dimic gestured to the crowd. "He wouldn't leave them with nothing. Otherwise, they'd turn against him altogether. There's always some water. It'll just take longer."

I nodded as he disappeared back into the crowd. I hoped he was right and that this wasn't a lost cause.

I ducked my head as my father swept past, his soldiers trailing behind him.

He didn't even eye me as he went by. Not that I should've expected it. Even I'd never really taken the time to look at the people on the streets. To see the way their shallow cheeks sunk or notice how many of their lips bled from lack of water.

I swallowed down the fire inside me, storing it away.

As soon as my father was gone, people spread out to fill the aisle he'd used. I let them push past me, fighting to get closer to the well.

Somewhere a guard shouted again to form a line. I scanned above the crowd. It didn't look like any of the soldiers stationed around the well had gone with my father like Cion had hoped. I prayed he was right that his boys could take on fifteen guards. Well, hopefully less than that after I played my part.

All I had to do was get them to chase me. Cion had drawn out a map that I'd tried to memorize, of the best route that would lead them far enough away while still allowing me to circle back and meet them at the gate.

My father's announcement had complicated that. If I went up there and announced myself hoping the guards would follow me, I'd have a mob on my hands. These people didn't know I was working with the Desert Boys. They'd turn on me as soon as they saw me. Two hundred ration coins would change their lives forever.

My palms grew sweaty as I debated what I should do. I scanned the crowd around me. I was walled in on all sides. I couldn't see Cion or any of the boys. Why hadn't I thought to mention it to Dimic?

The only thing I could think to do was weave my way out of the crowd and regroup, because they'd never get any water if there was a mob fighting to turn me in.

I turned and pushed back through the mass. People were just as unwilling to part for someone attempting to leave as they were for someone trying to cut in front of them.

I squeezed between pressed bodies while fighting to keep my gaze downward. Elbows rammed into my ribs. Buckets whacked my thighs. Someone careened into my side. I bumped into a man on my left. People were starting to shove each other.

The crowd shifted. Individuals crashed into me. I stumbled into a woman on my right.

I looked up to apologize, but the words froze on my tongue as a breeze ruffled my hair. My hood was puddled around my neck. The woman's eyes went wide. They stared directly at the golden cuff around my neck before going to the sword belted over my gladiator gear.

"It's you," she whispered.

"Please," I begged, trying to back away but getting nowhere.

"It's Princess Kateri," she squealed. "I found her." Her arm shot out and wrapped around mine.

I jerked out of her grip. But when I turned, a man grabbed me. I tried to run, but bodies pressed in around me. The man's arms snaked out and coiled around my neck, pulling me into a headlock. My golden neck cuff crushed into my windpipe, cutting off my air supply.

He strong-armed me toward the soldiers.

I let out a strangled cry and kicked at his knees while digging my fingers into his forearms. He responded by tightening his hold around my throat. I gasped for breath.

I squirmed and kicked, trying to tangle my feet with his to bring us both down. He wrenched my head back, squeezing even more. The air in my lungs burned hotter and hotter. The crowd hazed out of focus.

I clawed and pulled at his grip until my arms felt too sluggish to move.

The man shouldered and elbowed his way through. Hands reached out from every direction as though they thought just touching me would somehow entitle them to the reward. Hairs were ripped from my head. My cloak tore. Someone spit in my face.

Worse were the insults they lobbed at me: Snake. Palace rat. Murderer. Eventually their voices all ran together, a cacophony of noise that reverberated over and over in my mind with the sound of my rising heartbeat, which slowly drowned out everything.

We burst into the circle the guards were maintaining around the well.

The soldier who'd been on the well rushed over carrying his spear.

The man dropped me at his feet. "There's the princess. Now I want my reward."

I lay there, struggling for breath. I wanted nothing more than to get the golden cuff off my neck, to feel cool air over my skin. But I couldn't even bring my fingers up to undo the clasps.

"Shackle her," the soldier said.

I was rolled over and a knee pinned me to the ground. My hands were ripped forward and chained in front of me. Two soldiers yanked me to my feet, propping me up between them. They must've been fed a different story by Rodric than the one my father had spouted in the square if they knew I wasn't going to go easily.

"Move out," the soldier called. "Take her up to the palace."

"What about the well?" one of the soldiers holding me asked hesitantly.

"We're about to get promoted," the first soldier replied. "I don't care what happens to the well as long as we get her through this crowd and up to the palace."

"Where's my reward?" the man said, stepping forward.

The soldier studied the man for a moment. "Of course." Then he took his spear and rammed it into the man's stomach.

I cried out, watching while the man's wide eyes instantly turned to glass.

The soldier ripped the spear away and faced the crowd as the man collapsed in front of him, blood mingling with the sand. "Does anyone else want to claim the reward for Princess Kateri?"

The square had gone eerily quiet.

"I didn't think so." He turned back to his men. "Let's go."

The two soldiers dragged me in the direction I'd come from, which at least took them away from Cion's assigned location. Maybe he'd seen I'd been captured and made a run for it.

Then again, I was drawing all the soldiers away from the well. I'd failed at everything else, but maybe I'd done just enough and he'd risk the raid after all. If there was even water to be had.

But that meant I had to figure out how to get away on my own before we reached the palace, because every step we took was another second gone, another move closer to Rodric.

I took a steadying breath to drown out the pulsing in my head.

From what I could see, there were roughly fifteen soldiers around me. They hadn't thought to take my sword away, and they'd shackled my hands in front of me. If I could break free from one soldier, I could draw my sword. I wasn't sure how well I could yield it with my hands bound, and fifteen was a lot to take on at once. But if they wanted me alive, they might be reluctant to fight too hard. That would have to be my advantage.

I scanned the crowd up ahead looking for a break, for the right moment to try my luck. It wouldn't do any good to escape only to have the crowd converge on me again.

The soldiers in front shoved people out of the way with their spears, while the rest of the men closed ranks around me, keeping me from view, from grabbing distance. They didn't want anyone taking their prize.

Up ahead, I thought I saw a break in the crowd. I was just about to trip the soldier on my right when a familiar voice sounded.

"Why aren't you guarding the well?" Rodric barked at the guards.

If getting caught wasn't part of the plan, running into Rodric surely hadn't been part of any preparations. I tried to go for the soldier's leg. He buckled slightly, but he didn't go down or loosen his grip.

At the sound of commotion, Rodric pushed through the contingent of soldiers, the head soldier quickly at his heels.

A cruel smile spread across Rodric's lips. He crossed his arms across his chest.

"I knew she wouldn't last long outside the palace," Rodric said. "Even the famed Achran Flower dries up without water after too long."

I spit in his face.

He wiped it away with a swipe of his hand and leered forward. "I wondered how you survived out there all alone. Now I see it's because you're just like a yellow-spotted sand snake, attacking everything and hiding away in holes to stay alive."

"I survived," I replied, "because sand runs in my veins."

His hand squeezed around the cuff encircling my neck, making the edges dig into my skin. He brought his face up against mine. His acrid breath pounded against my face.

"Do you remember those cuts I gave you?" He squeezed harder for effect.

I tried to gasp. My shackles clanked as I brought my hands up to his, trying to pry it away.

He laughed. "I will do that to every inch of your body after you've given me a son or two. And I'll make sure you're still alive when I throw you into the desert. Then you'll really know what it's like to have sand in your veins." Sweat trickled down his forehead. "Only someone who comes from the desert, like I did, can rule this city."

As he squeezed, the veins in my throat felt like they were tangling around my airway. I dug my fingernails into his hand. He didn't notice. And he didn't loosen his grip.

The already hot air in my lungs felt like it was burning through my insides layer by layer.

He was actually going to kill me. He didn't care about the arena.

But then a voice cried out, "It's a raid!"

His grip loosened immediately as his eyes darted over my head. "No," he whispered. His eyes flew back to me, suddenly piecing it all together. "You're with them." He let out a cry of rage and flung me toward the soldiers. "Get her back to the palace."

I threw a glance over my shoulder. Cion was perched atop the well handing a filled bucket to a line of boys. The bucket was passed down the line, and the boy at the end grabbed it, snapped on a makeshift lid, and disappeared into the crowd so that the line got shorter.

Rodric and several soldiers raced toward the well.

The closest guard hauled me away from the square. I elbowed him and kicked the one on his left, which afforded me room to draw my sword.

The shackles awkwardly pulled against my wrists.

The circle of guards around me spread out. These men knew what I was capable of. Or at least they thought they did.

But after seeing those children and the Desert Boys gaunt with thirst, after watching Yeri take his last breath, after learning what my father had done to my mother and sister, to these people, fire was raging within me. Not fire. Heat. The very life of the desert itself. I let it loose on the guards. I struck out at the closest one, catching him in the leg. I didn't wait to see him go down. I twirled and met the attack of another, driving him backward until another guard came at me. I parried his attack and landed a kick to his chest. My world became a blur of metal and blood.

When the final guard went down at my feet, my chest was heaving.

At least I didn't have to worry about the crowd. They'd scattered as soon as Rodric pulled his sword. I could hear him shouting curses at Cion somewhere amongst the chaos of Desert Boys fighting guards.

Dimic appeared by my side. "Time to go." He grabbed my wrist and produced a piece of metal. He shoved it into the shackle keyhole. After a moment, it popped open, sending the chains clattering to the ground.

"Thanks," I said, shocked at how quickly he'd removed them.

"I'm the best lock picker out of all the boys," he bragged.

"I'm just glad you came for me at all," I said, rubbing my wrists.

Dimic gave me a sidelong look. "You're one of us. We always help each other."

We headed back toward the well where the fighting was the thickest.

Cion had Rodric pinned against the well. But more guards were pouring into the square. One headed straight for Cion.

"Cion!" I cried. He turned just in time to fend off a blow, but it also meant that he'd had to release his hold on Rodric, who used his bulk to smash into Cion's shoulder, sending him spiraling to the ground.

Without thinking, I rushed toward him. I stopped the arc of Rodric's blade before it could connect with Cion's neck. "Your fight is with me," I said. I pulled my blade back, drawing Rodric's attention with it.

"It would have been with you, if you hadn't run away," Rodric said. "I'm surprised you survived at all under the Desert Boys' water rationing system. I thought you would've dried up by now."

While he spoke, Cion struggled to his feet behind him. Dimic had appeared at his brother's side and deflected the attacks of the closest guards.

"You're going to regret coming here today," Rodric continued. He advanced toward me. I watched his wrists for any movement that might betray his next move. His arm twitched, and I brought up my sword to fend off a blow that didn't come.

Rodric's eyes went wide, his mouth gaping open.

Behind him, I saw Cion slice a small dagger across Rodric's side. Drops of blood stained the sand. It wasn't a deep wound. No worse than the one I'd gotten in the arena.

Rodric roared and swung his blade in a circle hoping to catch either Cion or me.

"Go," Cion shouted, using Rodric's unbalanced movement to knock him aside. Dimic ran for the other end of the empty square, but I couldn't leave Cion behind.

"Come on," Dimic shouted, frantically motioning with his hand while casting glances at the line of guards. "He can take care of himself."

As if to prove Dimic's point, when Rodric lunged for Cion, he sidestepped and let Rodric crash into the guards.

I didn't wait to see what Rodric would do next.

I ran.

Cion caught up quickly. He led us through a maze of streets before pausing at a squat building with an old barrel outside.

He leapt on top of the barrel and hoisted himself onto the roof. Dimic climbed next. Cion held his hand down to me, and just like during my initiation test, I took it and hauled myself up.

We jumped across rooftops and flew over alleyways.

When we reached the last house, I didn't turn back to look at the palace. I plunged off the edge with all the other boys and ran past the crumbling gates and out into the desert.

CHAPTER 17

By the time we'd made it back to the hideout, all the Desert Boys had returned from dropping off buckets of water around the town. And to my surprise, they were all clutching abandoned bits of wood or broken shutters.

"How many injured?" Cion asked.

Dimic stepped forward. "Liten got a bad cut on his stomach and Rivel got his nose bashed in, but Tania and Bala are seeing to them. Everyone is accounted for." He paused for a moment, tightening his grip on the wooden board he held. "Can we go?"

All eyes turned expectantly to Cion.

Cion seemed to be mulling something over. After a pause he said, "Okay."

A loud cheer arose from the Desert Boys, and they scuttled out one of the entrances like a pack of scorpions.

"Wait," Cion called. The boys froze. "Rodric will be angry after our raid today. Angrier than usual." Cion's eyes flicked in my direction before he continued. "No one goes into town until I say so."

He waited until each of the boys nodded in turn before tilting his head toward the door. The boys rushed out.

He turned to me. "You should come with us."

I didn't admit I'd been looking forward to resting after the raid. My throat still stung where the cuff had dug into it, and I was the only one not used to climbing up and down sand dunes on a daily basis. Even with all my training, it was difficult. Not to mention I felt like I could gulp down all the water in the oasis and still be thirsty. But I kept my mouth shut. I knew there were people worse off than me.

"Where are you going?" I asked.

"It's a surprise."

I rolled my eyes. He never made anything easy.

"I don't know if I can handle any more surprises today." My mind was abuzz with thoughts of my father now that my body was slowing down. I couldn't decide if it was better to keep moving, to keep going so numbness didn't overtake me, or if I wanted that numbness to drown out what I'd learned about my mother's death. "I'm worried about what my father will do now that he knows I'm working with you. Maybe we should stay here and plan."

"He can't do anything different from what he's done to us for years. We survived then, and we'll survive now," Cion said.

"How can you dismiss it that quickly?"

He offered me a small smile. "We never know what the king or Rodric is going to do. We only survive one day at a time. That's all we can do. That and celebrate our small victories."

"What victories?" It didn't feel like we'd won anything. Maybe some water, but at what cost? We'd lost Yeri, there were still so many without water, and my father had put a price on my head.

"We're still alive," Cion said. "We're still fighting."

"Yeri's not," I said quietly.

Cion hung his head. "We can't focus on what we've lost or the weight of it will bury us faster than the sand. We have to focus on what's still to gain. We have to focus on finding joy where we can." He tossed me a long piece of wood. "Here."

It stretched from my neck to my thighs and was wider than I was.

"What's this for?" I asked. I ran my fingers down the smooth lines in the grain. It was an old piece of wood, and I had no idea where he'd gotten it.

"Finding joy and getting your mind off your father," he said. He picked up another plank of wood and tucked it under his arm. Then he motioned for me to follow him.

I hesitated, but the longer I stayed still, the more my stomach rolled at the thought of my father. I wanted to push that pain off as long as I could.

If we were going to train, that would help more than anything. The world always melted away when I trained. Yet I didn't think we were heading to more training, not with all the boys tagging along.

I was right. After walking for about ten minutes, Cion paused at the bottom of a tall dune. Ahead of us, boys staggered up the hill like a reverse avalanche. Some had pieces of wood strapped to their backs. Others cradled them under their arms.

The first boy to reach the top of the dune triumphantly lifted his piece of wood above his head. Then he tossed it out in front of him, chasing it for a distance before hopping on. He stayed standing on the wood as it sped down the dune, leaving a trail behind him.

He wove back and forth. He zipped past several other boys still struggling upward. As I watched, more and more boys jumped on their boards and headed down the dune. A few of the younger boys lay on their stomachs on top of their boards rather than standing.

I'd never heard such shouts of glee as I did from the boys

coming down the hill. As soon as they hit the bottom, they snatched up their boards and headed back to the top.

"Sand surfing," Cion said. "It gives them something to look forward to after a raid. Come on." He began the long hike up the dune. Dimic slid past us, spraying us with a layer of sand. Cion put up his arm to block the spray; when he let it fall back down, a smile spread across his face. It made him look younger, and it erased the hardness that normally soured his features. And for the first time, I noticed two small dimples appear at the edges of his smile.

For a moment, I found myself staring. But then Cion took off toward the top of the hill shouting, "Just wait until I catch up with you, Dimic."

I raced after Cion. By the time I reached the top of the hill, I was out of breath.

"I'd try going down on your stomach first," Cion said. "It takes a while to get used to."

I wanted to hop on my piece of wood as I'd seen the other boys do, but I didn't want to make a fool of myself. I nodded and dropped my wood to the ground.

Cion instructed me how to lie atop it. "Try to pull up the end of the wood. Otherwise you'll get a face full of sand." He lay on his board to demonstrate the movement. His biceps flexed as he pulled up on the board and slid a few feet forward. "Arch your back slightly." He pushed off his board and waited for me to copy his movements.

Once I had, he moved behind me. "Good," he said. "Enjoy." And with those words, he grabbed my ankles and shoved me forward.

The slope of the hill fell out beneath me. My stomach went

with it. I tipped forward, and I knew I could have stopped by putting my feet down or plunging my arms into the sand. I didn't want to. I let my weight tip me forward over the edge.

I wasn't expecting the rush of wind. I snapped my eyes shut as sand sprayed my face. I couldn't be sure if the shouting came from me or from the wind whistling by.

"Close your mouth," someone shouted behind me. I snapped my lips shut as a wave of sand smacked my face. Remembering Cion's words, I pulled up on the front of the wood, which lessened the amount of grains that spit against me. I opened my eyes. Liquid sand sped past me as I glided over the surface.

Before I could even process what was going on, it was over. I was at the bottom of the hill. Only Cion hadn't told me how to stop, and I hadn't paid attention to how the other boys got off their boards. I'd been too preoccupied watching their flights down the hill. I skidded across the sand, rolling off the board until I came to rest at the base of the next dune.

Another board came to a stop next to my head.

Cion peered down at me. "That's an interesting way to get off your board. What do you call it? The Princess Plunge?" The way he cocked his eyebrow matched his lopsided grin.

I got to my feet, brushing away the excess sand. Then I gathered a fistful of sand and launched it at his middle. "I would have been better if you'd actually taught me how to stop."

The sand I threw collided harmlessly against his chest. He looked down at where it had hit him before looking back to me. "If you were aiming for my face," he said, "you missed."

"If I'd wanted to hit your face," I said, "I would have."

"Really?" His eyes brightened at the challenge. He dropped to the ground, rolled forward, and gathered sand in his hand all in one fluid motion. As he ended his roll, he tossed the sand toward me. I ducked out of the way.

"Sand fight," one of the boys called.

The next thing I knew, I was the recipient of handfuls of sand tossed in my direction. I snatched up my board and used it as a shield. I blocked one handful and let loose one of my own. It hit Dimic directly in the back of the head.

He spun and launched more in my direction. While he attacked me, another boy snuck behind him and poured sand down the back of his pants. "Larch," he called, ignoring me and going after the other boy.

While I was watching Dimic and Larch wrestling in the sand, I forgot about the cardinal rule of battle—always assume there is another opponent waiting for you.

A blast of sand hit my cheek. I turned to find Cion standing there nonchalantly. He raised his hands to say he had no idea where that sand had come from.

I drove one end of my board into the sand and dropped behind it. I scooped up handfuls of sand and launched them his direction. Instead of running away or returning fire, he raced toward me. Just when I thought he'd collide with my board, he did a front flip, landing behind me. He drained a fistful of sand from his palm into my hair.

With the board at my back and Cion in front of me, there was only one move I could make. I lunged forward toward his knees, tackling him.

He retaliated by flipping me over and pinning me in the sand.

"Ha," he said. "Got you."

His eyes were as dark as a desert night and just as unnavigable. Strands of hair fell around his face. He whisked them back with a flip of his head. "You shouldn't have left your back exposed."

My chest heaved from exertion and the adrenaline still coursing through me. "I know."

His eyes studied my face for a moment longer before he eased off me. I sat up quickly. I couldn't bring myself to look at him. Around us, most of the boys had ceased their sand fight and returned to the dune.

The warmth of the sand spread through my body, and the longer I sat there next to Cion, the worse it burned. I stood up and grabbed my board. I refused to acknowledge that the heat didn't go away once I left the sand behind. It flurried in my chest and tugged at my heart. I shoved it back down.

"Race you to the top," I called over my shoulder as I sprinted upward. I didn't wait to see if he would follow.

He still made it to the top before I did. I could have sworn he turned to make sure I was looking before he smiled, threw his board onto the sand, and hopped on. He surfed down the hill, his board spitting out sand behind it. He snapped his board back and forth to take him different directions. As he neared the bottom of the hill, he crouched lower, speeding up. He let his speed pull him up the next dune. He did a backward flip at the top. He landed and drifted down the rest of the hill with a grin on his face.

I rolled my eyes. If he could show off, then so could I. I tossed my board into the sand. I was now the only one at the top of the hill. At the bottom, everyone turned their faces toward me. Cion's grin had thinned to a smirk. He motioned for me to go ahead, then he crossed his arms over his chest, waiting.

Waiting to see me fall, but I wouldn't give them the

satisfaction. At least I hoped I wouldn't. I wet my lips with what little moisture I had and leapt onto the board.

It skittered out below me. It continued a few feet down the hill without me while I landed on my back. Landing may not have hurt my body, but it certainly hurt my pride. Laughter rang out from the boys. My only consolation was that from the bottom of the hill no one could see how red I'd gone.

I retrieved my board and brought it back up to the top. Squaring my shoulders, I leapt on again. This time I was ready for the whoosh of air that threatened to drag me backward. I leaned forward as I'd seen Cion do. I didn't pull my legs side to side as he did—it took all my strength to keep the board straight under my feet. Every bump in the dune left by another surfer tried to knock me off balance. I found by bending my knees I could absorb the blow.

I concentrated so hard on my feet that I didn't notice how close I was to the bottom of the hill. I looked up to see a small group of boys scatter before me. Behind them, Cion loomed large. My feet faltered. The front of the board bit into the sand. I launched forward. Right into Cion.

He caught me around the waist, somehow managing to keep us both upright.

I found myself laughing, smiling, cheeks still red from the wind.

His eyes were as bright when he spoke. "You may not know how to stop, Kateri," he said, "but you sure know how to fly." His arms released me, but his eyes didn't. His comment had been in jest, almost friendly. It was a tone not often used in the palace, and it made me want to retreat, to put up walls so thick that not a single grain of sand could find its way through, because as soon as one grain found a way in, it was only a matter of time before the rest of the wall eroded.

Pretty soon I'd be going back behind the palace walls. What was it about Cion that made me keep forgetting that?

I took a few steps backward. "When do we train again?" I turned my gaze toward the top of the hill and absently smoothed back the hairs that escaped from my braid.

"Tomorrow."

I nodded. I knew his eyes were still on me. Though mine were on the top of the hill, my mind was imagining the way his arms had felt around my waist.

CHAPTER 18

The sun had nearly set by the time we made it back to the hideout.

"Everyone, take three ladles of water before bed," Cion called as the boys clamored inside with cheeks red from both sun and sand spray.

I gulped down my share. It wasn't nearly enough. My lips had started to crack, and my skin was starting to feel as wrinkled as the leather of my gladiator gear.

Dinner was a quiet affair of bread passed around so everyone could rip off a chunk.

Cion handed me my share. It barely filled my palm. Still, he'd given me a bigger piece than all the rest. I wasn't sure if that was because he thought I couldn't survive on what the other boys did yet or because he thought I'd need it to survive his training. Either way, my stomach growled too much at the sight of the bread to question him. I shoved large fragments into my mouth. They took longer than normal to chew because of how dry my mouth had become. Swallowing it was like swallowing rocks.

I should've copied the other boys, who'd taken one ladleful of water before eating, one during, and one after they finished. I guess those were the things you learned over time.

I thought I'd be exhausted, but when I lay down for bed later that night, I couldn't get to sleep. Despite the bread, hunger gnawed at me, almost as though the bread had awakened my stomach, reminding me that it did need to eat. Now it wanted more.

I rolled over and wrapped my arms around my middle and tried to think about something else. The only problem was, the thoughts that came to mind were worse. Everything from Yeri's yellow skin to the abandoned children to the smile on Rodric's face to what my father had done.

Especially what my father had done.

After an hour of letting my anger build and build and my stomach clench in on itself, I knew I needed to release it if I was ever going to fall asleep.

I needed to train. That was the one time where the rest of the world melted away. It became just me and my blade.

It wouldn't help the pains in my stomach or the harsh ache in my throat, but I'd rather face those than my thoughts. I shoved back my blanket. The evening chill settled around me as I wandered through the tunnels looking for an abandoned room.

After a few wrong turns that led nowhere, I finally found myself in a decently sized alcove with firewood stacked inside. This would do perfectly.

I lit a few torches and balanced several logs end to end on top of one another. I slipped the knives from my sandals and threw them at my makeshift target. One thunked in right about mid torso. The other missed.

I collected them and threw over and over again. The even thuds when I hit the target weren't enough to drown out my thoughts. I slipped one dagger back into its sheath and pulled out my sword. I still felt unbalanced without a shield. But Cion was right that I needed to learn to fight without it.

I charged forward.

Fighting an unmoving target wasn't the same as fighting Cion. My goal was to leave a scratch on the logs and roll out of the way before they toppled over. I carved mark after mark into the sides of the logs. Ripping through where ankles would be. Jabbing right into makeshift ribcages. Diving out of the way.

Over and over again, I shaved away chunk after chunk from the logs until the world melted away. Until I melted away. I spun, I leapt, I plunged forward. Striking first with my sword and then with my dagger, drilling hole after hole, wound after wound, until my arms were numb.

"What'd that log ever do to you?"

I whipped around to find Cion leaning against the mouth of the tunnel.

My chest heaved. My cooled sweat clung to me in the dampness of the cave. I wiped it from my brow with my arm.

He pushed off and sauntered over, stopping in front of the logs. "I think you successfully killed it."

"I'm sorry if I woke you," I replied. "I couldn't sleep."

"Some of the boys and I were still up." His eyes moved from the logs back to my face. "I'd thought you'd be exhausted."

"Me too." I rubbed my neck where the golden cuff cut into me.

"You'd have a better range of motion if you took that off," Cion said. "You'd be able to whip your head around faster, see more quicker."

I slid my fingers back and ran them over one of the clasps. If I took it off, he'd see the scars. Everyone would. Yet, keeping it on felt like I was still shackled to my father, still chained like a tiger, ready to fight, to destroy whoever he told me to.

I was done with that. I was done being afraid.

"Here," Cion said. "Let me help."

He stepped forward and gently pulled my fingers away from the clasps, then snapped them open.

He was standing so close I could feel the heat rising off his body. His fingers trailed along my neck as he removed the cuff.

I caught it as it fell forward and turned to face him.

I half hoped the weak light from the torches hadn't highlighted the raised scars. But his eyes went right to them. He leaned forward and lightly touched each one. "Who did this to you?"

My lips opened, but no sound came out. I felt exposed. I felt weak.

"Was it your father?"

"Rodric."

The torches cast soft light across his face. His brow was scrunched in concern. "Is that why you wear this?" He took the cuff from my hands. "To hide them?"

I crossed my arms over my chest. "If my father saw the marks, he would've known Rodric was stronger than me. He'd know I was weak, that I failed, that I wasn't strong enough." Although it hadn't mattered in the end. My father had chosen Rodric anyway.

Cion shook his head. "It's not weak to bear scars. It shows you were strong enough to survive." He handed the cuff back to me.

"Or too weak to fight back," I countered. I ran my fingers over the metal. Dents marred the surface where Rodric had strangled me.

"Scars tell their own stories," Cion said, "and out here, we listen to them. Because if one boy has a scar from a guard across his stomach, he tells the story of how he got it to the other boys so they can be better prepared. If one boy cuts his hand on something on the rooftops, we tell everyone else about that spot. We use scars to learn. So you see, they make us stronger in the end."

I stared down at my distorted reflection. Orange and black shadows played across my face. The light was too faint to make out the scars on my neck. But it was the first time I'd seen myself since leaving the palace. My hair was matted to my head in a mix of sweat and sand. My chapped lips faded into cheeks hollower then I remembered. But the grime covering my skin somehow made my eyes stand out. They shone brightly, reflecting the torchlight, showing that I wasn't broken. I hadn't given up.

I looked up at Cion and tossed the cuff back to him. "Sell it. Use the money to buy food or something."

Cion caught the cuff. "Spoken like a true Desert Boy."

"Well, I am one." There was no going back now. "I certainly look like one, anyway," I joked and gestured to my tattered clothes.

He laughed and motioned for me to follow him back into the tunnels. "Let's get you to bed, or you won't have any energy for training tomorrow."

I groaned. "Only if you teach me how to survive on so little water. I'm starting to think half the boys are part camel."

Cion shrugged as he led me down the tunnels. "I know it's tough, but rationing water is the only way we stay alive and the only way we can help people escape this place."

Something sparked in my mind. "Was that the rationing system Rodric was referring to?" I asked.

Cion stiffened. Slowly, he nodded.

Somewhere up ahead, I heard some of the boys who weren't yet asleep shouting over each other, eager to brag about the soldiers they'd fought at the well that day or to explain the mistakes that had given them the injuries they bore.

"How did Rodric know about that?" It hadn't struck me at the time, but Rodric knew a lot more about the Desert Boys than he let on.

Cion paused. He turned and stared down the tunnel behind us, to where the voices of the other Desert Boys drifted out of one of the alcoves.

"I guess sleep can wait a little longer," he said and turned back, taking me down a side tunnel. "Follow me."

I glanced to where light filtered out of the common room, not understanding what he'd seen that I hadn't. And not able to figure it out, I followed after him.

He led me down a dark tunnel. Sand squishing ahead of me was the only indication that Cion was still there. After a few moments, he stopped. There was a rustle, and light flooded the narrow tunnel. He'd pulled back a thick flap to reveal a small square alcove.

He motioned me inside. It was surprisingly warm compared to the hallway. Smoke had collected in a haze at the top of the room from the single torch anchored to the back wall.

A woven rug lay across the floor. Two blankets were stacked in the corner. Their red-and-black stripes were typical of the blankets made by the women in the city. A pillow lay in one corner of the room.

I sat on the ground to escape the smoke. Cion dropped the flap and followed suit, facing me. The room wasn't long enough that we could both keep our legs extended, so I curled mine in close to my chest.

I waited for Cion to speak, but he seemed in no hurry. He

tucked the pillow behind his torso. His head fell back against the wall, and he closed his eyes. Although I'm not sure how he could stand it. The small bumps and spikes of the rock wall dug into my skin, and I kept shifting position.

The silence in the room was accented by the crackle of the torch as bits of fire shot out and fizzled.

"Why won't you talk about Rodric?" I finally said.

He opened his eyes. "It's not that I won't talk about him," he said. "It's that I don't know where to begin."

"You could start with how Rodric knows so much about you."

He sighed. He ran both hands through his loose hair, pulling the tangled strands away from his face. He looked younger in the torchlight. The shadows played across his high cheekbones, making them appear more sunken in than they did in direct sunlight. "Rodric used to be one of us."

His words were so simple. Individually, they made sense. Together, they refused to adhere in my mind. "Rodric couldn't have been a Desert Boy," I said. "He hates you." He was the only person I'd ever known who hated them as much as I had.

"You don't think he stumbled out of the desert knowing how to fight like that, do you?"

He'd never really said where he'd come from besides the desert itself. I always assumed it meant he must've come in with one of the caravans. But thinking about it now, I knew it was untrue. No one takes a caravan into the city. Everyone was trying too hard to get out.

I put a hand down to steady myself as another thought ripped through me. Suddenly, it felt like the flap was preventing any fresh air from coming in, and the room had gone stale. I clenched my fist around the edge of the rug for something to hold on to.

I forced myself to meet Cion's gaze while my stomach collapsed inward, sucking what little breath I had with it. "You trained him." It came out as a statement, but I so desperately wanted it to be a question. A question whose answer I didn't already know.

He nodded. A simple, unassuming nod, as though he hadn't just thrown away all our plans. "Cintric trained us both until he left. Then I took over."

He'd probably spent years training Rodric. I had less than a month. There was no way I could compete with Rodric. I'd been hoping to show up with an arsenal of new moves. I had no advantage now. He would know them all.

"Were you planning on telling me this?" I asked. I leapt to my feet. The heat from the torch dripped downward and the smoke clouded my vision.

"Would it have made a difference?" he said.

"Yes."

"How?" he snapped. He rose to his feet and towered over me. "Either you have what it takes to beat Rodric or you don't. And I wouldn't be helping you if I didn't think you could do it, because believe me, I'm the only person who wants Rodric dead more than you do."

There was so much fire behind his words. I took a step back. "Why?"

He pushed his hands against his forehead. He kept them cradled there as he spoke. "Because he killed my brother."

I realized my mouth was hanging open, and I shut it. Hadn't Rodric said as much when Dimic and I were cornered in the alleyway? I hadn't known Dimic was Cion's brother then, and I hadn't given the conversation much thought afterward. Rodric killed a lot of Desert Boys. "I'm sorry."

"You don't even know what you're sorry for." Cion slowly slid down the wall, the anger gone from his body. He just looked tired. "You don't even know what he did or how cowardly he did it."

He buried his face in his hands.

I knelt down on the floor. I didn't know if I should reach out to him or if that would somehow make things worse.

"Rodric started out like the rest of us," Cion's muffled voice sounded from between his hands. He let them fall onto his lap. His eyes were unfocused. "He was a street orphan with no place to go. His parents had both been killed by the plague. We took him in. He showed more skill with a sword than most. He and I were the only ones Cintric gave private lessons to. It drove Rodric crazy that I was better than him though, that I became his trainer when Cintric left me in charge. But he was the best guard any of our caravans ever had." He paused. "At least until he started stealing from them himself.

"At first, we wrote it off as misplaced goods. Things sometimes get blown away in sandstorms, but more and more items started going missing. I actually enlisted Rodric to help me catch the thief. That's how much I trusted him." Cion leaned back, clenching his jaw so the muscles stood out.

"About a month later, my brother Remy saw Rodric stealing from the caravans. When Remy reported it to me, Rodric called him a liar and said I was standing by my brother simply because he was family.

"I saw it then, the anger and jealousy that drove him. I knew Remy had to be right. Rodric had often spoken of how we should keep more goods for ourselves, how we could use the money to build our own army to take down the king. He would say that the desert had chosen us, and it clearly wanted us to rule. None of us loved the king and the poverty he forced on us, but I didn't want a war that would cost the lives of the rest of the Desert Boys, so I ignored it. Even from the start, the Desert Boys had always been about helping people, not about war.

"After Remy brought his accusations forward, I had no choice but to kick Rodric out. I thought that was the end of it, but Rodric was never one to give up easily. He snuck back in that night and slit Remy's throat. He would have slit mine too if I hadn't woken up in time.

"I fought him all the way to Scorpion Hill. I'd trained him well, but I had rage to spur me on. I cut him across his side. It was a deep wound, deep enough to kill him. He stumbled backward over the ridge into the scorpion pit. I left him there to die." He balled his hands into fists. "I don't know how he survived, and there's not a day that goes by that I don't regret not staying there, not making sure he was dead. I owed it to Remy." He exhaled deeply, like he was letting the words out for the first time. Maybe he was.

"It wasn't your fault Remy died," I said.

He exhaled. "I wasn't just his leader. I was his brother. I was supposed to take care of him." He grabbed a handful of sand and flung it at the wall. It splashed outward and trickled down over the rug.

"You did everything you could. You led the other boys to safety and have continued to keep them from harm. Rodric didn't find anything when he broke into your last hideout."

There was a crazed look in Cion's eyes when he looked at me. "I made the boys pack up everything and move to a new cave because I couldn't stand to stay in the place where Remy bled out. It was sheer luck I picked a hideout Rodric didn't know how to get to, because this place had once been solely for initiations, and the only one Rodric had the patience to attend was his own. And he was led blindfolded then like all the other boys." His eyes roved about the room, and I realized it wasn't wildness and anger I saw in his eyes. It was tears. He was fighting to hold them back. "It's one of the few he didn't know how to find."

"You couldn't have known what he'd do, what he'd become." I'm not sure where the gesture came from, but I moved forward and put a hand on his.

Cion seemed just as surprised. He started to pull his hand away but didn't. "I should've known. I owed it to them. All of them. Every time I watch one of them die, I think back to how I could've prevented it if I'd killed Rodric when I had the chance. Yeri would still be here. They all would."

"I used to think that my mother's death was my fault," I said quietly, "that if I had been stronger . . ." I swallowed. "I blamed myself for my mother's death, but I was wrong. Even if it had been the Desert Boys and not my father, it still wouldn't have been my fault."

He brought his eyes up to mine. The golden flecks were hidden behind the rim of tears reflecting the torchlight, but it was impossible not to see the pain floating beneath the surface.

"Sometimes you can't stop people from doing terrible things," I said. "All we can do now is stop Rodric and get justice for Remy and Yeri and all the others."

My words seemed to solidify Cion. He nodded. "You're our hope now." He clenched my hand tightly in his, as if by letting go he might lose that hope.

I gave his hand a squeeze in return. "I will bring down

Rodric and then help find the water controls and destroy them. Together, we can fix this city." It would take more training than I imagined possible to beat Rodric now that I knew who'd trained him, but we could do it. Maybe not alone, but together it was possible. It had to be.

"In that case," he said, finally releasing my hand, "you should get back to your own room. You'll need rest before training tomorrow. I've kept you up long enough as it is."

"Whose room is this?" I asked. The smoke dried my already parched throat, but I liked the privacy here.

"Mine," he replied.

I looked at him sideways, trying to see if he was joking. "I thought you'd sleep closer to the other boys."

"I like the solitude better. And the lack of light trained me to rely on my other senses. I know every whisper the sand makes when it moves and shifts. No one can sneak up on me here."

With those words, he quickly rose. He threw the flap aside and escorted me back down the long tunnel toward my room, where I lay awake listening to the sand trickle into the cave long into the night.

CHAPTER 19

The next morning the caves were in chaos when I awoke. Boys ran frantically in all directions carrying bolts of fabric, water skins, bags of dark red kana fruit, baskets piled high with curled talon berries, and more jars of preserved jamma beans than I'd ever seen in my life.

My first thought was that Rodric had found us and we were abandoning the cave.

I grabbed my sword and ducked into the hallway. I followed the throng of boys until I heard Cion's voice echo down the cavern. He was shouting about where to put new goods and yelling at someone else to stay in line to load the cart.

I followed the noise to the large cavern.

Hardesh, Tania, and Bala were sitting on the back of a sizable cart loaded with barrels of water, cages full of green-spotted lizards, firewood, and an assortment of other clay jars with their lids tightly shut. Two large camels waited at the head of the cart.

Bala sat with her legs dangling off the back. She smiled kindly at me.

I wanted to ask her about my mother, my sister. But I couldn't bring myself to. So instead, I smiled in return.

Thankfully, Hardesh didn't throw a fit when I moved toward him. His face looked better, but he sat in a daze.

"Hardesh," I said, slowly approaching him.

"Careful," Tania said.

I paused a few feet from the back of the cart. "I just wanted to wish you all luck," I said. "And once I kill Rodric, I hope you'll think about returning."

"Thank you," Tania supplied for the group. "I'm sure we'd all like to return someday, but many more things would have to change to make that possible."

I nodded. "I will do my best to make the city what it once was."

"I believe you will," Tania said.

Her words surprised me.

"Everything's loaded and ready," Cion said, coming up next to me while speaking to the cart's occupants. "We'll send Hardesh's daughters as soon as it's safe."

I caught Bala's eyes moving between Cion and me. I took a step to the side under the pretense of kicking some sand from my sandal.

"My boys will deliver you safely," Cion continued. He bent down and picked up a handful of sand. He blew it over them. "May the desert recognize you as one of its own and allow you safe passage."

Bala wiggled off the cart and scooped up her own handful of sand. She emptied it into Cion's still-outstretched hand. "And may the desert return to you the kindness you've shown us."

Cion clasped the sand in his hand, touched it to his heart, and then released it before helping her back into the cart.

The caravan was about to creak away, but Hardesh suddenly looked up at me. "Wait," he cried, the word echoing around the chamber. He stared at me, his eyes round.

He motioned me forward.

Warily, I stepped closer.

Hardesh grabbed my shoulders and yanked me toward him. "You have to understand."

"Understand what?" I tried to pull away, but his fingers dug into my flesh, refusing to let go.

"Your father chose me as a competitor because he thought I'd killed my wife. But I loved her. Larina was the only thing worth living for." He choked over the name, sucking in large breaths of air to steady himself. His grip on my shoulders tightened. "Your father asked me if I was strong enough to kill you if your rule was plagued by weakness."

"It's okay," Tania said. "Let her go." She rubbed her hands in small circles on his back. "Why don't you rest?"

He shook her away. His eyes were wide and wild, with bloodshot veins streaking through them. "I didn't kill Larina, but I told him I did because I had to fight you. I had to win for my daughters, for the only piece of Larina left in this world. Your father and I both knew I wouldn't win, but I had to try. I had to."

"I understand," I said. "We do what we have to in order to survive."

"No." He clenched down harder on my shoulders. "I would've killed you to save them. I'm sorry. I'm so sorry. I'm no better than him. You have to forgive me."

"Shh, Hardesh," Tania soothed, getting him to release his grip on me and pulling him farther into the cart.

But he kept shouting, "You have to forgive me."

"I forgive you, Hardesh," I said.

He nodded his head repeatedly as though I'd exonerated him from his greatest crime. But he wasn't a criminal. He was the victim. Another victim of my father.

I tried not to let his words show their effect on me, but I was shaking.

My father thought Rodric was of the desert, chosen by the

desert, and that's why he deserved to rule. Well, I'd show him that the desert had accepted me too. It made me want to train all the more. Because once I was done with Rodric, I was going to face my father.

I would demand justice for his crimes. I wasn't going to abandon him to the fate of the arena. I would deal with him personally. I would be the desert's justice, mightier than any tiger.

Tania waved as the cart started to creak away, led by several of the Desert Boys. More boys raced to open a pathway set so deep back into the rocks I hadn't even known it was there. They shoved away two wide sheets of metal that were so cumbersome, it took three boys to push each one aside.

"Safe travels," Cion called as the carts disappeared into the sunlight that lay beyond.

When the boys pulled the metal sheets back into place, the cave felt even darker than it had before.

"Let's go train." Cion said.

As the rest of the boys were busy sorting out the new supplies the arriving caravan had brought, Cion and I slipped back through the tunnels. After getting a few sips of water, he picked up a yellow sun fruit from an open bag and cut small slits in the pointed joints sticking out from the bulbous center before tossing it to me.

"You're going to need that," he said.

"We're heading to the shifting hills?" I asked as I peeled away the hard outer casing of my breakfast.

He nodded. "I think you can make the walk in the heat now."

I swallowed my groan along with the sticky pieces of sun fruit. Now more than ever, I'd do anything I could to beat Rodric, so I followed Cion out into the blazing sun.

We encountered two different sets of guards on our way to the hills. We were able to easily slip past the first group by crawling over dunes while they were down in a valley several hills away. The second set made enough noise that we heard them before we saw them.

"If the king cuts off access to the wells, we'll all be killed in the revolt," one soldier said as Cion and I ducked into a dune's shadow.

I looked questioningly at Cion. Cut off access to the wells? I wouldn't put it past Rodric and my father. Not anymore.

"As long as we keep receiving extra water rations, I don't care what the king does," a second voice said. "My wife just gave birth to our second son, and I need all the water I can get."

Sand shifted. They were getting close.

I eyed Cion, waiting to see if he'd give the signal to run or attack. He held up his hand for me to stay where I was. There was still a chance they could bypass our little valley.

"At least if he did cut access, they might finally force the princess out, and we'd stop having to search out here for her."

The voices were going around us, growing fainter.

"You'd think they would've stopped sending us after the first six men died."

Whatever the other guard said in reply was lost to the sands as they moved farther away.

"That was close," I said after they were gone.

"Too close." He watched the direction the men had disappeared.

"Do you think my father will really cut off well access?"

Cion shrugged. "I don't think he's so desperate he'll risk turning everyone against him. Not yet, at least."

These patrols made Hardesh's words even more real. These soldiers were proof of how much my father and Rodric needed me back, of how both needed me to secure their place in the monarchy. My father couldn't be seen as having two children taken by the desert. And I knew Rodric well enough to know he wanted to beat me in the arena in front of everyone. He couldn't leave a question in anyone's mind that the desert had chosen him.

All that would just drive them to excessive cruelty to get me back. Hadn't my father said during his speech at the well that there'd be consequences, that things would only get worse if I wasn't found?

"What if he does cut off access?"

"We'll find a way to get water," he replied. "We always have, but I'll get in touch with my source in the palace and see if they can find out if there's any truth to what the soldiers were saying."

I didn't like not having a plan, but for now, that was the best we could do.

Cion and I had just trudged up to the top of the dune when a voice cried out, "There they are."

The two guards we had overheard stood only a dune away. They must've stumbled upon our footprints and followed them nearly to us. They dashed down the dune directly toward us.

I started to go for my sword, but Cion stopped me.

"Run."

I remembered what he'd said about not killing the guards the first time we'd come across them in the desert, so I shoved my sword back down and took off after him.

We raced up one dune and down another, but so did the guards, their sword hilts clanging as they ran.

They hadn't been living on only a few sips of water a day, and with each dune we climbed, they grew closer.

I forced my legs to move faster. My lungs burned.

Cion easily leapt up the dune ahead of me, cresting over the hill.

I stumbled as something pulled at the sandal strap around my ankle. I plunged forward into the sand.

I turned just in time to see the soldiers crest the dune and slow as they approached me. I scrambled backward.

That's when I noticed what I'd stumbled over.

I slowed my pace.

"Just come with us nice and easy," one of the soldiers said. He had one hand up as though I were a wild animal he could tame. The other hand held his sword.

He took slow, measured steps forward.

He inhaled sharply, his whole body going rigid.

I looked away.

He dropped his sword and stumbled backward into the other soldier, blood dripping from his foot where a spike from a spiral cactus had gone straight through.

I rose to my feet and pulled out my sword just as Cion reappeared over the hill with his sword in hand.

The second soldier seemed to realize he was outnumbered now that his partner was injured. "Let's get out of here," he said, helping his friend hobble away.

Cion and I stood there a long time with our chests heaving and our swords out just to make sure they didn't reappear.

"Do you think we should head back?" I asked.

He shook his head. "I'd rather them think we went this way. It'll lead them farther from the hideout."

I sheathed my sword and followed him, but I couldn't help glancing over my shoulder every few dunes, praying we'd make it through a few more weeks, that my father wouldn't cut off well access. I needed more time until I was ready to face Rodric. But I had a sinking feeling I wasn't going to get it.

CHAPTER 20

It was late by the time I finally pulled myself from the tossing surf of the shifting hills and collapsed next to Cion.

"Better," he said.

"But good enough to beat Rodric?" I asked. Because that's what I needed. And fast. Especially after overhearing those soldiers.

He looked at me sidelong. "If you got him mad enough that he focused more on his rage than his training, then yes."

"So really, that's a no." I sighed.

"Rodric thinks his strength will carry him through any fight. His weakness is dismissing those he sees as weaker opponents. Remy once got Rodric's sword from him in a training fight by pretending to be injured."

"So Rodric can be beaten," I replied, hoping that was the message I was meant to take away.

Cion shrugged. "It was only a mock fight. It's hard to say what would've happened in a real one."

"I guess I'll get to find out."

"I'd trade places with you if I could," Cion said, "but I don't think I'd look as good as you do in that gladiator gear."

I looked down at my clothing. My skirt didn't even reach my knees. One of the leather flaps arranged to flare out over the base when I spun around had been torn away while I was in the shifting hills. The leather of the breastplate was beginning to fray. Dirt and dust covered everything. My legs looked darker because of it, and a swipe across my scalp proved sand still matted my hair. Not to mention the small cut above my ankle where the spiral cactus spike had scraped me.

"I don't look any different than any of the other Desert Boys," I said.

Something in the way Cion looked at me told me that wasn't true.

I tried to ignore his gaze. No one had ever looked at me like that before. It wasn't the greedy look Rodric always gave me. It wasn't the weighing look my father always judged me with. He was simply looking at me. And yet, it felt like he was the first person to ever see me. Not the gladiator. Not the princess. Just me.

"Come on," he said, pulling me to my feet. "I've got a surprise."

I ignored the way his hand clasping mine sent a tingle up my arm. "A surprise?"

"You'll like this one," he assured me.

I rolled my eyes but followed.

It was late by the time we arrived back at the cave, which thankfully meant the soldiers had cleared out for now. I congratulated myself on being able to pick out the dune from several peaks away. I never would've found my way back on my own, but I was learning.

Cion led me through an entrance to the large cavern where the caravan had departed. Several mounds of supplies and goods still lay where they'd been unloaded.

Cion moved toward one of the piles and started looking through them. But he seemed to have trouble locating whatever he was looking for.

"What are you trying to find?" I moved toward the pile of

bolts of fabric and pulled a silky bundle off the top. It was a rich red color, the same as many of the blankets the women in the marketplace sold.

"I saved you a woven dress so you could get out of your gladiator gear for a while," Cion said from beneath the stack. "But it looks like one of the boys must've put it with the ones we were sending into town." He dropped the bolts of fabric back down and straightened.

"What's this?" I asked as I unrolled the fabric I held. A portion slipped to the ground. The part I still held turned out to be a pair of thin pants.

"That's a sand dancer costume that got sent by mistake. We can't sell those because no one can afford them, and if we gave it away, Rodric's men would know where it came from and try to torture our location out of the recipient."

He picked up the top I'd dropped and shook the sand away. "You don't have to wear that. You can stay in your gladiator gear for the celebration tonight."

"Celebration?" I wasn't aware we had anything to celebrate. In fact, I was more worried than before after overhearing those soldiers and wondering how I'd find enough new moves to beat Rodric.

"Every time a caravan arrives, we celebrate. It's tradition."

"Is there anything you don't celebrate?" I asked.

"When life is as hard as it is out here, you celebrate as often as you can."

I looked at the gauzy red fabric in his hands. I hated wearing those outfits back at the palace, but that's because they were meant to please my father.

I stroked the silk pants.

My mother had worn something similar when she caught my father's eye during one of her performances. She'd taught me the steps when I was little, but the lessons had died with her. Though I could still remember one lesson with my mother. She'd taken my hands and guided me through my steps, shown me when to point a toe and when to dig my heel into the floor.

"You'll be a master yet," she had said, adjusting the position of my arm. "You'll be better than me."

At the time, all I'd wanted was to be her. I wanted to shimmer like she did when she danced. I wanted to twirl like she could because that's when she was happiest, when she locked herself away with me and spent hours dancing. It was the only time I saw her smile and heard her laugh.

At the end of each lesson, we'd clasp hands and spin around until we ended up in a heap on the ground, laughing. But after this lesson, we'd sat in front of her wardrobe, and she'd pulled out her only remaining sand dancer dress.

The shimmering green fabric had been so vibrant. So alive.

"One day, you'll wear this," she'd said. "Maybe you'll catch a man's eye." There was sadness in her voice. "I pray you'll find a kind man. A generous man."

She'd kissed me on my forehead and returned the dress to the back of the wardrobe. She thought I didn't see when she wiped away several tears.

My mother had died a little more than a year later.

"I'd like to wear the costume," I said to Cion, pulling the top from his fingers.

"Are you sure?"

I nodded. Not only did I really want to get out of my gladiator gear, it was time I reclaimed more of my mother. More of myself.

CHAPTER

21

It took me nearly a full hour to get dressed. Mostly because the costume was way more complicated to put on then I'd first suspected. It had multiple pieces that were supposed to loop and connect, and none of them seemed to match up the way I thought they should.

I bet if Latia were here, I'd have been ready in five minutes.

One veil-like piece was sewn into the shoulder seams. It draped down my front, ending in a triangular point below my exposed belly button where it met my pants. Two other pieces hung down my back to my ankles. Some dancers crisscrossed them over their stomachs, but it hadn't looked right when I'd tried it. So I let them hang loose.

I'd spent the rest of the time running my fingers through my hair. I'm not sure it looked presentable by the end, but it at least looked better than it had since the shifting hills had gotten ahold of it.

The cavern passages were deserted by the time I emerged. I only took one wrong turn on the way to the cavern.

Eventually, I simply followed the smell of smoke.

All the escape routes concealed in the cavern walls had been thrown open to let out the bonfire smoke. I worried Rodric would see it but realized we were too far out from the city for our celebrations to be seen. And if the Desert Boys knew enough not to go out at night, then Rodric had to as well. I also knew Cion wouldn't risk the bonfire if he thought it was unsafe.

Groups of boys danced in front of a large fire while others lounged on cushions, rugs, and blankets.

"Whoa," Dimic said when he spotted me.

All the other boys stopped and turned to stare.

Thankfully, the flickering light of the flames hid the embarrassment in my cheeks. I must look like a mess. I crossed my arms over my stomach and turned to go back, but Dimic's words stopped me.

"She's the prettiest sand dancer I've ever seen," he said.

"She's the only one you've ever seen," another boy shot back.

A shadow pulled away from the bonfire and moved toward me. Cion.

"It looks good on you," he said quietly.

I tugged at the transparent fabric covering my stomach. "I'm not even sure it's on right."

"Does that mean you don't know how to sand dance?" Dimic asked, disappointment staining his voice.

"I used to." I was so used to regular performances at the palace, I'd forgotten that to them, such entertainment must be a rare treat. So I knew what was coming next.

"Will you dance for us?" one of the boys asked.

My immediate response was to tell them no, but more of the boys crowded around, begging.

"I've always wanted to see a real sand dancer," one called.

My eyes went to Cion.

He stood unmoving, the fire reflecting off his face and dipping into the small grooves of his dimples as he smiled at me.

His eyebrows were arched slightly as if to say that the decision was up to me.

Sand dances were originally meant to be performed for your loved ones. I'd never gotten to perform for my family. And this group of boys was the closest I had to family now. They'd taken me in. They'd protected me. They'd fought for me.

The least I could do for sharing their home, their water, and their food was give them this one gift in return.

"All right," I said before I could change my mind. "I'll dance."

A shout of glee went up from the boys. They ran off to every corner of the room, dragging jars and ceramic pitchers with them as they sat in a circle away from the fire. They pushed and shoved each other for better positions.

Now I had to figure out what I remembered and what possible dance I could perform. The first one every girl learned was how to scrawl her name in the sand. But that seemed too simple for the eager eyes before me.

The one I'd seen performed most recently was the celebration dance, the one the girls would perform whenever I beat an opponent in the arena.

That's the one I would do. It had always been my favorite. And we were celebrating anyway.

After I took up position in the middle of the circle, I sprinkled sand over my feet, asking both the desert and my mother to guide my steps.

Slowly, the boys drummed on the objects they were holding, creating a steady beat even with the rhythm of my heart.

I let the music build, letting them all join in. Then I swooped my hands down, scooping up handfuls of sand. My hands formed a basket over my head. I spun. Sand flew out from between my fingers, showering the boys around me.

My mother had explained that it was meant to represent rain. For there was no greater thing to celebrate than water.

The boys shouted with glee. I spun faster.

Once all the sand had escaped, I moved toward the edge of the circle. I kicked up my feet, spraying every third boy. Although I gave a little extra spray toward Dimic, who laughed and held up his arms defensively.

If this had been a true performance, the sand would've been evenly laid and each swipe of my foot would've left a deep groove. My marks were uneven and not precisely spaced, but they looked a little like the sunrays they were supposed to be. I ran my foot in a circle inside the marks while my arms waved back and forth.

The next part was the trickiest. I hopped on one foot while the other drew a wavy line, representing the obstacles we'd overcome. I continued the pattern, spinning and weaving until the untouched sand shrank and shrank around me. I drew one last circle with my toes. I was in the small center, and the pattern lay around me like a woven rug.

The tempo increased.

I let it take me.

I spun in circles in that tiny space. Around and around and around. The world became a blur of darkness on one side and light from the bonfire on the other. It was said you could tell a good sand dancer by how well her pattern was executed and by how long she could spin without growing dizzy and tripping into the outside pattern.

I don't know how long I spun. But eventually, the world fell away. There was nothing but me and my breathing. There were no expectant faces. There were no suitors sizing me up. There was just me.

I pictured my mother's face. Her laughter wrapped around me as I spun. I let my arms go wide like a bird floating on the breeze I'd created.

I spun for her. I spun for the sister I'd never gotten to meet. But most of all, I spun for me, for the years I'd never get back. I spun away from the woman I didn't want to be.

I'm not sure when the tears started. They were just there as I spun. Clinging to me and then letting go. I let them come. It was the first time I wasn't ashamed of their presence.

I let heaving sobs take me. They pulled at my body, throwing me off balance.

I spun until I couldn't hold breath in my lungs, my legs gave out, and I fell to my knees in the middle of the circle.

The drumming cut off.

I covered my face with my palms and sobbed. The sound echoed around the cavern.

It sounded like weakness. But I didn't feel weak. For the first time, I felt strong. The strength my mother had been talking about.

What had Cion said? That it was right to return our tears to the earth?

I think my mother would've agreed. She'd said that strength didn't always come in the form of a sword arm.

I wiped my eyes and looked up at the dirt-stained faces around me. More than one was crying. I thought I even caught a glint in Cion's eyes before he rose to his feet, clapping. That broke the spell over the boys. They jumped to their feet, applauding.

I rose to my feet and bowed as steadily as I could.

Every pattern had an escape route that was supposed to be visible to only the dancer in the middle. Mine was a little crooked. I weaved through the lines so as not to disturb anything.

By the time I found my way out, some of the boys had returned to the fire. Others had moved off to the side and were trying to make their own patterns.

Cion waited at the edge of the sunrays. "That was beautiful."

"It's been a long time," I replied. I was suddenly conscious of how blotchy my cheeks must be. I ducked my head and rubbed at my cheeks using the dangling fabric wrapped around me.

Cion surprised me by lightly touching my chin and pulling it back up. He wiped away a tear with his thumb, sending warmth through my body.

The golden flecks of his eyes pulled in the warmth of the bonfire as he smiled down at me. How could I have misjudged him so? He wasn't the cold-blooded killer I'd always pictured. He was gentle, kind, understanding. He was so unlike anyone at the palace that he seemed more like a mirage than something I could believe was real. Then again, hadn't my mother possessed his same optimistic spirit, that same drive to stand up for her people?

"Thank you," he said. "You gave these boys something they will always treasure."

I wiped away another tear. "I'm sorry I ruined it by crying. I was thinking about my mother."

"Ruined it?" He shook his head, sending his untamed hair even further astray. "You made it personal, real. You made us feel what you were feeling."

I smiled up at him. But there was sadness in his eyes.

He dropped his gaze. "I want to show you something," he finally said. He took my hand and pulled me away from the boys dancing around the bonfire and led me to a small passageway hidden behind one of the stalagmites ringing in the room. The tunnel was entirely dark. He let go of my hand so I could focus on my footing as the pathway slanted upward.

His breathing was the only thing that signaled he was still in front of me. The air became colder around us. At first, I thought it was due to the absence of the fire, but the farther we climbed, the colder it got. We started to encounter more loose sand. It made the climb more difficult, and I had to shove my feet into it to gain any sort of traction.

Cion stopped in front of me, his shape silhouetted against a cascade of sand. He plunged through it.

I wasn't sure what I'd find inside, but I followed him.

I took a breath and pushed forward. I stumbled into a small circle of light. Cion caught me, his arms lingering on my waist as he set me gently on my feet.

Above us was a hole wide enough that I couldn't touch either side. Sand trickled in around the edges, forming a curtain around us and covering the floor.

"Where are we?" I asked.

He pointed to the sky visible through the hole. "This is the best spot for watching shooting stars. It's not always accessible, but a sandstorm usually clears it out."

Across the visible sky, the stars hazed in and out of focus like lanterns in a faraway town. Even from my balcony ledge they'd never looked that bright before.

As we watched, one fell away from the others, dragging itself across the sky and leaving a trail of light behind. Then another dripped from the heavens. They shot toward the horizon, chasing one another.

There was an old myth that the sun was made up of stars. When the sun rose during the day, bits would break off and linger in the sky, visible at night. People believed there was one star for every person. The day you were born was the day your bit of star would break away to decorate the sky. The day you died was the day your star would shoot across the sky, going back to the horizon, returning your light to the sun so that it could go on supporting the living.

Cion released his hold on me and motioned for us to lie down.

I sank in next to him. Sand filled around my hips and back.

I expected Cion to speak. He didn't.

But the silence was peaceful, nothing like that first day out here when I couldn't think of a single topic besides training that we could talk about.

We just lay there, our bodies almost touching as we watched the sky go round.

"Do you believe in the story about the stars? That there's one for each of us?" I finally asked.

He shook his head. "I came up here the night Remy died, and there weren't any shooting stars. Everything was as still and lifeless as his body had been."

"So you don't think the stars mean anything," I ventured. I looked over at him, but he was only looking up.

"The first night I came out here to be a Desert Boy, I saw a shooting star. And to me, it meant that I was on the right path. That's what I believe now. That they show you when you're going in the direction you were meant to follow."

I'd never heard that explanation before. But I liked it. "So you think those two we just saw mean we're both on the right path."

"I hope so," he said.

Sand whispered silently around us. Cutting us off from the world.

"I always come here when I think about Remy," Cion said quietly. "This was our spot. I've never brought anyone else here before. Not even Dimic."

I studied him. "Why me, then?"

He was silent for so long I didn't think he was going to answer. "I feel like you understand loss the same way I do. That you feel it as deeply as I do. Tonight, you let it show. I know it must kill you inside to have discovered what you did about your own father. I thought you might want a place to be alone with your thoughts."

He was mostly right. Except for the being alone part. The more I thought about it, the more I realized how alone I'd been all my life. No mother. A father who didn't love me. Not even a sibling to share the burden with.

"I think it's easier," I said, "never having known my . . . sister. And I was always so busy trying to impress my father that there was never any time to truly love him."

"Were you lonely in the palace?" Cion picked up a handful of sand and let it slowly drain from his palm.

"No."

He cocked an eyebrow.

"I didn't know what loneliness was back then. That's just how life was. But now . . ." I met his eyes. "Now that I've seen what it's like to have people care about you, I would be."

"Well, you can always find a Desert Boy in the dungeon," he said, only half joking.

"I'm sorry," I said. "For what my father's done to you. For what Rodric's done to you. For what I've done to you." I pictured the day Dimic was in the arena, how I wanted so badly for a tiger to tear him apart. How I wanted to tear him apart.

I clutched at the sand around me. "Sometimes I'm glad my mother is dead so she can't see what I've become, how I've treated her people."

"She'd be proud if she saw you now," he replied. "You're going to beat Rodric. You're going to save our people."

I wasn't sure I believed him. Not yet. "Would you disband the Desert Boys then?" I asked.

"If you stop restricting the water levels, probably. But most won't have anywhere else to go."

"If they know the way through the desert, why don't they just leave?"

He shook his head. "It's hard to leave the only homes they know. And starting over is easier for the women we help. We can find them jobs weaving or making pottery. The boys struggle to find work when the only skills they have are stealing and fighting."

I stared up at the stars. "What if I disbanded the royal caravans and opened the marketplace to anyone who wanted to import and sell? Your boys could have a booming business. And if they didn't want to do that, we could open a training school for soldiers."

"They would never fight for your father," Cion said, "but they would fight for you." He pulled his gaze away from the stars once more. "I would fight for you."

His words hung heavier than the stars above us, and his eyes gleamed just as brightly.

I was suddenly aware of how close our bodies were. Our shoulders were touching. Our faces mere inches apart.

I'm not sure what would've happened if I'd kept my face turned toward him. I was too afraid to find out, afraid to admit what I saw in his eyes was mirrored in my own.

I swallowed. "I'll need a new captain of the guard once Rodric is gone," I said, finally breaking his gaze. That was the most I could offer. For now. Because for the first time, I'd found someone who didn't want to be master of me. Because I'd never loved someone the desert hadn't taken away—and I couldn't chance adding Cion to that list.

That scared me.

Out of the corner of my eye, I caught him turning away to stare once more at the sky.

I thought I'd sense disappointment in his voice, but I didn't.

"If the position requires killing the previous occupant," he said, "then you can count me in."

"You'll have to get in line," I replied.

He laughed.

That broke the awkwardness between us. He stood, brushing sand from his loose pants. "Let's head back before we freeze to death. You've got training in the morning, and if we're lucky, the boys might still have saved us some dinner."

Oddly, I hadn't even felt the cold when I was next to him, but I took the hand he stretched toward me.

I caught sight of two stars as they rushed across the sky before I followed him back through the sand and down the tunnel.

CHAPTER 22

The next morning, Cion woke me early for training. I changed back into my gladiator gear. The fabric itched after the softness of the sand dancer dress.

Neither of us spoke about the previous night as we left the hideout behind after our usual small cup of water and a spiked kana fruit. Part of me wanted to apologize while the other half shouted not to bring the subject up. I was here to train. I should focus on that and be on the lookout for roaming soldiers.

"Are you sure it's safe to go out?" I asked.

"We're going to a different part of the desert today. It's unlikely we'll encounter any soldiers. Rodric knows there's no place to hide in that direction, so he wouldn't waste time having it searched."

I nodded and followed him.

I must've finally adjusted to so little water. My body didn't protest quite as much as we walked.

Cion didn't stop until the sand dunes leveled off. A wide stretch of smooth sand spread out before us. The sun beat down on us without the occasional valley in which to hide from its assault.

"What is this place?" I asked.

"We call it the plateau," he said simply. "It's the closest thing we have to your arena."

He strode out to the middle, and I assumed he wanted me to

join him. He stopped after a few steps and faced me, pulling out his split blade. "If you can beat me, you can beat Rodric."

He didn't wait for me to pull out my weapon. He pushed forward, nearly taking off my arm. I spun out of the way and rolled to the side. As I stood, I unsheathed my sword. It looked small and thin compared to his. I fumbled for one of my daggers, freeing it just as he pressed his attack.

His blade bit into mine with enough force to shove me onto my heels.

I recovered quickly and tried an attack of my own. I spun my sword low toward his ankles. He jumped over the attack and brought his sword hilt down hard against my shoulder. I faltered, pain spiraling down my arm and back.

Cion didn't even give me time to recover. A foot connected with my backside. I collapsed forward.

I scrambled up. Cion attacked. I ducked under his blade and arced my sword toward his midsection. He parried the blow, pressing me back. I managed to stay on my feet, but if this had been a real fight, I'd already be pressed against the arena wall. Trapped.

His sword kept coming. The reverberations rippling down my arm hurt less as I focused on nothing but his blade swirling through the air. Again and again, I blocked it, but I couldn't advance.

I tried several of the jabs he'd taught me with my dagger while our swords were locked. He dodged each one.

Beads of sweat appeared on his brow. Eliciting that felt like an accomplishment in some way. It gave me hope. I may not have been able to touch him, but I was tiring him out.

His blade faltered. He was too slow in bringing it up, and I lunged toward his right side, disarming him.

His sword dropped to the ground, and his body followed after. He lay there for a moment. I leaned over his face. His eyes sprang open, and his hand darted from his side, spraying my face with sand.

I coughed and stumbled backward, waving my hands in front of my eyes.

The next thing I knew, hot metal slid against my throat, and my head jerked back. "If I were Rodric," Cion said, his breath warm against my neck, "you'd be dead."

I groaned when he released me. I could barely make out his shape as I rubbed my eyes. I blinked a few times to try to clear the grit away.

"Did you have to do that?" Rodric had thrown sand in my eyes before, and for some reason, I thought Cion would be different.

"I want you to win," he said. "Thinking Rodric will fight fair is like thinking the shifting hills will stop moving. They won't. He knows all our moves. So you must be better than him, faster than him. You need to prepare for whatever he throws at you, and right now, you rely on your sight too much."

I would've rolled my eyes if it wouldn't have ground the grains further against my pupils. "At the shifting hills, it was all about sight, all about anticipating."

He nodded. "Yes, and you've mastered that. Now you need to master fighting when you can't see where the attack is coming from."

I scowled, but I'm not sure the look had the full effect I wanted, because tears rolled out of the corners of my burning eyes. "A blindfold would have worked just as well," I said, unable to keep the sarcasm from my voice.

"I needed you to experience it first, so you knew how quickly you could be brought down without your sight," he replied. "And"—he took out a strip of cloth—"now that you're aware of that, we can use the blindfold."

I didn't protest as he tied it over my eyes. When his fingers were done knotting it behind my head, his hands rested on my shoulders. Then he pushed me forward.

I spun back to where he'd been standing.

A piece of metal thumped against my back. I whirled around, swinging my sword out. Another blow ripped the blade from my hand, followed by the flat edge of a sword against my calves.

I dropped to the ground, swinging my arms out widely, searching for any hint of my sword.

"I've already stabbed you at least ten times by now," Cion's voice called from my side. I slid a leg around hoping to connect with some part of his body. Nothing. He laughed.

I stood up and dove toward the sound. I landed on more sand. Metal tapped against my shoulder.

"Eleven," he said.

I moved to rip the cloth off, but one of the points of Cion's blade poked into the back of my hand, stopping it.

"You're not trying hard enough," he said.

"How can I stop you if I can't see you?"

"Learn to hear the sand. Start by standing still," he said. "The sand has a language all its own." The words wrapped around me. He walked in circles around me. Close enough to touch if I reached out my hand. "Listen."

I didn't move. His footsteps continued. Near and far, left and right, until I could tell the distance. I slowed my breath. I let the sun's warmth soak into my body as it rose. I let the wind whisper over my skin.

I could smell Cion. Underlying the smell of smoke was the slippery scent of body heat rising against the sweet coolness of the desert breeze. It reminded me of twilight.

"Now come find me," he whispered. His voice floated on the wind.

I took a step forward, my arms cast out in front of me. I kept walking. Sand sprayed forward with every step. I walked several feet and encountered nothing.

"Wrong way," Cion said.

His voice came from behind me. I whipped around, but already he was moving. Sand scattered, but I couldn't tell in what direction.

I started back toward where his voice had come from.

There was the smallest murmur, like an inhale, as sand sunk downward. I raced toward it, but by the time I got there, Cion was gone. And my own loud footsteps had drowned out any hints of where he'd gone.

"Listen harder," he said from off to my left.

This time I didn't leap toward the noise. I waited. Sure enough, he began to move. His footsteps were hard to hear above the wind, but there was the smallest crunch where his full weight came down on the sand.

I waited until the noise stopped. I crept forward. I flung my arms out. Nothing. I dropped my hands and balled them into fists. I took one more step forward.

I faltered. There was nothing there. I stamped my foot into the dirt and waited for him to give me another clue as to where he'd moved.

None came.

Maybe he was reclining somewhere, laughing at me going in circles.

"This isn't working." I yanked the blindfold up.

To my surprise, Cion stood right in front of me. My nose almost poked into his chest. His face was as close as it'd been last night. So close I blushed at the memory.

He looked down at me, his lips tugging up mischievously at the ends. "Really? I thought you were finally catching on." There was a softness to his features that wasn't normally there. I hadn't seen him this relaxed since I'd met him.

"You were really standing right there?"

He nodded.

A breeze blew across me and then him, confirming why I hadn't been able to smell him. Though I could feel heat rising from his skin. I wasn't sure if I should move away. I told myself I didn't want him to think that I was one to back down.

But it was more than that. Being near him was a welcome warmth. The sun didn't pound my shadow into the ground quite so fiercely when I was focused on his eyes. Even the coarse sand being whipped against my skin didn't sting quite as much.

"You should've trusted your instincts," he said. "Rodric's no doubt spent months teaching you not to, to trust your sword and eyes instead. He's wrong. Honed instinct is worth more than a honed sword in a fight, and the desert is the best trainer. If you can't distinguish a yellow-spotted sand snake hole from regular sand, you won't survive. And if you can't distinguish one of Rodric's feints from his real attacks, you won't win."

"Right," I said, trying to sound interested in what he was saying and not betray that I'd been watching the wind drag his hair across his face and had almost reached out to swipe it back.

I dropped my gaze and cleared my throat.

"Don't worry. We'll make a Tamlin out of you yet." Cion's

hands darted forward and pulled the blindfold down over my eyes. Then his hands were on my shoulders, spinning me around so he could pull it tight once more. But all I could focus on was the way his body pressed against mine as he leaned in close and said, "Now try it again."

He gently shoved me away.

The blood pounding through my body covered up the sounds of his feet. I forced myself to focus, to listen. I found his path and chased after him. I crashed into his side. After glancing off, I managed to regain my footing.

"Good," he called. "Again."

Over and over, I listened until I heard the trail he left trickling in the sand. I could tell when he shifted his weight while waiting for me to find him. I began to recognize when he was creeping along and when he was running.

I'd chase after him. Sometimes he'd catch me as I dove at him. Others he'd let me fly face-first into the sand as he'd dodge my advance. Then he'd slink away laughing.

After about the fifth time of hearing him chuckle, I ripped off the blindfold and tossed it into the sand. "You're doing that on purpose!"

"What?" he asked, with his hands held in mock innocence. "I can't help it if you're not fast enough to catch me." He had a roguish grin on his face. One I planned to wipe off.

"We'll see about that." I launched at him. He moved out of the way easily. I ended up rolling across the sand. I gained my footing quickly, and it became a game of chase.

We kicked up waves of sand as we ran after each other across the plateau. Wind splashed around us, spraying us with granules.

There was something freeing in the chase. There was no skill to it. We were just running in one of the last wild, free places on the earth. Here, nothing could hold us down. The sand could be shaken off. I almost felt like we could have outrun the sun, beating it to the horizon it retreated to each night.

I sped up as Cion changed direction and called over his shoulder that I'd never catch him. I'm sure he was used to that being true. He moved as one with the desert, encompassing both the ferocity of sun and the litheness of the sand.

But after months spent training in full gladiator gear, I was faster.

I tackled him into the ground. He grunted in surprise as we crashed down and rolled across each other, ending up about a foot apart. We both gulped in a mixture of sand and air while we watched the blue sky float by above us.

"You're not what I expected," Cion said after finally catching his breath.

"Why? Because I'm faster than you?"

He scoffed. "Because you actually might know how to have fun."

The heat from the sun weighed down my chest. "It was different when my mother was alive. She would show me how to paint with colored sand, and she's the one who taught me to dance. She could make the most beautiful sand arc with her foot and trace the most intricate shapes. My feet were always too big for my body."

"You mean you weren't born with a sword in your hand?" He said it lightly, because there was no way he could know what my past was like. Especially since I'd never told anyone. There'd never been anyone to tell. At least not anyone who'd care.

"My father didn't speak to me until after my mother died. I

was the daughter he never should have had. It wasn't until after she died that he took notice of me." I sighed. "But that was only because I was his last chance to hold on to the monarchy."

He sat up and looked down at me. "Then why did you stay and fight for him?"

I sat up as well and swirled the end of my sandal through the sand. "I thought my father cared, and that was why he wanted me to train so hard. Plus, I promised my mother I would watch over her people." I met his eyes.

It was surprising how easily we could talk about anything now. I'd thought all those days ago that we didn't have anything in common. But we'd both suffered under my father, and neither of us had let it break us. We'd both been raised as if we were orphans, our training driving us onward. We both wanted to save our people. No, Cion and I were more alike than I ever imagined. And if there was anyone in this whole desert I wanted to be like, it was him.

Besides, his obvious strength with a sword, his underlying kindness for those he met, his willingness to give them everything he could, made me want to do better. To be better. When I was with him, I finally felt like I was living up to my mother's expectations. It was more than that though. I finally felt like me. Not a princess, not my father's puppet, not Rodric's tiger on a leash. Me.

He studied me a moment before offering me his hand and pulling me to my feet. "Then let's make sure you can fulfill that promise to your mother."

"Right," I said, playfully nudging him, "we wouldn't want the vultures getting any ideas if we laid here any longer."

"Very funny," he said, unable to hide his smile. He pulled out another blindfold and tossed it to me. "Again."

By the time we collapsed from thirst, the sun had risen nearly to its peak. We slowly walked back across the hills, Cion and I trading the stories we remembered about our mothers.

His used to hum while she tended the fire. Mine was always tracing some pattern with her foot under the table at big feasts when she thought no one was looking. I used to make a game of trying to guess what she spelled.

And both our mothers had instilled in us the old saying, "When bouncing sand blows, a sandstorm grows."

"My mother used to huddle us inside during sandstorms," Cion said. "We'd sit there, and she'd make up the most amazing stories for us. She talked so loudly we couldn't even hear the wind."

"Mine read to me when the sandstorms came. I'd curl up in her lap and look at the gilded pages. Books were her favorite thing after sand dancing."

Cion smiled down at me, genuinely interested, as we walked easily in step. I caught myself returning the smile.

It was nice to finally have someone to talk to about my mother, someone who missed theirs like I did mine. My father never allowed me to bring her up. And it was comforting to know the memories were still there, that the more I talked, the more I remembered—like that she often smelled of sweet jasmine or how she'd pluck the flowers off the garden cacti to wear in her hair. Sometimes I'd even catch her giving out the flowers to the thin, dirty hands stuck through the back gate, along with a few coins and the water she'd secretly disperse.

She'd be proud of me now. Win or lose in the arena, she'd be proud.

And I had Cion to thank for that, for showing me how I needed to truly help my people. For showing me who I could be.

I was about to ask him what stories his mother used to tell him when we heard voices.

We froze. Cion crouched down and crept up a dune. I followed after him.

A few dunes away, Rodric stood with several soldiers.

"They like to hide in caves hidden under the sand dunes," Rodric said. "Use your spear like this." He demonstrated by ramming one into the sand over and over again. "If you hit rock, alert me." He tossed the spear back to the nearest soldier. "Spread out."

The men fanned out across the surrounding hills and started jabbing their spears into the earth.

Cion and I slid back down the hill so as not to be seen by the soldier who'd picked the next hill over.

Cion motioned for me to follow. We crept backward, clinging to the shadows of the dune. There was no way we could get over the next sandbank without Rodric seeing us.

And after running across the plateau, I wasn't sure my legs would carry me much farther if we had to make a run for it, which was the better option than facing Rodric with soldiers at his back.

"What do we do?" I whispered.

Before Cion could answer, a shriek echoed across the sand.

My heart leapt in my chest.

"I told you what a yellow-spotted sand snake hole looked like," Rodric's voice cried.

"Go," Cion whispered.

We dashed for the next hill, crouching low. I threw a glance over my shoulder. All the men converged into one of the valleys, where a man was screaming in pain.

"You two, get him back to town," Rodric commanded. "Then you better return immediately."

Cion and I dashed over several more dunes, using the screams to cover our movement.

The cries grew more distant as the man was taken away. Men started climbing back up onto the hilltops with their spears.

Thankfully, none of them glanced toward where we were. They were all looking too closely at their feet, at the sand around them.

We moved diagonally back the way we'd come. Only after the men were well out of sight did we start angling toward the hideout. To mask our footsteps and ensure we left no trail, our route took us farther out into the desert.

My throat burned, my feet ached, and my legs were numb by the time we finally reached the hideout. But I reminded myself it was nothing compared to what would happen if Rodric found me.

He was bringing more men out into the desert, becoming more desperate.

That made him more dangerous.

CHAPTER 23

The next few days were a blur of training. We stuck to the hideout because too many guards had been spotted in the desert. It also wasn't safe for the boys to go in and out as they used to.

It wasn't long until everyone found the cave stifling, and water began to run low. We'd have to do another raid soon, but according to Cion's sources, Rodric had increased the number of guards around each well and started doing random patrols along the old, crumbling city wall. At least we hadn't heard more about the wells being cut off entirely.

Cion left me in the care of the younger boys while he went out to scout and talk to his source. We practiced sword maneuvers. Some of the boys were surprisingly good despite their small size and emaciated frames. I'd take them over the palace guards any day.

On the days Cion was there, he and I would eventually end up facing each other, attracting a ring of boys around us, which spurred Cion to fight harder so as to not make a fool of himself. Occasionally the boys rooted for me, but I think that was simply because they liked seeing someone who could go blow for blow with Cion. Though I never could beat him.

But I was getting better. Even if I couldn't always stop his attacks, I could tell when he was actually going to hit me and when he was feinting to aim at my other side. Fighting without a shield was starting to feel more natural as well.

Most nights, I fell into my blanket exhausted and woke up with sore reminders of muscles I didn't know I had. I'd fall asleep listening to the sound of footsteps shuffling through the sand outside my room. I learned to pick out Cion's from all the rest. His were the quietest.

It was one such night when my eyes had just shut and sleep was speeding toward me like a sandstorm when I heard his soft patter.

I sat up.

His shadow appeared in the alcove doorway. "Your hearing's getting better."

"Maybe you're just getting louder."

He laughed, and I relaxed back against the wall. "Please don't tell me you've come to take me to do some night training. I don't think my muscles can handle it." I already had a bruise forming on my arm where Dimic had smacked me with a wooden sword while I'd been fighting Cion. The whole exercise was supposed to show how you needed to be aware of your opponent while still noticing what was around you.

And I definitely noticed Dimic's practice sword after it crashed into me.

"No training," Cion said. "Now, I need your mind."

I groaned. "I'm not sure that's in good shape either." I'd been trying not to think for days. Only react. And learn. Otherwise the weight of my father's betrayal would suck me downward until sand choked off my screams.

"It'll have to do," he said.

I tried to stifle the moans caused by stiffness that emanated from my muscles as I stood and followed him out of the hideout into the cold night air. I would've thought it would be refreshing after so many days cooped up in the cave, but I'd never liked the desert at night. The desert sun might roast you, but its absence would immobilize you. The chill snaked in around you, slowly seeping into your skin like poison from a yellow-spotted sand snake bite. You'd shiver until your muscles cramped up, useless.

There'd always been something about staying still, about not moving forward, that I didn't like.

Cion set a quick pace across the desert. I wasn't sure if that was because he'd finally seen I could keep up with him or if he did it to stave off the cold.

"So where are we going?" I asked.

"I can't tell you," Cion said.

"Why not?" I tried to hide my feeling we were past the point of not trusting each other.

But Cion must have heard it in my voice because he stopped and turned toward me, saying, "This is the most closely guarded secret I have. Only Dimic knows. I'm only bringing you because I think you could help. In case something happens to us on the way there . . . well, the less you know, the better."

He turned away and continued walking across the steep dunes, and I was even more confused than when we'd left.

I trudged after him, my mind too worn out to think. I was so exhausted I thought I was seeing things when lights appeared on the horizon. I'd never heard of anyone having night mirages, but maybe after what I'd been putting my body through, anything was possible.

As we neared the light, it wasn't the greedy wisps of the sunlight claiming the sky once more. It was softer. Lantern light. We were close to the city.

Cion came to rest in a valley with a good view of the unguarded main gates to the city. The crumbling city wall ran away on either side, circling in Achra. It was easy to see the top of the arena just past it. It looked smaller than I remembered.

"We'll wait here," he said. He hunkered down in the sand, wedging out a space for himself using his backside.

"Did you even look for yellow-spotted sand snakes?" I asked as I plopped down beside him.

"You can hear them coming," he said.

I gave him a sidelong glance. "I doubt even sleeping in your isolated sleeping quarters gives you enough training to hear a sand snake."

"They hiss about every five seconds during the heat of the day and about every ten seconds at night."

"There's no way you can hear that," I repeated. Maybe I wasn't the only one capable of suffering night mirages.

"The sound is different from sand falling. It's wetter."

I shot him another look, but I'm not sure it really came through in the dark.

"Trust me," he said, "when you live every day on a few sips of water, and you hear anything that sounds even remotely close to water, you'll take notice."

I rolled my eyes. It was followed by a shiver. It was scary how quickly body temperature plummeted in the open air.

"I forget you city dwellers can't stand the heat or the cold," Cion said.

"I'm fine," I said, but my body betrayed me by shivering again.

"Here." He wrapped his arm around me and pulled my side close to his, tucking me under his embrace. His muscles pressed against me and warmth surrounded me, like somehow his body had been absorbing all the day's sunlight for this very purpose.

I couldn't help but press further against him in response.

There was something comfortable and safe about being with Cion, something that made the tension drain out of my muscles that were normally so poised to respond to an attack.

"Warmer now?" Cion asked. His voice was quiet, like the wind glancing off the tops of the dunes.

For some reason, my voice didn't seem to want to work, so I merely nodded. I couldn't take my eyes from his.

His head inched closer to mine. He paused, licking his lips.

If I turned away again like I'd done several nights ago, I wouldn't get another chance.

But would the desert take him from me too? That thought slid through my mind, threatening to build up the wall I'd created after my mother's death, the wall Cion had managed to start slowly tearing down.

No. I shoved the thought away because we both belonged to the desert now. Somehow we'd managed to find each other in this maze of sand. The desert had given him to me, and there was no way it would rip him from me.

His gaze leapt from my lips to my eyes.

I waited, staring back, refusing to turn away this time, daring him to draw closer.

He inched forward.

Then his body went rigid.

Sand scattered behind us, and Cion leapt to his feet. I whipped around as a figure emerged from behind the dune.

Cion visibly relaxed and hurried toward it.

A rush of cold air washed over me, highlighting the spot against my ribs where his warmth had been.

I was glad for the darkness. It hid the blush staining my cheeks and the smile spreading across my lips at the thought of almost kissing Cion. The memory warmed me enough to get to my feet and follow.

The figure was shorter than I was, probably another Desert Boy, but it was hard to tell beneath the hood concealing his face.

Cion threw back the hood. I caught a glimpse of a long braid before Cion wrapped the figure in a hug.

I draped my arms around my torso to keep from shivering.

"I got your note," Cion asked. "Are you well?"

"Yes." A female voice.

Not just any voice. One I knew well.

I pushed around Cion, certain it couldn't be who I thought it was. But there she stood, her arms wrapped around him.

Latia.

CHAPTER 24

A strange pain shot through my chest at seeing her next to him.

"Latia?" I asked, not quite believing what I was seeing.

Her eyes went wide when she recognized me. "You brought her?" She tried to pull away from Cion, but he wouldn't allow it.

"It's okay," he soothed, squeezing her hand and moving off to the side so she could get a better look at me.

There was something off about her. About the way she carried herself. Or maybe it was that she wasn't backing down and was meeting my gaze. She was challenging me.

I took a step back. That couldn't be right. This was demure little Latia, who wouldn't even look at me in my gladiator gear because I frightened her so much. The intensity I'd seen in her eyes must've been a trick of the moonlight.

"Latia is my source in the palace," Cion said. "She's been trying to figure out where the water controls are and feeding me information about what Rodric and your father have been up to."

I should've been pleased we had someone inside the palace who could help, but feelings of betrayal crept up my body. So did some vomit when I saw he still hadn't let go of her hand.

I took a steadying breath. No, she hadn't betrayed me. She'd betrayed my father, the same thing I'd done, and yet it still stung because I thought we'd been some version of friends.

I nodded, numb, taking in the way his hand grasped hers with such familiarity, such comfort. No, more than comfort. Affection.

I shook the word from my mind. That couldn't be right. Could it?

Latia was in love with a soldier back in the palace. The one she drew little rendezvous maps for. The one she would sneak out at night to meet.

My stomach tightened.

Hadn't I seen Cion pull out a crumpled parchment and head off into the desert the night Dimic and I had played Skips? Hadn't he gone off on his own several times since then?

Maybe Latia hadn't been writing notes to her lover. Maybe she'd been giving Cion detailed maps of the palace.

But did she really fake those small smiles and blushing cheeks whenever I asked her about her soldier?

No, even then I'd known she was in love. No wonder I'd never been able to get the name of the man from her. Because it wasn't a soldier.

It was Cion.

I swallowed down the lump in my throat. I took deep breaths of the frigid desert air in the hopes it would breathe life back into the parts of me that suddenly felt as if they were dissolving and numb the strangled feeling wrapping around me.

Even the small part of me that wanted to hope I was wrong knew I wasn't. If she was out here helping him, there's no way she'd let herself develop feelings for a soldier in the palace, for the enemy.

As if to prove my point, she glared at me and said, "Are you sure she can be trusted?"

I scoffed, as much in reply to her question as to hide that I needed a few more moments to be sure my voice wouldn't betray any emotions. Besides, she was one to talk about trusting people.

She studied me from beneath long eyelashes. The kind of eyelashes any girl would be jealous of.

I'd never taken the time before to really look at her. She'd always seemed to dislike attention. But out here in the desert, she seemed to have bloomed like a cactus flower. Her large eyes stood out in the moonlight. In any setting, she'd be considered a beauty with her soft features, and standing next to Cion's muscled body made her only look softer, more feminine.

I looked down at my own arms. Honed muscles stood out.

I couldn't believe I thought Cion was going to kiss me. He must think I was a fool, sitting there staring at him with eyes as wide as moonstones. I wanted to grind my foot into the sand until all my anger drilled away. I wouldn't let him, or her, know they'd had any effect on me. I had to be as cool as the desert. I straightened my shoulders and forced myself to look at her, face as stoic as my father's as he waited for the accused to pick a door in the arena.

"We can trust her," Cion replied. "She's helped us with a raid and hasn't run back to Rodric yet."

"Only because she wouldn't be able to find her way back," Latia said.

I stiffened but stopped myself from going for my sword.

Cion must have sensed that. He sighed. "I was hoping you would get along for once. For all our sakes."

"We've always gotten along," I clarified, not taking my eyes from Latia.

"It's easy to get along with someone when they have to do everything you say," Latia spat.

"Now's not the time," Cion said, holding her back.

"Then when is?" She turned on him. "She doesn't get to escape without paying for what she did."

"For what I did?" I demanded. "What did I ever do to you?"

Her body stilled in Cion's arms. Her eyes narrowed. "You took my mother from me."

"The sun must have addled your brain," I said. "I have no idea what you're talking about. You said scorpions killed your parents."

"That was a lie to cover up what your family did to mine. Your father gave the order . . ."

I charged toward her. "My father did a lot of things I don't approve of, like kill *my* mother. So if it's him you want to go after, you'll have to get in line. Don't blame me."

"As if you didn't blame the Desert Boys for years and sit by while they died in the arena?" She lunged toward me, but Cion easily held her back.

"Kateri isn't the enemy," he spoke softly into her ear. "Not anymore."

Latia stopped fighting him, but she didn't stop glaring.

After a few moments, he released her, and she stood with her arms crossed.

"And we won't be able to stop the king and Rodric unless we all work together," he said. "Why don't you tell Kateri what we know about the controls so far?" He raised his eyebrows at her, waiting for her to speak.

Latia flipped her braid over her shoulder. With one last sigh, she said, "I've searched nearly the entire palace, and I can't find them." She glared at me in accusation, as if I had been the one to hide them somewhere.

I shook my head. "I don't know where they are." When Cion had suggested the water controls existed, I'd tried to think of where my father could hide something like that. But I'd come up empty.

She shot me a look laced with more poison than a scorpion sting. "Are you sure?"

"I didn't know my father controlled the water levels until a few days ago," I said, "so I have no idea where he'd control them from."

Latia rolled her eyes.

I closed my eyes, trying to think. Once my mother was gone, I hadn't spent much time exploring the palace. I'd been too busy training.

I opened my eyes and shook my head. "I don't know where it could be."

"She's as useless out here as she is in the palace," Latia said. "I'm better off searching more on my own."

"Once I beat Rodric," I supplied, "I'll find the controls and destroy them."

"We don't have time for that," Latia snapped. "Rodric's going to cut off all access to the wells until you're returned. Your father warned things would get worse, and now they have," she said, her eyes burning like flames.

"Are you sure?" We'd heard that rumor days ago and nothing had appeared to come of it. Maybe she was wrong. She had to be wrong. I needed more time.

"He's tired of his soldiers dying in the desert," Latia intoned. "He knows Cion cares about these people. Your father's counting on the fact he'd rather give you up than watch them all die of thirst."

Cion was lost in thought. "We've been in worse situations before."

"We've never had all access to the wells cut off like this," Latia said.

"The people will revolt," I said.

"It won't do them any good," Latia replied. "The wells will be empty unless we can break the controls."

Cion paced back and forth, running his hand through his hair. "He's flushing us out. It feels like a trap to me."

"Of course it's a trap," Latia said. She pulled at the end of her braid, and for the first time since arriving that night she resembled the unsure girl I was used to. "Kateri should just give herself up now."

Cion shook his head. "That won't help anything. We need a plan."

"We don't have time for a plan," Latia replied.

"Then we have to go tonight," Cion said. He eyes swung to the sky, heavy with stars. "If we left now, we could break into the palace and search for the controls."

"It's suicidal," Latia said. "You can't get into the palace. It's not like the city wall that's unguarded. Its main gate is manned, and the only time the palace wall is fully patrolled is at night. I can get in, but I can't get the rest of you in with me."

Cion dug his foot into the sand.

I stared off toward the city lights and the arena that rose above them.

"The arena," I whispered.

Cion and Latia turned their attention to me.

"What?" Cion said.

I pointed. "The arena has an access tunnel to the palace to

transfer the tigers in and out. It'd be a lot easier than trying to make it over the wall. It would bring us in on the lower levels."

Cion studied the shadow in the distance. "How many guards would we be facing?"

"There aren't any soldiers guarding the arena." No one was stupid enough to want to go in. "There are maybe one or two locked doors we'd have to pass through, and there might be some tiger trainers in the small prep room off to the side of their cage. Once we're past that, it'll be pretty quiet down there."

Cion looked to Latia. "What do you think?"

"It's too risky," Latia said.

I stepped forward. "All we have to do is pick the lock and face a few soldiers."

"We?" Latia asked. "I didn't know you could pick locks too."

"Dimic," I said, remembering how he opened the lock on my shackles. He'd said he was the best lock picker out of all the boys. I switched my focus to Cion. "He could do it. I could take the Desert Boys through the tunnel in the arena."

"You're quick to volunteer others for a cause you've only been championing for a few days," Latia snapped. She crossed her arms and leered up at me. "The Desert Boys aren't just pawns you can use. They're actual people. Dimic is Cion's brother. Did you ever stop to think that he could get hurt? Or caught? Rodric won't let him go again." Her cheeks were aflame and her eyes bright with anger.

"I think Kateri is right," Cion said. "We need to get in and destroy the controls once and for all."

Latia opened her mouth to interject, but Cion silenced her by continuing on. "But I do think it's too dangerous for all the boys to come. We need a small group. It'll be just us and Dimic."

"No," Latia said. "He's not coming."

Cion sighed. "He's the best lock picker, and you know it."

"I don't care," she said. "He can't come." She chewed the side of her cheek so violently I thought she'd bite through.

"Latia . . ." Cion started.

"Don't," she said. "You weren't there when he was caught last time. You didn't have to hear him screaming. I won't go through that again. I won't let him go through that again." Her voice broke. She turned away to stare back at the city.

Cion moved toward her and pulled her into a hug.

She melted into his arms, burying her face against his chest.

I couldn't help but shiver at the memory of how much warmth that embrace brought. I shoved the thought away. He clearly had feelings for Latia. I'd been stupid for mistaking kindness for affection, but I guess when you're not used to either, it's easy to mistake the two.

"We're not going to lose him," Cion said. He stroked her hair.

"I don't think I could take it again. Not after Remy . . ." She trailed off. "The only reason Rodric let him go last time is because he knows Dimic is reckless and would likely lead him to the hideout. He won't release him again."

He cupped her chin and forced her to look at him. "I won't let anything happen to Dimic."

She wiped her eyes and nodded, renewed by the conviction in his voice. "What do you need me to do?"

"Nothing," he said. "I want you out of harm's way. You should go back to the hideout. You'll be safe there."

She shook her head. "If I don't go back, Rodric might get suspicious. We can't risk that."

"If anything went wrong, Rodric might suspect you since you went out tonight." Cion pressed his lips together.

"I just hope you know what you're doing then."

"It's the best chance we have." He stared down at her.

They seemed to have forgotten I was there. I cleared my throat.

Cion had the decency to look a little sheepish as he took a step away from Latia.

"I still don't like this, Cion," Latia said.

"They'll suspect something tomorrow if we don't turn Kateri in and don't attack the wells. It has to be tonight."

"Please be careful," she said.

"You too," he replied. He stared down at her for a moment, then something sparked in his eyes. "Oh." He reached into his pocket. "I know you refused to leave on the last caravan, but I think it's finally time you have this." He pulled out a small object wrapped in cloth.

She looked questioningly up at him.

"Please," he said. He pushed it toward her.

Reluctantly, she took it in her hands. She unwrapped the cloth, but I couldn't see what it hid.

Her eyes went wide. She looked up at Cion. Her hands were shaking.

The cloth that had been concealing the object fell back. Gold glinted in the moonlight.

It took me a moment to recognize what I was seeing. A bracelet. And not just any bracelet. An engagement bracelet.

My heart dropped.

"It's time for you to leave the palace," he said.

She shook her head in disbelief and appeared to be blinking back tears.

"Just keep it for now," he continued. He curled her fingers

gently around the bracelet. "We can talk about it later, after we destroy the water controls. Things will be different after that."

She looked up at him. Her mouth opened and closed several times as she tried to speak. Finally, she said, "I hope you're right." She tucked the bracelet into her pocket and wiped her eyes. "But I still don't want you to do this."

"I know," he said gently, "but Kateri is offering us our best chance yet."

Latia shot me a hard, studying glare, like she was reliving every moment we'd spent together, weighing if I would be up for the task. Then she turned back to Cion. "I only hope you know what you're doing."

"I do."

They stared at each other for a few moments. Finally, Latia lowered her gaze and nodded. "All right."

He pulled her into one last hug.

I turned away, offering them what little privacy I could while ignoring the tightening in my stomach. It's not like I had any claims on Cion. He was my trainer, nothing more. Besides, I had bigger things to worry about.

I never even wanted to wear one of those engagement bracelets. Shackles, I had called them.

Only, maybe I was wrong. Maybe they didn't chain you down. Maybe they chained you to someone. Someone you never wanted to lose.

Cion released Latia, and she wiped away a tear, pulled up her hood, and to her credit, walked with her shoulders thrown back until she faded into the desert shadows.

Cion watched her go for a long time. Eventually, he turned to me. "I wanted to tell you about Latia," he said, "but—"

"I get it," I said. I didn't need him to explain. I didn't want him to explain.

Just like my father kept the location of the water controls secret, Cion had kept her a secret. You did that to protect the things you cared about most, the things you couldn't afford to lose.

"Let's go before we lose any more time," I said as I cut a path across the desert, revealing along the way everything I knew about the arena tunnel and tiger cages to drown out the aching in my chest.

CHAPTER

25

The hideout was quiet when we returned. I heard the slight whispers of breath as we passed by small alcoves where boys slept and in the main room, where Dimic and a handful of other boys were also fast asleep.

I stayed in the entryway while Cion crept over the boys to his brother. He woke him with nothing more than a tap on his shoulder.

Dimic rubbed his eyes and sat up. He must've understood the need for silence since he followed his brother out into the hallway without a word.

"We're going after the controls tonight," Cion said. "I need you to use your lock-picking skills to break into the palace."

Dimic's eyes went wide. "I'm assuming you have a plan."

Cion filled him in as we double-checked our weapons. Then Cion handed me a ladleful of water. I let the coolness slip down my throat. I dipped the ladle back into the bucket and held it out to Dimic. He didn't take it.

A mischievous smile spread across his face. He grabbed the bucket at our feet and started chugging water.

"Dimic," Cion hissed.

Dimic released the bucket and wiped his sleeve across his face, getting rid of dirt and water droplets but not his smile. "What? Either we break the controls tonight and get all the water we want, or Rodric catches us and we never get to drink again."

"Thanks for your vote of confidence," Cion said. He took the ladle from me and drank. I could see the makings of a smile tugging at the corners of his mouth.

As we carefully made our way across the still-dark desert, Dimic regaled us with everything he was going to do once he had all the water he could dream of.

"First, I'm going to take a bath," he said. "Then I'm going to build a moat around our house," Dimic continued. "Big enough to swim in."

"You should probably learn to swim then," Cion cut in.

Dimic ignored his brother. "And I'm going to have a fountain I can drink from whenever I want. It'll be taller than the palace. Everyone will come to see it."

I was glad for Dimic. His dreams blocked out the reality of what lay ahead of us.

But by the time the city wall came into sight, even Dimic had grown quiet.

The barest ring of light formed a halo around the horizon, hinting that the sun was eager to spread its heat once more.

The city gates lay unguarded, as they had since being blown off their hinges by a sandstorm before I was born. The only things worth guarding in the city were the wells anyway since no army could make it across the desert without kicking up a cloud of dust we'd see miles away.

The arena lay not too far past the wall.

After checking to make sure Rodric hadn't posted any guards, we ducked toward it. There was just enough light to see by.

A thick bolt secured the gates I'd left the arena from just a handful of days before—I shuddered at how little regard I'd paid the people clinging to those bars then. Maybe they hadn't been looking to me just for water. Maybe they'd been looking to me for hope.

Dimic knelt down in front of the lock and stared through the keyhole. After a few seconds of consideration, he pulled up his thin shirt to reveal various sizes and shapes of metal. He pulled one out and shoved it into the lock. After a few moments, there was a click and the bolt retreated.

The hinges groaned against the sand trapped in them as we moved inside. I led the way down the tunnel, past the prep room.

The tunnel was cool and quiet. Our feet scraped against the sand-littered floor.

I stopped at a heavy wooden door. Again, Dimic selected a tool and went to work. This door took slightly longer, and he put more effort into shoving the metal into the lock.

I couldn't help casting glances down both ends of the tunnel, but no one appeared.

Once we entered, I was as blind as they were in our pitch-black surroundings. I'd never been in the tigers' tunnel before. I kept my hand on the wall, where every few feet there were deep grooves. Claw marks.

I tried to gauge how far through the city we'd moved. We were probably between the southern and eastern well. We were sloping up, which was a good sign. We were getting closer.

Sooner than I expected, a light appeared. It silhouetted the doorway in front of us, the one leading to the tiger trainers' prep area. My breath caught at the chance someone was in there at this hour.

I slowed my approach and crept toward the door, trying to keep my footfalls softer than those Cion made.

Peering through the tiny window in the door, I saw ropes and the long poles used to control the tigers lining the walls. A table sat in the corner. Bits of leftover meat dripped blood onto the floor. A long stretch of the small room sat empty, presumably so the tigers could be walked through.

"It's empty," I said. I tried the latch, and this door was unlocked.

I snuck into the room and heard the others follow. We moved quickly to the door across from us and threw it open.

Despite the two torches lit on either end of the room, I shivered in the cold.

Both tigers leapt up at our appearance.

Dimic jumped and plastered himself against the wall opposite the cages. Cion stared at the tigers, as though he were finally getting to come face to face with an enemy that had always stalked him unseen.

The closest tiger launched its claws at the bars. Cion didn't flinch.

Slowly, he pulled himself away from the tigers and moved toward the door that led to the hallway. "Let's keep going before all this noise attracts attention," he said.

Dimic eagerly scurried after him.

Cion motioned for me to follow, but something tugged at me.

I spun around the room. Cion's words from the desert came back to me. When you went so long without water, you learned to recognize when it was around.

The air down here wasn't just cold.

It was moist.

I'd always thought the tiger cages had to be kept cool to keep the tigers from overheating. But what if that wasn't it?

I scanned the room and came to a dead stop in front of the cages.

There through the bars, straight across from me, stood a

small wooden door. The same door I'd thought as a child you'd have to be crazy to go through because you'd have to make it through the gauntlet of tigers.

I turned around to the wall, to the small keyhole.

But the trainers didn't have the key to pull back the tigers by their chains. Only my father did, and it never left his sight.

He only used to come here to pick out which tiger he wanted present at an arena trial. But more and more recently, he and Rodric had been going together.

I wandered closer to the cage. A tiger leapt at me, but I ignored it.

If I didn't hate him so much, I would be oddly impressed at how well my father protected his controls.

"Kateri," Cion whispered. "The hall's clear. Let's go."

"I found the controls," I replied, pointing to the door.

Dimic peeked back into the room and shook his head. "Uh-uh. I'm not going in there. I don't look good with slashes down my body."

I moved aside to reveal the keyhole. "Can you pick that?"

"And let the tigers free?" he asked incredulously. "I think the lack of water has gone to your head, Kateri."

"This pulls back the tigers' chains," I explained. "We should be able to walk right past them."

"You're sure that's where the controls are?" Cion asked, coming to stand next to me in front of the cage.

"If Latia's searched as much as she can down here, this makes sense. She wouldn't have been able to search back there. My father has the only key."

Cion nodded and motioned Dimic forward. "It's worth a try then."

Dimic reluctantly knelt down, pulled out a bigger piece of metal, and went to work.

Cion took up position by the door leading to the rest of the palace.

The tigers paced the length of the bars, studying our movements. Their eyes sparked with intelligence, understanding. They knew what that keyhole did. And they were waiting, ready to strike, to fight for their freedom, before the chains dragged them backward.

The torches made the shadows of the tigers play across the wall. Up and up they rose, surging across the ceiling.

I shivered and shut my eyes. Did they always keep the lanterns lit? I fingered my sword hilt. I wish I'd spent more time down here to know. I kept waiting for some trainer to come through the door at any moment. Every growl of a tiger made me freeze, listening for boots running toward us.

After what seemed like an eternity, Dimic cried, "I got it."

A great cranking echoed through the room. The tigers fought against the chains around their necks, but slowly they were pulled backward toward the walls. There was just enough room between where their paws could reach for us to walk single file through the room.

Dimic opened the door to the cage as quickly as he'd gotten my shackles off.

Cion was the first to step into the cage. He held his sword at the ready. The beasts tugged at their collars, but they couldn't reach him.

Dimic and I hurried after. Long claws fell just short of our shoulders. Teeth glinted against the light. But for the first time, I noticed the missing fur and scarred skin around their necks where their collars had dragged them back so many times. My father was choking the life out of them, out of the desert itself, as much as he was the rest of us.

The tigers' sides heaved with effort as they continued to pull at their chains. Their ribcages were visible since my father had kept them underfed to make them more aggressive in the arena—just like he hadn't fed me the truth about my mother in order to motivate me to fight.

I looked away before the pain in their eyes reflected too much of my own.

Dimic scooted forward and unlocked the door faster than any of the others, probably because he didn't like the tigers being so close.

We all pushed through the door, eager to be away from the tigers. We ended up on a ledge overlooking a vast underground lake contained in a bowl-shaped ring of rock. The whole cavern had to be at least four or five times the size of the palace grounds. I could barely make out the ceiling above us. A narrow staircase of about thirty uneven steps led down the side of the ledge, toward the lake.

What a lake it was. I'd never seen so much water in my life. From one tunnel at the far end of the cavern, even more water poured into its depths.

"A waterfall," Dimic said in awe.

The end of the lake closest to us had a gap in the rock face about the size of two of my arm spans. Ten or so long beams of wood and clay dammed it up. A small amount of water trickled over the beams and down into one of four grooves, each leading toward a tunnel about the size of a doorway.

Those must lead to the wells.

All of the tunnels had slabs of thin rock raised to various heights that, once the dam was removed, would allow a certain amount of water through. The slabs were held in place by ropes that looped upward toward the ceiling of the cavern and down to a spot below us.

There were a few more unblocked tunnels situated around the room, but I doubted they went anywhere important since they weren't blocked off. They were probably just tunnels carved out by the water over time.

A few torches cast light around the area.

"Dimic," Cion said, "cut those ropes." He pointed to the ones holding the slabs in place. "Kateri, come with me. We're going to chop through those beams blocking the rest of the water."

"I don't think you are," a voice called.

A figure meandered out of one of the unblocked tunnels and into the light.

My heart stopped.

Rodric.

Soldiers followed him.

"Run!" Cion shouted.

I turned just in time to see a guard in front of the keyhole. A large clanking reverberated through the room. Chains clinked to the ground. The tigers sprang to life. I was barely able to slam the door closed before one raked its claws right toward it.

I leaned back against the wood, my heart hammering in my chest.

We were trapped.

CHAPTER 26

Rodric sauntered closer. "I didn't think you'd actually find this place," he said. "But after I followed a little birdie into the desert tonight, I had to see for myself if you could figure it out. I couldn't resist being here if you did."

"No." Cion went pale.

"Latia." Dimic let out a whimper.

"Come on, Cion." Rodric spit the name. "I always thought you were smart. I followed you when you used to meet her in the desert when I was still one of you. I knew she'd come in handy someday. And I was right." He leapt over the small trickle of water flowing into the tunnel he'd emerged from. "I thought Dimic would be the one to lead me to you, but Latia was so much easier to follow."

I couldn't imagine what Rodric had done to her. I didn't even know if she was still alive. Maybe she was somewhere bleeding and hanging from one of the towers.

I shook away the image. We needed to get away from Rodric before we could search for her.

But Cion couldn't let it go. "What did you do to her?" he raged.

Rodric shrugged. "I made her sing."

"You're going to wish you were bitten by a yellow-spotted sand snake instead of facing me."

"That's funny," Rodric replied. "I always thought of you as a snake—the way you crawl through the desert with that ridiculous sword of yours."

Cion let out a cry and leapt off the ledge. He rolled forward, meeting Rodric's blade.

The pack of soldiers gathered around the bottom of the ledge, staring up at Dimic and me. Several moved toward the stairs.

"I'm Princess Kateri," I said to the soldiers. "If you throw down your arms now, you'll not be punished. But any who stand with Rodric are traitors and will be dealt with as such."

The men didn't stop their advance.

"That worked well," Dimic quipped beside me.

"It was worth a try."

"What do we do now?" Dimic asked.

"We fight."

"You fight," Dimic said. "I'm going to cut through those logs and fill up the wells."

Before I could stop him, he leapt off the ledge as his brother had done. He took out one guard by sliding his blade across the man's leg as he rolled by. Then he was off, running toward the dam stopping the water flow.

Soldiers moved to stop him, but I didn't see what happened next because a barrage of them reached the top of the staircase.

My position proved an advantage. Only one could fit up the stairs at a time, so I dispatched them each quickly in turn. At least until the last three grew wise and huddled at the bottom of the stairs, waiting for me.

I leapt down the stairs, kicking one in the face and elbowing another. I got my sword up to block the third one's blow.

He swung. I knocked it aside.

I went for his knees. He blocked.

I circled around the soldier. He matched me step for step.

I took every skill Cion had taught me and rammed my sword over and over again toward the soldier's chest. His blocks became sluggish. Fear played about his eyes.

That look was still on his face when my sword slid into his stomach. He gasped and fell to the ground.

I pulled my blade free and turned to assess the situation.

Cion was holding his own against Rodric.

Dimic was hacking away at the beams of wood stopping up the lake. It looked like he'd already gotten through one and was fighting the current of water to hack at the next.

Water cascaded over the beams and hit the slabs full force before pooling back into the room.

If I didn't get those slabs moved, then the water would just trickle wastefully down the open tunnels.

I raced to where the ropes wound around wheels, waiting to be raised or lowered, and swung through the ropes holding up the first slab.

There was a loud crash as one of the slabs fell to the ground and keeled forward. Water flowed over and around it into the tunnel leading to one of the wells.

It was swiftly followed by three more.

Rodric screamed in frustration.

Before the echo of the last slab settling in place had died out, I was already running toward Dimic. His thin body wouldn't be able to stand up to the increasing current for long.

Worse, as I got closer, I spotted the soldier he'd cut across the leg climbing up the beams toward him. He was hidden under the stream of water. Dimic couldn't even see him.

"Dimic, look out!" I called.

He turned in time to avoid the soldier's blade from running through his side, but he lost his balance on the beam. He splashed into the water behind him.

"Dimic!" I screamed. I swallowed the bile creeping up my throat. My heart thudded in my chest. He couldn't swim.

I dropped my sword and leapt onto the beams. Clay had dried between the logs. Chunks of it had eroded over the years, leaving easy handholds. I pulled my way up toward the soldier, grabbing his ankle and pulling him down. He tried to kick me. I tugged harder. He lost his grip and thudded to the ground below me.

I fought against the water pouring above me and got ahold of the highest beam, pulling myself up. I scanned the water around the dam.

There was no sign of Dimic.

I shoved wet hair from my face.

"Dimic!" I shouted.

I searched for any sign of bubbles. Any ripples.

The cave was too dark to see much of anything, but I sensed something moving in the water.

My heart leapt.

Dimic's head peeked above the surface. His arms flailed weakly. He tried to gulp in air but got water instead. His head drifted under.

I dove in.

The water was colder than anything I'd felt before.

My muscles seized up.

I plunged my arms forward into the darkness.

I spotted him several feet below the surface. His legs were kicking but he wasn't moving upward.

I swooped in and grabbed him around his stomach. I kicked upward until his head broke the surface. He gagged and coughed as I swam back to the dam with one arm around him.

I heaved him up onto the rocks.

He turned on his stomach and coughed up water. "Is that what a bath feels like?" he choked out.

"Real baths are much better," I said, hauling him to his feet. "And I promise to make sure you have one as soon as we get out of here."

"Good," he said, "because I think I know how to bring down the wall." He slipped the two daggers out of my sandal laces and tossed one to me. "There's no way we can chop from above with all that water. But if we can wedge enough cracks in the clay in between the slats, the water might do the work for us."

I stared down at the wall. His plan just might work. "Stay here. I'll do it," I said. "If that wall comes crashing down, I don't want you getting caught in the wave."

I moved to the edge of the dam and positioned myself so I was hanging off the ledge. From there, it was easy to duck under the pouring water and climb midway down the wall. I rammed my dagger into the clay, rotating it back and forth. Water spurted out. I moved further down the wall and repeated the motion until a steady stream of water slipped through.

The wood groaned.

So did someone behind me.

The noise tore through me.

"Cion!" Dimic called.

Leaving one dagger wedged in the clay, I let go of the wall before I could even think. My feet thudded against the wet earth. I dashed through the water.

By the time I got close enough to see what was going on, Rodric had Cion wedged in one of the channels. He was holding him under the water with his foot against Cion's chest. When Cion struggled to get free, Rodric kicked the sword from Cion's hand.

"Finally enough water for you?" Rodric taunted.

I switched my remaining dagger to my left hand and scooped up my sword as I ran toward them. I swung my blade toward the middle of Rodric's back. He must've heard me coming because he turned to meet the blow. Our blades met midair. The clang resounded through the cavern.

Just as Cion had taught me, I moved my dagger upward, nearly catching Rodric under his ribs, but he brought his other arm down and caught my wrist, squeezing until I let go. Then he released my wrist, flinging me backward.

I stumbled a few paces away.

The whole time he'd kept his foot on Cion, keeping him below the water. Cion had stopped struggling.

"Maybe I should give you gills again and see how well you can swim," Rodric said.

"You can try." I moved several steps back in the hopes he'd follow.

He did.

And as he moved, his foot released Cion.

Rodric slowly advanced toward me.

It was hard to keep focused on him. I kept getting caught in crevices or tripping into puddles as I moved backward. And with water gurgling everywhere, it was impossible to tell how close the next channel of water was. If I turned to look, Rodric would strike.

"What chance do you think you have?" Rodric asked. "Not even Cion could beat me."

"I'm not dead yet." Cion, dripping wet, swung his blade at Rodric, who ducked under the blow and whirled several steps back to keep us both in view.

Over his shoulder, I caught sight of Dimic on the dam, drilling my other dagger into the clay.

My view lasted only a moment as Rodric charged forward, his blade soaring toward my neck. I knocked it away, but Rodric's foot caught me in the knee.

I stumbled backward as Cion moved forward.

"Is that the best you could teach her, Cion?" Rodric asked. "I think you made her worse. At least she'll be easier to beat in the arena."

Cion didn't respond. He kept his focus on the battle, but I could tell he was exhausted. His blocks were sloppy. His footwork was hindered by the slippery terrain.

"But you," Rodric continued, "you I can kill now." He took a long swipe at Cion, who leapt back. Rodric laughed. The sound echoed around the cavern. "Even together you can't beat me."

Cion drove his blade toward Rodric's arm. Rodric spun away from the blow and responded by swinging his sword toward Cion's face. "I couldn't stand taking orders from a weak leader like you. Cintric should've given me that sword. He should've left me in charge. I'm the one chosen by the desert."

Cion's blade met his in the air, and they pushed against one another. "I'm not weak."

"Tell that to Remy. And to Latia."

Cion put his full weight into shoving Rodric back.

Rodric stumbled a few feet away. "Too weak to save them

both." He shot a look over his shoulder to where Dimic was still punching holes in the clay. "Maybe I'll keep you alive long enough to watch Dimic die too."

Cion roared and moved forward.

I moved to stand shoulder to shoulder with Cion. We became a whirl of blades. One of us would advance while the other tried to move a little to the side to get around Rodric, to force his blows farther apart by having to turn more to defend himself.

But Rodric's attacks never faltered. Each blow against my sword radiated down my arm. My bones hurt. My muscles groaned. I was used to having a shield to absorb those hits.

Then it happened.

He hit me with so much force it ripped my sword from my hand. I faltered forward.

Miraculously, Cion was there to stop the blow that would've cut down my arm, but it cost him.

He'd left his entire side exposed.

He inhaled sharply as Rodric's blade sliced across his ribs.

"No!" I screamed.

Too late.

Cion fell to his knees. His sword splashed against the rocky channel.

Rodric pulled his blade back once more.

I scrambled forward, reaching for Cion's sword. Before my hand got there, a crack sounded through the cavern.

All eyes went to the dam towering above us. Spouts of water burst through the clay. Several beams bent outward.

I spotted Dimic's shadowy figure under the falling water. "Get out of there!" I screamed, but the sound was cut off by the splintering of wood and a roar unlike anything I'd ever heard.

I dove toward Cion, wrapping my arms around his neck. I barely had time to take a breath before the wave hit us. Then we were tumbling, being tossed in too many directions. I felt like I was in the shifting hills.

I smashed into rock. The force of it stole my air. I lost my grip on Cion and tumbled underwater. When my head broke the surface, I spotted him ahead of me.

He was flapping one arm in the water, but the effort read across his face.

I let the current take me closer to him.

"Hang on," I cried, catching hold of his arm.

We were at the front of a wave racing down one of the tunnels, and the current had a firm grip on us. I prayed that it was a tunnel that led to a well. Otherwise, we'd drown when the water collided with a dead end.

Cion winced every time the tossing waves pulled us apart, forcing me to tug on his arm. We choked and gagged as water sprayed us. I couldn't even feel the chill of the water because I was too focused on searching for any hint we were headed toward one of the wells. My free arm scraped along the edge as I fought to stay afloat. Ahead, the tunnel brightened just enough to become visible.

"The well," I shouted between blasts of water hitting my face. It had to be. It was that or Cion was growing paler by the minute. Maybe both.

One final push shoved us forward. We swirled upward.

Light.

We were being pushed up one of the wells. Green moss gave way to thick stones. We were nearly to the top of the well when we slowed.

Our bodies bounced back and forth between the walls as the water settled into place. Cion cried out with each impact.

I grabbed onto a mossy patch of rock and surveyed the situation. The water around Cion swirled red. His face was ashen and his eyes cloudy. His head dipped dangerously close to the waterline. It was taking all his energy to hold it that far up.

I transferred his grip on me to the wall so that I didn't keep jostling him around every time I moved, but without the current holding him up, he was sinking steadily.

I looked up at the circle of light above us.

We still had probably fifteen feet to the top.

There was no way I'd have time to climb up and lower the bucket to him to pull him up. Not before he sank and drowned.

There was only one other option.

"Can you climb?" I asked.

He let out a small noise that I couldn't tell was meant as a yes or a no. But he started pulling himself up the wall.

His eyes scrunched shut. His knuckles turned white, and yet he continued to move upward.

If it'd been anyone but Cion, I doubted they'd have the strength.

I waited until he made it a few stones up before climbing up after him.

He kept having to pause to catch his breath. His entire side was covered with blood, which stained the wall as it slid down into the water.

"Keep going," I urged. "You're almost there."

His breaths were labored when he made it to the ledge. I hopped over first and pulled him the rest of the way up. His fingers were clammy and could barely grasp mine. His eyes rolled back in his head.

We landed with a thud in the sand.

"You're not giving up now," I said. He looked even paler in the morning light. His lips were nearly blue. He started shivering.

I knelt next to him.

Already the sand beneath his side was turning red.

I pressed my hands against the wound. It was nearly the length of my entire hand. And it was deep.

"Come on, Cion," I pleaded. "You can't give up on me now. Not when we've made it this far."

"Dimic," he moaned.

"He's fine," I said. I knew it was a lie, but it was what he needed to hear. "He will meet us back at the hideout." I shoved wet strands of hair away from his forehead.

I knew Dimic couldn't swim. The image of Dimic's shape against the beams when the dam burst haunted me. I couldn't let Cion see that; he needed to believe his brother was alive. That hope might be the only thing holding him together.

Because the desert couldn't take that from him. Not Dimic. He'd never even gotten to take a bath. And I couldn't imagine a more horrible way for a Desert Boy to die than to drown in the very water he'd been deprived of his whole life.

I shoved the thought away. I'd get Cion to safety and then scour the wells looking for Dimic. I would find him. Alive.

"I need to get you to an apothecary."

"No," Cion wheezed. His eyes fluttered open, unfocused. He tried to sit up and fell back. "Most of them . . . Rodric's spies."

"There has to be someone here who would help you," I pleaded.

He shook his head. "Can't risk it. Get back to the hideout. Sew it shut with a cactus spine."

I didn't like it, but I nodded. I prayed he'd last that long.

"Thank you," Cion murmured. His hand shook as it stretched toward my cheek, resting there for a heartbeat before falling away.

That heartbeat was enough. Because the warmth his touch sent through me was nothing like the unrelenting heat of the desert sun. It was gentle and welcoming. And I knew even if his heart belonged to Latia, I couldn't live in a world where that warmth didn't exist, even if I never got to feel it again.

I pulled Cion to his feet and propped his arm around my shoulder only to realize we were surrounded by a wide circle of guards and a crowd of people looking for water.

CHAPTER 27

People stood gaping at us over the guards' shoulders.

The guards ringed us in on all sides, standing about twenty feet from the well to keep people back. But as they slowly turned to face us, they hemmed us in.

And I didn't have a single weapon on me.

"Cion," someone whispered.

The name raced through the crowd.

The guards moved their circle in closer around us.

I scanned the faces of the soldiers, looking for one I knew. One I'd fought before. One I knew I could easily rob of his weapon.

I didn't recognize any of them.

I was about to run back for the water bucket as my only available weapon when the first ration coin flew from the crowd. It smashed into the helmet of the guard directly in front of us.

Then they started coming from all directions.

The people were throwing away their most important possession. For Cion.

Buckets started flying out of the crowd as well.

I heard Cion's name chanted over and over again.

Soldiers threw up their arms to protect their exposed faces. As soon as one of the soldiers went down, I hauled Cion toward the opening.

The crowd parted for us and closed in behind us, not allowing the soldiers to see our path.

Cion weighed down my body. Each step took more and more effort.

We made it through the crowd and into the streets. I scanned up and down each looking for a landmark I knew. But I'd never spent much time on the streets, and I didn't even know which well we'd bubbled up in.

I tried to find the sun to navigate by, but I still got lost in the maze, full of the knowledge that every wrong turn could cost us. Could cost Cion.

"Which way's the main gate?" I called desperately to an old woman sweeping sand from in front of her shop.

She looked me up and down before gazing at Cion.

"Two streets down," she said quietly. "Take a left."

I nodded and repositioned Cion's arm over my shoulder.

After following her directions, the broken gate leading out into the desert loomed ahead.

I leaned Cion against the wall as we passed.

His eyes wouldn't focus on my face.

I grabbed both his cheeks in my hands, trying to force him to look at me. "Cion, which way is the hideout?" I scanned his face for some recognition.

Sweat dotted his brow. He mumbled something I couldn't make out. His head rolled forward. I fought to keep him upright.

I switched my gaze to the sea of hills. I couldn't risk wandering around in the desert while the sun continued to rise. Already, I couldn't tell if I was still wet from the well or if the sun had dried me and I was dripping sweat.

"Come on, Cion," I pleaded.

Every moment I hesitated, the sun rose higher, and he lost more blood.

His eyes closed, and he sagged against me.

A blood beetle burrowed out of the sand and scuttled toward Cion. I kicked it away. But if we didn't move quickly, more would come.

I pounded my fist into the crumbling wall. The desert wasn't taking someone from me. Not this time.

I looped his arm back over my shoulder and shuffled forward. I prayed that if the desert really did respect its masters, it would show me the way.

I didn't even have energy to be proud I'd successfully spotted a sand snake hole and navigated around it, because if I'd thought Cion had been heavy before, it was worse pulling him up sand dunes. Once we made it to the top of one, we half stumbled, half fell back down. Then I'd start the trudge upward once more.

On one such dune, I was about to lean forward and tumble down into the next valley when something made me look back.

A dripping wet Rodric stood at the gate with a pack of soldiers. He pointed right toward us. And then they were racing across the sand.

I forced my legs to move faster. Cion took about one step for every four of mine until eventually his feet simply dragged behind me.

My shoulders groaned. My arms ached. My heart thudded so loudly in my ears that I couldn't hear the sand. I couldn't hear how close they were getting.

My lungs burned so badly it felt like I was underwater again.

I kept my focus on getting up each sand dune as it appeared before me. But every time we crested one, the figures grew closer. Rodric drew closer.

Hot sand scorched my calves and shins as I dug my legs into the dunes to get enough leverage to pull Cion up.

We reached the top of a dune just as Rodric and his men crested the one behind us.

Rodric leapt into the valley between us.

"Nowhere to run now, Kateri," he said.

He started up the dune toward us.

I glanced down into the next valley, praying there was someplace to hide. Something to use as a weapon. Some sign that if I shouted, the Desert Boys would come running.

What I saw before me wasn't unending sand. It was a sea of black. It had to be some sort of mirage.

I shook my vision clear, certain the effort of dragging Cion had caused my vision to haze, that I was moments from blacking out.

No matter how many times I blinked, the sand ahead of us remained black.

Rodric's feet pounded into the dune. The whisper of the sand wrapped around me, warning he was getting closer.

The sound was echoed by something else. Soft clicking. At first, I couldn't figure out what it was. Until the sand in front of me shifted without the wind blowing it.

Because it wasn't sand.

It was scorpions.

Scorpion Hill.

The thought jolted through my mind. I'd stumbled upon the very place Tamlin had run through on his way to save the kingdom.

If he'd made it through unscathed, maybe I could.

I swallowed down the thought that no one had ever survived

a scorpion sting, telling myself I shared Tamlin's blood. I could make it.

Rodric's heavy breathing signaled he'd neared the crest of the dune. I knew what he'd do to Cion. We were dead either way. The most I could hope for was to get Rodric to follow me out there. To take him down with me.

"I'm so sorry," I whispered to Cion as I took an unsteady step forward.

Several scorpions scuttled away as a wave of sand hit them.

I hoisted Cion as far as I could against my hip and kept going. I sent small kicks of sand forward to get scorpions to move. I took slow, measured steps.

"Still running away?" Rodric laughed. But his laugh cut off when he crested the hill and saw what waited before him. "Scorpion Hill," he breathed.

I could hear the fear in his voice. "Think about what you're doing, Kateri. Get back here while you still can."

"If you want me," I panted over my shoulder, "you'll have to come and get me." I'd made it to the first valley between the dunes. I turned to stare up at Rodric. Half because I wanted to draw him out. And half because I wasn't sure how much longer I could hold Cion up.

Sweat greased my grip on him. His head rolled against my shoulder with every step I took. I just needed him to hold on a little bit longer. Either I was going to find a way out of this, or it was all going to be over very soon.

I'd created a makeshift path in the mass of scorpions. A few had filled in some of the gaps, but it wouldn't be hard for Rodric to follow me.

He eyed me.

"You're not Tamlin," he said.

"Then prove you are," I called. "I've made it this far without being stung. Prove you're better than me. Prove these creatures recognize you as the king of the desert that you claim to be, that my father thinks you are. Prove once and for all that this desert is picking you and not me."

I could tell he was mulling it over in his mind. His soldiers joined him on the ridge and considered their leader.

"Didn't Cion tell you where he left me to die? It was here." He stomped forward, crunching scorpions as he went. "He left me right here on this ridge, and the scorpions didn't sting me. This desert chose not to kill me. I am the desert king."

"You're not a desert king," I called. "You couldn't even survive in the desert like the rest of us can. You fled back to the city. But not us. No, these creatures won't touch us. They know the desert has accepted us, embraced us."

"I am the only master here," Rodric said. He raised his sword and used it to flick scorpions away in big, sweeping swipes, clearing a wide path.

Every scorpion he sent flying landed atop another one, agitating it. The mass came alive. The sound of legs clicking against hard bodies and tails was overwhelming.

I turned back to the dune in front of me. I kicked sand up it, but the scorpions only had one direction to move—down, toward me. I couldn't clear a path.

Every swipe of Rodric's sword signaled he was getting closer.

I kicked more and more sand up the dune. Nothing happened.

The scrape of Rodric's sword was right behind me.

I didn't know how long it would take for scorpion poison to set in, but maybe it'd be long enough to let me get Cion to safety.

Abandoning my method, I dug my feet into the dune. Scorpion bodies squished under my sandals, a sickening crunch.

Then I felt it.

I inhaled sharply. It felt like a cactus spine rammed into my ankle. And it was on fire. I lost feeling in my foot. I tried to take another step. My leg buckled. I landed on my knees.

Stingers sliced into my calf and lower thigh. The whole left side of my body burned as though someone had bottled the sun and poured it on me. The pain was so great I couldn't cry out. Not a sound passed my lips.

I lost my grip on Cion. He rolled down the dune and lay at Rodric's feet.

Miraculously, it appeared not a single scorpion stung him. They actually seemed to be moving away from him.

Rodric picked up Cion by his collar. "And I thought killing you would be a challenge." He pulled his sword back and readied it to run Cion through, but then a small smile slid across his face. "No, I've got a better idea." He shoved Cion's limp form to the guards who'd ventured warily into the path he'd cleared.

I struggled to get my body working. My muscles wouldn't respond. None of my fingers would bend. I couldn't even blink.

Get up, I told myself in a desperate mantra.

"I always knew the desert would pick me," Rodric said. He pulled my braid, and I fell into the sand at his feet. He crouched down to look at me. "And the Desert Boys will have to be held responsible for your death, just like they were your mother's, because your father won't want it known his weak daughter died on the same hill Tamlin escaped. The same hill I've survived twice now." He patted me on my cheek and disappeared from view. "Take them back to the palace," he called to his soldiers.

The fire in my left side spread to my right. It seared through my lungs. I wasn't sure if I could breathe or not. Everything in front of me spun around, a mix of golden sand and black scorpions.

It swirled and swirled until everything went dark.

CHAPTER 28

Fire ripped through me. It knotted my veins. It tore my muscles from the walls of my body. It turned my bones to ash. And just when I thought it would melt through my flesh, it turned to ice.

Beads of sweat froze on my skin. My bones hardened, and then repeatedly cracked as the ice spread through them. Splinters broke off and threatened to ram through my flesh.

Everything began to itch. I could feel the scorpions crawling on me, burrowing into me. I screamed for someone to get them off me.

And I heard voices.

"Remarkable she's still alive."

"More strength than I thought possible."

They faded. I returned to a world of darkness, too tired to fight off the scorpions any longer.

When I woke, light streamed in through a high window.

I bolted upright. Everything in the room spun. I tried to put my hand to my head to steady it, but shackles prevented me.

"You're awake," Rodric said, sliding into the room. "It only took you three days. Although, really, I'm surprised you're alive at all."

I tried to lunge for him. The chains held me back.

"Save that for the arena," he said. "Your birthday will be here soon."

"I'm going to kill you," I spat.

"You can try," he said. "But you and Cion have already failed more times than I can count."

"What did you do to Cion?"

He crossed his arms over his chest and a self-satisfied smile spread across his lips. "I have big plans for him. And for you." He gestured to the practically empty room around us. "I hope you like your new chamber. After we're married, it'll be yours. Your father has his tigers as his pets. I'm going to have you. But," he continued, mock sadness marring his voice, "in your weakened state, it won't be a surprise if you succumb to the ailments the Desert Boys will give you mere hours after bearing me a son."

I glared at him. My fingernails dug into my palms. If I wasn't chained, I would've gouged his eyes out.

"But that will come later. For now, you should rest," he said. "You're going to have a big decision to make tomorrow."

"What do you mean?" I hated the glint in his eye.

He smiled. "You'll see."

I pulled against the chains.

He laughed and left.

"I'll kill you," I screamed until the door opened a few minutes later.

A portly older maid walked in carrying a bowl of soup and a glass of water.

"Latia," I said. "Where's Latia?" I couldn't have lost everyone.

But for once, I couldn't blame the desert. I'd done this. I'd put them all in danger.

The woman ignored me. She placed the bowl and glass on the small table next to my bed. She then sat in the chair next to it, dipped a spoon into the soup, and then cradled it gently toward my mouth.

"Please," I said, "you have to help me."

She instead tried to force the soup into my mouth. I jerked my head away.

"Please, I have to get out of here."

She tried again.

"No," I shouted. "I have to stop Rodric. He's going to bleed this town dry. Whatever he's promised you, he's lying. It was all lies—the drought, everything."

Again, she tried to get the spoon into my mouth. Soup spilled down my chin as I clamped my lips shut.

"Rodric is going to cut off water to the wells unless everyone obeys his every command. He's going to be worse than my father. I can stop him, but I have to get out of here. I have to find the Desert Boys."

She silently refilled the spoon and tried again.

"Aren't you listening?" I pleaded. "Don't you have people out there who are dying without water? I can help them. I can help you. I'll protect you from him."

She leaned forward with a cross look on her face, like I was child that needed to behave, and when she did, her hair shifted. Where her ears should've been, two long, puffy scars lay. They were fresh.

"No," I said, gasping.

Her eyes pleaded with me just to eat the soup. And while my mouth hung agape looking at her scars, she slid the spoon into my mouth.

I gagged and swallowed.

The soup settled like sand in my stomach.

I silently let her feed me the rest and pour the water down my throat. It should've felt good after so long without it, but I had to fight not to gag on every mouthful.

Tears slipped down my cheeks. I tried to hold them back because I was going to need my strength. Because no matter how long it took, I was going to kill Rodric.

CHAPTER 29

My new maid, whose name I'd probably never learn, woke me at sunrise the next day. She wiped away the dirt, dust, and sand and smoothed my hair. Then, while I was still chained to the bed, she stripped off my old gladiator gear and maneuvered a clean, gauzy dress onto me.

The last time I'd worn such fabric, I'd performed the sand dance.

I blinked back tears.

I didn't know if any of those boys were still alive. Especially Dimic. I'd been the one to involve him in the plan. It was my fault he was dead.

Latia was right. I didn't know what I was getting them into.

And what about Cion? Whatever he was going to face was because of me. Because I sought him out. Because I couldn't face my problems on my own. No wonder the scorpions had stung me. I wasn't strong enough. I wasn't Tamlin. The desert hadn't chosen me.

The door to my room squealed open to reveal Rodric carrying another pair of shackles.

He secured them around my feet and produced a key. "Now," he said, wagging the key in front of my face, "you can either be released from your hand shackles and come with me, or I give the order to have Cion killed right now without giving you the chance to save him."

I studied his face. I didn't really see I had a choice in the matter, and if my hands were free, I'd have a better shot at finding a way to attack.

"I'll behave," I said.

"Good." He slid the key into the shackles and freed me. "Then let's go."

Several guards waited in the doorway. Rodric motioned for me to take my place between them. The chain around my ankles scraped against the floor as I walked, but it wasn't visible under my long dress.

Guards fell in around me. One of them was Sievers. He gave me the slightest of nods, so slight I wasn't sure I'd seen it at all. Maybe he'd help me escape. Maybe that nod was his signal to me to keep strong until he found the right moment to help.

But he was so rigid standing there I started to wonder if I'd imagined him nod. Was I still delirious from my scorpion stings? All of this could be a dream.

No, a nightmare.

I kept wanting to glance at Sievers, but he was stationed behind me. And Rodric had taken up his position at the very rear. No doubt because it would offer the best view of me going for any of the guards' spears or swords.

Instead of moving up through the palace, we moved down. All the way to the tigers' cage.

I had one moment of panic that Rodric was going to throw me into the cage, but we breezed past it into the tunnel leading to the stadium. My heart dropped when I spotted that one of the tigers was missing.

"I'd much rather you be publicly seen in my company so soon after my gallant rescue of you from your captors," Rodric said, "but I couldn't trust those desert rats not to make one last rescue attempt. So the tunnel will have to do."

It wasn't as dark as I remembered. Someone had lit torches at even intervals. They played against the long claw marks running down the walls. Fire-legged flies buzzed over spots of dried blood caked to the walls.

We moved down the rest of the tunnel in silence and emerged near the room I used to prep for my arena fights.

I caught the vague scent of coconut. Ahead, guards pulled a small figure into that room. A figure with a long braid.

"Latia?" I called. It had to be her.

Her head rose ever so slightly, but as soon as she saw Rodric, her eyes immediately shot down.

But not before I saw her face. Freshly cut lacerations ran down her visible skin. Dozens clouded her face. I didn't recognize her. Only the eyes betrayed it was the same girl.

"No." I shook my head.

"Don't worry," Rodric said, coming up behind me and whispering in my ear. "Yours won't be so visible. At least at first."

I jerked away from him. "What's she doing here?"

"All part of the show." He motioned for the guards to take me up a side staircase and into the arena seating area.

The crowd erupted the moment we appeared.

I looked out into the empty arena. I swallowed down the lump that rose in my throat when I thought about the insults I used to toss at the Desert Boys brought here.

Rodric waved to the crowd as if he was a kind, benevolent ruler. What I always thought had been cheers morphed into jeers. Though it was more akin to general screaming because no one wanted to be singled out for disparaging Rodric.

Except for one man.

He jolted forward from the crowd. To my astonishment, it was the Lorian man I'd saved at the well. As he tottered forward I saw his face was flushed, his steps unsteady. If I wasn't mistaken, he was drunk. He matched Rodric for size, but most of his weight was centered around his middle and not regulated to his muscles. Lister, I think Dimic had said his name was.

"There he is," Lister shouted. "The desert's greatest coward."

"Are you looking to be next in the arena?" Rodric asked. "All that weight would go a long way in feeding the tigers."

Lister moved so quickly I barely registered it. He crashed right into Rodric, driving him against the railing. The force loosened a section of the railing, sending the metal bars dangling into the arena.

Rodric managed to keep his balance by grabbing onto the part of the railing still anchored and used it to shove Lister off.

All but two of my guards rushed to help as the man attempted to charge Rodric again.

Sievers was one of the remaining guards. Was this his plan? Should I make a run for it?

But then I'd never find out where Rodric was keeping Cion. Nor could I get Latia away.

Then, I felt it.

At first I thought it was just the crowd pressing around us, but it was more than that.

Someone tugged at my shackles. I looked down to find a small figure huddled over my feet. As soon as I'd felt his hand, it was gone. So were my shackles.

"Is that a Desert Boy?" Sievers voice rang out.

My heart dropped. I thought he was going to help me, not

betray my rescuers. When my head swung around, Sievers was pointing in the complete other direction from where I stood, distracting the other guard.

Whoever had freed my shackles popped up in front of me.

Dimic.

My heart leapt.

He winked at me before disappearing into the crowd.

I had to be hallucinating, but here he was. Alive. I had to bite my lip to keep from crying out in joy.

The soldier behind me said, "That's not a boy at all. That's a girl."

"My mistake," Sievers said.

The other guards formed rank around me. Two of them had Lister in custody. They pulled him back through the stadium. The crowd roared.

He gave me a wink as he went by.

I cast my head down so Rodric wouldn't suspect anything.

The absence of my clanking shackles wasn't missed over the noise of the crowd, but I tried to keep my walk awkward, like I was still tethered.

Rodric eyed the crowd as my guards escorted me toward my father. But instead of seating me in my normal spot at my father's side, Rodric took that seat. I was shoved down next to him, farther from my father.

My father didn't acknowledge me. He instead crushed a fire-legged fly where it landed on his arm and then flicked the lifeless body away, never taking his gaze from the arena. To him, I was no more than a failed experiment, no more than the fly he'd just crushed, a woman as weak as his wife. My only use now was as an easy path for Rodric to the throne.

But I was going to show him that my mother was right, that true strength didn't come from wielding a sword. It came from having your people be willing to follow you.

I scanned the arena. If Dimic was here, that meant other Desert Boys may be as well. I could only hope that when the time came, they'd help me get a weapon. Because I could only imagine that Cion was going to be pulled into the arena. And that tigers were waiting behind both doors.

I'd only seen one tiger missing from the cage, but they'd had plenty of time to go back for the other.

Suddenly, the arena doors opened. Guards pulled a figure forward, confirming my fear.

Cion's hands were shackled as they led him to the post. His skin was ashen, and he looked thin. But he was alive.

I leapt to my feet.

Rodric yanked me down.

My hands were shaking. They went to grasp my sword hilt, which wasn't there.

"See how kind I was," Rodric said over the cries of the crowd. "I kept him alive for this moment."

"Why?" I had to admit he looked stronger than I expected. He walked unaided. He managed to hold his head up.

"Because the people need to see that even Cion falls before me. They need to be reminded who the desert has chosen."

The guards shackled Cion to the short post in the middle of the arena with several lengths of loose chain between him and the post, just enough so the accused could think he could dodge the tiger, just enough to give my father a show.

Cion turned, and his eyes sought mine. He seemed to relax a little.

I knew the feeling. I leaned forward as far as I could before Rodric pulled me back by my braid.

My father stood. The crowd quieted.

"My people," my father started, "we have before us an accused Desert Boy. But not just any Desert Boy. Their leader, Cion, who Rodric dragged from the desert."

It took several minutes to quiet the crowd. The whole time, Cion's eyes never left my face.

I tried to glean anything I could from his gaze. Was he in pain? Had Rodric tortured him? Did he know Rodric's plan? My heart broke to see him standing where I couldn't reach him. He straightened his shoulders under my gaze. I hadn't given up, and neither had he. He shifted his gaze toward my father.

"He is accused of stealing water, leading illegal caravans into the city, and kidnapping Princess Kateri."

"That's a lie." My words were cut off by Rodric grabbing my throat.

He yanked my face toward his. "Say that again, and I release the tiger right away."

He dropped his hand.

I sputtered for air. By the time I recovered, the crowd had quieted.

I forced my eyes back to Cion. His face had taken on a darker look. His hands were clenched in fists as he stared at Rodric.

Rodric smiled and turned to me. "Behind the door on the left," he whispered, "is the tiger. And behind the door on the right is Latia."

I eyed him. "Is it supposed to be worse now that I know?" Because my stomach already felt like sand was rubbing against it, dissolving it layer by layer.

He sighed like I was a child who didn't understand. "If the door reveals Latia, I promise to let them go free together. They'll be on the first caravan out of here."

"You'd never let him go."

He leaned back in his chair. "I would if it's the only thing that would make you more miserable."

"Nothing could be more miserable than being near you."

"Not even watching Cion with another woman? Knowing they're going to go off and have a wonderful life while you're stuck here with me for as long as I choose to keep you alive." He smirked down at me. "I saw you with your arms around each other when I followed Latia into the desert. But go ahead, deny you have feelings for him. Tell me you don't care if he marries Latia."

I crossed my arms and refused to answer. I never again wanted to experience the gnawing inside me when I saw Cion giving Latia an engagement bracelet. But he'd chosen her.

"Oh, and there's one more thing . . ." His face beamed. "I'll let your father tell you."

My insides turned to ice.

My father said, "While it's customary for the accused to select the door, today, Princess Kateri will pick the door instead."

Rodric shoved me to my feet.

I caught myself on the railing. It jiggled loose in its moorings, the metal burning my palms.

Only my breathing sounded through my ears. Every eye in the arena was on me.

Including Cion's.

For the first time, something like hope sparked in his eyes. And I so desperately wanted him to hold on to it.

My eyes swung back and forth between the doors. I wanted to point to the door with Latia, but I couldn't figure out if Rodric was tricking me. Thoughts flew through my mind at an alarming rate.

If I picked the door with the tiger, I knew what was going to happen. But I doubted if I chose the door Latia was behind he'd let them go. He'd probably have soldiers escort them to the desert and kill them there. Was it better to let them die quickly here?

And for all I knew, Rodric had already lied. Maybe Latia wasn't even behind one of the doors. Or maybe she was, and he'd purposefully told me wrong. But if Latia was behind the door I picked and Rodric didn't keep his promise, maybe it would be enough to incite the people to fight back.

"Decision time, Kateri," Rodric said. "Is it the lady or the tiger?"

Cion's gaze stayed steady on me. He appeared calm and collected, which was the exact opposite of the sandstorm brewing in my stomach.

My heart clenched.

I hadn't thought love could truly exist in this desert. I thought it was the biggest mirage of all. Something meant to trick those who sought it out, to distract them from their miserable lives, the ones without futures.

But it wasn't. It was about hope. It was about having a future worth living.

I'd known from the moment Cion had given that bracelet to Latia that he would never be mine. I just hadn't admitted how much I'd wanted him for my own. But watching him stand there, knowing no matter which door I picked it would be the last time I'd see him, broke something within me.

The wind caught wisps of his hair and pulled them across his forehead. Even in the arena he still managed to look wild and untamed. He managed to look defiant. Free.

And I wanted him to stay that way. With Latia.

I took one long last look at him, at the gaze that I would never be able to claim as my own. I let it burn into my memory.

Then I steeled my face and pointed to the door on the right.

CHAPTER

30

Rodric waited a moment before signaling for the door to open. "I should've told you that I made sure Cion knew that you knew what was behind each door, that he knew you held his fate."

He signaled for the door to open.

It creaked inward.

A tiger charged right toward Cion.

"You liar!" I screamed at Rodric.

"Of course they both had tigers. Did you honestly think I'd let him go?" Rodric laughed.

My thoughts raced. So did my heart.

I did the only thing I could think of.

Before Rodric's laugh had even died out, I'd switched my grip on the railing. I kicked my feet off the bench and flipped over so my back would've hit the other side of the railing if I hadn't let go.

I landed and was running before the sand settled around me. Gasps escaped from the crowd, followed by cheers.

I didn't even turn to see Rodric's puzzled look over where my shackles had gone. My sights were aimed at the tiger. It loped across the arena, leaving a trail of dust behind it.

My dress wrapped around my legs. I kicked through it, running faster than I ever had before.

Out of the corner of my eye I saw another body jump through the broken section of railing not far from me and angle toward me.

Dimic.

He had two swords in his hands.

"Kateri," he called. He heaved a sword toward me. I caught it as I kept running.

"Free Cion!" I threw over my shoulder.

The tiger locked eyes with me and charged forward as though it knew it was in a race for its prey.

Cion had pulled his chain taut as far from the tiger as he could get. I could only watch as the tiger's paws pounded into the sand and it leapt over the post, straight at Cion.

He rolled forward out of the tiger's path and ducked around the post, back toward the doors.

The tiger recovered quickly, turning back and snapping, narrowly missing Cion's arm. Cion whipped the small amount of chain back and forth, trying to keep the tiger at bay.

The beast didn't care. It moved forward, forcing Cion to dive around the post again. His body shuddered as the length of chain ran out, and he was jerked around. He landed at an awkward angle, momentarily tangled.

I was nearly there, nearly to him, but I wasn't going to make it in time. The tiger tensed, ready to jump on its stunned victim.

I forced my legs to move faster.

Just as the tiger's front paws left the ground, I leapt.

A roar ripped from my chest as I jumped over Cion, landing one foot on the post he was chained to. I bounded off it and met the tiger midair.

I rammed my sword through its chest as we collided.

The tiger's weight drove me backward as we crumpled to the ground together. The beast's paws were around me and trying to detract enough to claw me. I didn't have room to pull my sword free, so I rammed it in farther and twisted. The tiger let out a heavy breath and stopped fighting. I rolled the tiger away and disentangled myself from its limbs.

The tiger moved a leg before it fell still. A small breeze ruffled its fur.

The crowd cheered.

But one voice stood out above the rest.

"Open the other door!" Rodric screamed.

The door I hadn't chosen slid open. Another tiger roared out.

I pulled my blade from the tiger's chest and turned to face the new threat.

Out of the corner of my eye, I saw Dimic already at work picking the lock. I just needed to buy him more time.

The second tiger snarled as it ran forward.

It leapt as it reached me, throwing its paws around. Its teeth snapped inches from my face. Hot breath washed over me.

Its paws ripped into my dress, tearing through the bottom half.

It took all the skills I'd learned while being hit from all directions in the shifting hills to keep the tiger's claws from biting into my flesh.

I threw my sword in an upward arch to block both front paws at once. The tiger put more weight behind its attack. I could barely hold my sword up against the force as it brought its weight down.

It threw itself forward, and I fell backward. I rolled out of the way just as a paw dug into where my head had been.

The tiger would've snapped at my neck if a pair of shackles hadn't smashed into its skull.

It whipped around, hissing.

"Over here, you flea-bitten mongrel," Dimic taunted. And then he took off running.

So did the tiger.

I rolled to my feet.

The tiger was gaining on Dimic as they raced to the edge of the arena.

Dimic leapt onto the fallen bit of railing, balancing on the thin beam and climbing up, disappearing into the crowd.

But the tiger didn't stop. It pounced over the railing and into the crowd too. People ran everywhere.

I moved toward the chaos.

Cion, free from his shackles, was ahead of me, running to make sure his brother made it away safely and that the tiger didn't hurt anyone else. He clutched the sword Dimic had been carrying in one hand and had the other wrapped around his still-healing side. I raced to catch up with him. I wanted to tell him to get away from the arena, but I knew he wouldn't go. Not until Dimic was safe. Not until everyone was safe.

The tiger was tearing its way through the stands. Several guards had spears pointed at it. It leapt forward, breaking a spear with its paw and biting into the guard's leg. The tiger whipped the man around, knocking him into the other nearby guards.

I lost sight of Cion and Dimic as I hauled myself up the broken railing into the stands and ran through the wake the tiger created.

I raced along several rows below the tiger, dodging fleeing bodies. I saw the path the beast would take and dashed up a staircase to cut it off.

Halfway up the stairs, I nearly ran straight into my father. I skidded to a stop.

My chest heaved from running and my breaths were uneven.

He stood staring down at me, just as he'd always done, as chaos filtered around us. His lips were tight, his eyes colder than I'd ever seen them.

I'd done what I'd always feared. I'd made him look weak.

Yet I didn't feel weak in response. I felt strong. As strong as the desert.

"The people will have to pay for what you've done," he said. He pulled his sword from his scabbard. The hiss of the metal echoed around us.

"They've suffered enough under your rule," I spat back. I raised my sword and pointed it at him, my chest shaking with rage at the thought of how many third children—tiny babies like the ones Insa cared for—had died because he'd been too afraid to lose his throne. "Your fake drought, your two-child law, your tiger trials. It all comes to an end now."

"You wouldn't even have people to rule if it weren't for my actions. When the water returned years ago, I knew they'd all want to leave if I gave it to them." He slowly advanced down the stairs toward me.

I took measured steps back, keeping him in my sights because I knew the height gave him the advantage.

"How long?" I asked, fighting to keep my voice level. "How long has the drought really been over? How long have you kept these people chained to you when you knew there was plenty of water, when you knew you could've ended the two-child law?"

"It doesn't matter," he spat. "The desert started the drought so that I could continue it, so I could continue ruling over my people." He glared down at me. "That's what you never understood, Kateri. If you don't control the people, you don't control anything." The crown atop his head gleamed in the early morning sun as he continued his slow, regal saunter down the steps. "Do you really think any of them would stay now if they had enough water to cross the desert?"

"Achra could've rebuilt. It could've become even greater under your rule—under our rule." My back hit the railing. The heat of it burned through my dress. I kept my sword aimed at his chest. "But you never wanted me to rule."

He sneered. "You were weak, like your mother. I constantly had to bandage your wounds, to make sure you'd be capable of fighting again. But even a rat like Rodric who crawled out of the desert could beat you."

"Is that why you adopted him to be the son you were never able to have after you killed your own wife and daughter? You chose a Desert Boy over me?"

"Prove it to me," he said. "Prove I should've picked you over Rodric. Prove to me that the desert didn't send him to us because he was the better choice." He swung his sword toward my chest.

The railing behind me shook as I blocked the blow and knocked it to the side.

Again and again he swung at me.

"Show me," he screamed. The crown shook on his head. His blows started coming faster and faster.

I swung my sword at a dizzying pace to keep his from biting into my flesh.

Gritting my teeth, I braced against the railing. After his next hit, I shoved off. He wasn't prepared for my attack. He stumbled backward, tripping over the steps.

I knocked his sword away as he lay sprawled across the

stairs. I pointed my blade at his collarbone. My chest shook, and my heart raced. "Is this proof enough for you, Father?"

His eyes narrowed. "I should've realized long ago the desert gave me those tigers to make up for you, for your weakness, because if you were truly my daughter, you would've already killed me."

I took a deep breath as his words struck me. "You're right," I said. I pulled my sword away and took a few steps back.

Just as I did, a woman to my left screamed.

The tiger had torn a gash across her stomach and was barreling right toward us.

I threw myself backward, dropping over the railing into the sandy arena.

My father stood.

The tiger turned toward him.

He'd always thought he was master of the tigers. Maybe that's why he didn't even go for his discarded sword. Maybe he honestly thought the beast would recognize him as its superior.

But the tiger headed straight toward him, as though it had been looking for him. A paw rushed forward, raking down my father's chest.

My father crumpled forward and lay there as blood pooled around him. His head was turned toward me. His crown rolled away. His eyes stared, unblinking. That was the closest they'd ever come to holding any warmth.

I clenched my teeth and refused to shed a single tear over his death. He wasn't worth returning water to the earth over.

The tiger bounded over him to chase a guard up the bleachers. I spotted Cion in pursuit.

I moved to follow him, but a figure dropped into the arena in front of me.

Rodric.

His eyes swung up toward my father's lifeless body.

"I guess that means I'll be king sooner than I expected," he said.

I brought my sword up between us. Sunlight glinted off the blade. "You'll never be king."

"Why wait for your birthday? Let's find out now." He pulled out a sword. But it wasn't a normal blade. It was Cion's sword. "Like it?" he asked. "I found it in the tunnel leading to the southern well after my men worked tirelessly to block off the tunnels once more."

My throat was dry. My legs ached. My muscles felt as empty as my stomach.

This was the moment I'd been dreading since I ran away. But I wasn't that same girl.

I threw myself into an attack.

My sword glanced off his. I positioned for another advance. I watched his body for slight movements like I had in the shifting hills.

He went straight for my neck. I knocked the attack away.

He alternated stabbing at my right and left side, but each time his shoulder hinted which direction he was going.

He let out a frustrated grunt as I knocked aside another hit.

I lunged toward him. He stepped to the side and then brought his arm crashing down on my outstretched one. The weight of the blow loosened my sword, and it fell to the dirt. He swung at me. I rolled under the blow, grabbing my sword as I went. I ended up in a crouching position facing him. And just as I brought my eyes up, his foot launched forward, spraying my face with sand.

It burned into my eyes. I resisted the urge to rub them. Instead, on instinct, I dove to the side.

A sword thunked into the sand where I'd been crouching.

I blinked, trying to clear my vision, but that only made more tears appear.

I clamped my eyes shut. It was nearly impossible to hear anything above the din of the crowd.

There. A footfall coming from my right.

As soon as I sensed he was close enough, I whipped my foot out, tripping him. He thudded onto his back. I rolled the opposite way and got to my feet just as he did.

"I see Cion threw sand in your eyes too," Rodric said, giving a clear indication of where he was.

I ignored his words and focused on his feet. I scrambled backward every time I heard him come forward. But I couldn't let him drive me all the way to the wall. We were nearly back at the post Cion had been chained to.

My vision cleared enough to make out his shape coming toward me.

I lunged forward, hoping he wouldn't be expecting an attack.

He knocked the blow aside and rammed his other elbow into my throat.

My back slammed into the ground. Sand burned my exposed skin.

I gasped for breath.

Rodric slammed his foot down on my arm, breaking my grip on my sword. He picked it up and tossed it away.

Between fits of gasping, I searched for another weapon as Cion had taught me. The slain tiger lay only a few feet from me.

Sand scraped my eyes as I scanned the area. Something glinted.

And I remembered what Cion had said about Remy. About how he'd gotten Rodric's sword away from him by faking an injury.

Only I didn't have to fake it.

"Please," I gasped. "Please let me go." I wrenched my arm away and slowly crawled backward toward the tiger.

Rodric laughed. "I don't think so."

I collapsed by the tiger's body.

Rodric crouched near my head. "You may've survived the scorpion sting. But I'm master of the arena."

"No, you're not." My arm shot out, grabbing the shackles lying just behind the tiger's head. I swung them as hard as I could into Rodric's temple.

Surprise flashed across his face.

I didn't wait around to see what other emotions surfaced. I leapt to my feet and scrambled toward my sword.

Rodric was swift behind me.

He took one long swing at me just as I grabbed my sword. He put all his weight behind that swing.

Cion had been right. Not only had Rodric been counting on his sword as the only weapon he needed, he didn't think I'd know how to wield a blade with my shield hand.

I waited until the last possible moment to duck under the blow and toss my sword to my left hand. As his momentum exposed his entire right side, I rammed my sword right under his ribs. Just as Cion had taught me to do with my dagger.

Rodric's momentum carried him a few feet away. He fought to stay on his feet as his sword arm dropped to his side. The twin tips of Cion's sword dragged in the dirt. He took a few stumbling steps back toward me. Blood dripped out of his side and left a trail. He attempted to raise his blade. Instead, it fell to the dirt. He crashed down next to it.

I watched his body until I was certain he wouldn't rise.

My chest heaving, I picked up Cion's sword from where it had landed and turned back to the chaos of the arena. People were streaming toward the exits, but amidst the chaos I spotted Cion in the stands. He'd acquired a spear somehow. But he wasn't pointing it at any threat. He was screaming something and pointing it at me.

No, behind me.

I turned just in time to see the remaining tiger heading right for me.

I dove out of the way as it snarled past. I rolled to my feet, sword at the ready to attack.

But when the tiger turned back toward me, there were no bars separating us. I could look directly into its eyes. No reflections of flames stared back. Instead, all that was reflected was me—crouched low, sword in hand, ready to pounce.

I inhaled, watching the tiger's paws in the sand, waiting for the smallest movement hinting that it was about to leap forward. But the tiger made no move toward me. It stared as if it were judging me, as if it were looking through my eyes into my spirit. No, not my spirit. The spirit of the desert that swirled inside me. The one I'd brought back with me when the desert sands had sent me back into the city. The one it recognized because the same spirit lived in it as well.

Slowly, it lowered its gaze, staring at the sand. The longer it stood there, the more and more its sides heaved. It panted, exhausted from the day's events and the desert heat. Or maybe it was simply as tired of fighting in the arena as I was. It lay down in the sand only a few feet from me, its white whiskers pulling back as it sucked in air.

It wasn't meant for this weather. It wasn't meant for the desert. And yet, the desert had let it pass through all those years ago when my father had captured it.

And I wondered if this is how my father had stumbled upon the tigers, weak and depleted. No wonder he'd been able to capture them so easily. But the longer I watched the creature lying there, the more I realized that the tigers had never bowed before him. They'd cowered from the desert like everything else.

He'd thought he was their master. He'd thought he could tame them, but my father had mistreated them, forcing them to fight in the arena to survive, just as he'd made me do. He'd tried to bend the desert to his will instead of realizing we're all at the mercy of these sands.

I wouldn't make the same mistakes because I didn't need tigers to rule these people. My own strength was enough—the strength of the desert inside me was enough. So even though it only would've taken one swipe of my sword to kill the tiger lying at my feet, I let my sword fall to my side. The desert had taken enough from me, and I had killed one of its tigers in turn. The bloodshed had to end somewhere. It had to end now.

The tiger and I were both done fighting in this arena. Because I'd beaten every opponent. I'd won. For the first time, my future was finally my own. And I was going to make the decisions that should've been made years ago, the ones that didn't shackle the people to me out of fear. It was time to cut the last of the chains linking the desert to my father and his terrible rule. It was time to set the tiger free.

I let it lie there undisturbed as I turned to face the crowd, and this time when I raised my sword to signal the fight was over, I wasn't raising it to my father—I was raising it to the desert itself. I let out a roar and pumped my hand in the air until it began to ache because after all this time, it was truly over.

A cheer went up all around from the people still scattered inside.

Cion leapt into the arena and jogged toward me. And then his arms were around me. I exhaled for what felt like the first time.

He pulled back. "Are you okay?" His eyes flickered back and forth between me and the tiger, but the beast made no move to get up. It rolled into the sand, seemingly content to lie there.

Breathlessly, I nodded. "Are you?"

"Yes." His eyes were bright. His smile was so big it made me want to laugh. "You did it." He lifted my face toward his. "You really did it." His hand lingered on my cheek. And then he was pulling me closer to him. His lips pressed against mine. Heat shot through me. He tasted like the cool desert night.

His hands moved upward, entwining in my hair, pulling me against him until our chests touched, making me never want to let go. I responded, wrapping my arms around him. He deepened the kiss, pressing his lips against mine with more ferocity than a tiger. It was like being in the shifting hills. The world tumbled away around us. All there was were his lips on mine, the small gasps of air we snuck, and our heartbeats.

Thoughts of how I never wanted him to stop, of how I could ever have thought I didn't want this rushed through my head until one final thought sliced through them all.

I pulled back. "Latia," I said, trying to catch my breath, "she's alive."

His arms didn't drop away. "I know. Rodric made sure I saw

her before I was taken into the arena. He probably wanted me to think she was behind one of the doors."

He leaned forward like he was going to kiss me again.

I didn't move, confusion playing across my face. "You gave her an engagement bracelet . . ."

"What?" Then understanding dawned in Cion's eyes. "You thought I was in love with Latia?"

I ducked my face. "What was I supposed to think?"

"She's my cousin," he said with a laugh. "Bala is her mother." He shook his head, sending wisps of hair over his eyes. "Latia's like my sister."

"Then why did you give her the engagement bracelet?"

"You know it's a tradition for a mother to give hers to her daughter. Bala wanted her to have it, but Latia refused to see her, knowing she'd try to get her to leave on the caravan with her," he said. "Bala thought if Latia would get married, maybe she'd give up this idea of getting revenge. Both Bala and I thought it was too dangerous for Latia to keep working in the palace, but she refused to stop searching for the water controls. Her mother was hoping if she had her engagement bracelet, it might change Latia's mind."

I nearly cried in relief. "You could've told me that."

He looked puzzled. "I tried right after she left us alone in the desert. You said you understood. I thought you did."

It felt like he'd pulled me out of the shifting hills again, and I was back on solid ground. This time, I didn't stop myself from brushing the hair away from his eyes, and when he kissed me, warmth shot through me hotter than the blazing desert sand.

The roaring of the crowd was what finally drew us apart. My cheeks blazed when I remembered just how many people were watching us, but they didn't seem to mind the idea of Cion by my side.

"I guess since I defeated Rodric, that means I get to pick who I marry," I said, eyeing him and thinking maybe I wouldn't mind wearing my mother's engagement bracelet at all.

A smile slid across his face. "Does that mean you're rescinding your offer to make me your captain of the guard?"

I shoved his arm playfully. "It looks like you escaped Scorpion Hill without being stung," I pointed out. "Some would say that makes you chosen by the desert and worthy of following in Tamlin's footsteps."

Cion laughed. "The only reason I didn't get stung was because I rubbed my legs in the juice from a spiral cactus last week," he said. "Scorpions hate it."

"What?" I said.

He shook his head. "You think us Desert Boys would let our biggest secret reach you palace folk so you could come searching for us anytime? I'm the only one who knew what it was, so not even Rodric could've told you. That's probably why he didn't get stung when I chased him out there after Remy died.

"I give it to the boys every two weeks," he continued. "If I'd known you were going anywhere near there, I would've doused you in it four times over, even if it does leave you with a rash for several days every time." He took my hand. "I didn't want to put you through the pain. It's always the worst the first time. You wouldn't have recovered in time to get in any useful training."

"You really do have everything about the desert figured out, don't you?" I couldn't help but marvel.

"Achrans always have been survivors. Although, I've always thought that Tamlin must've figured it out. It's the only way he would've made it through untouched. But you . . . nobody survives a scorpion sting. You must really be chosen by the desert. Not to mention even the tigers—the desert spirits themselves—recognize you as their queen." He kissed my hand. "And so I pledge my loyalty and my heart to you, my Tiger Queen." He bowed low.

And to my astonishment, the crowd did the same. They started chanting, "Queen Kateri."

I spun around, taking in the crowd. The Desert Boys had the guards cornered in one area of the stands. Later, I'd have to sort out who was loyal to me.

That would be the first of many changes, because it was time to open up the country. We had water. We could be a crossroads, an oasis in the desert once again. No more restricting the caravans. I knew there'd be many who'd want to leave now that they had water, but others would stay, and they would be looking to me to lead them.

As I looked around the crumbling arena with Cion at my side, I knew it was time to start rebuilding. It was time to claim my mother's crown as my own. And it was definitely time to finally get Dimic that bath.

EPILOGUE

I released the tiger into the desert after fattening it up for whatever journey the desert had prepared for it. The beast looked back only once, its eyes meeting mine, before it raced forward—its orange-and-black stripes fading completely into the desert landscape, as if it was a true spirit of the desert that had finally been reclaimed.

Then I focused on my people.

The unnaturally bad sandstorms that had been plaguing the kingdom started to dwindle, and caravans were coming and going once more.

Latia was the first one to claim a place in the caravan across the desert. She'd only remained after her mother left because she wanted revenge against my father for forcing her mother to flee all those years ago. Now that he was dead, she wanted to reunite with her mother. And she needed time to heal. So while I wished she would stay, wished for a chance to get to know the brave girl she'd hidden for so long, I respected her decision to go.

A handful of the Desert Boys elected to go with her, but most decided to stay. Many had joined my newly created soldier training program. If we were going to open our gates to the world, we'd need to be prepared to defend them.

I lifted the ban on only having two children, and I removed the water restrictions. That made Dimic the happiest of all. On most days, Cion had to drag him out of the bathtub, which surprised me since Dimic had recounted how he'd been sucked into one of the wells like we had when the dam exploded. Except he'd managed to grab a shard of wood from the dam, and when the wave took him, he used the wood just like he was used to doing on the desert hills. He surfed his way along until the force of the water shot him straight out of the well closest to the palace. He kept claiming it was the greatest moment of his life. He was the only Desert Boy who'd surfed on water and not just sand.

As for Cion and me, we spent most of our nights watching sunsets from the palace. He called me his Achran Flower, and I grew to love the nickname just as I did him. And I already knew no matter if we had sons or daughters someday, there'd be no more fighting in the arena. Because my mother was right. While I was sure all our children would learn to fight, they would also be taught that it takes more than just skill with a blade to rule a country. We needed to band together in order to survive, in order to grow stronger.

Hopefully all the generations to come would learn from my example, from my legend, as I was told my story was quickly becoming. For I may not have been able to make it across Scorpion Hill without being stung, but I'd survived.

In some ways, that made me stronger than Tamlin ever was, for I knew the poison the desert held. I had it flowing in my veins, making me part of the desert itself. And for now, the desert had chosen me to lead these people. That was enough for me.

ACKNOWLEDGMENTS

Once again, I give all glory and honor to God, Jesus, Mother Mary, and the angels and saints, who have all guided me along this path. A special shout out to Saint Kateri for inspiring me and for letting me borrow her name to inspire my character.

I also could not have written this book if it hadn't been for my family and their love and support. So thank you to my amazing family—Dad (John), Mom (Meg), Katie, Patrick, Michael S., Danny, John, Maggie, Michael K., James, and Mittens—for always being there for me and making me who I am today. I love you all!

My parents have always supported me and my dream of writing, and for that, I am forever grateful. They've also helped me see the world, which inspires my writing more than they know.

To my sister Katie: thanks again for always being my first reader. Thankfully, it wasn't as many drafts as *A Touch of Gold* this time. I don't know what I would do without you.

To my buddy John, my Magalicious Magpie, and my godson Michael: thanks for keeping your EE young and inspiring me every day. I love you!

Thank you again to my extended family for not only promoting my books, but for all your continued support.

To my agent, Christa Heschke: thanks for being with me every step of the way and helping release this story into the world. I can't wait to see what the future holds for us. Also, thank you to Daniele Hunter for her help!

To my amazing editor Hannah VanVels: this book would not be what it is without your guidance and help! Thank you for believing in the story and in me. I can't wait to work on more books with you in the future.

To everyone at Blink—Annette Bourland, Jen Hoff, Ron Huizinga, Londa Alderink, Jacque Alberta, LaTasha Estelle, and so many others. This book wouldn't be out in the world without you. Thank you for being such big supporters of my work.

To Liz Osisek: thanks again for being such a great critique partner. Your insights always bring my characters to life. I couldn't do this without you.

Also, thank you to fellow writers and authors Jessica Fair Owens and Rebekah Snyder for stepping in to help when I needed it.

To Eileen Bos, who created an absolutely stunning book sculpture for *A Touch of Gold*. You are truly gifted, and I am blessed to have found you!!! Everyone should go check out Enchanted Couture by Eileen Bos on Facebook.

To my friends who put up with me even when I can't hang out with them because I'm on a deadline: Carolyn Johnson, Anna Vorsilak, Amy Dreischerf, Rose Jindal, Vinaya Bahatia, Brynn Hollingsworth, Emily Gorrell, Julia Stern, Nikki Mousdicas, Vivian Liechty, Marija Stankovich, Joe Geisinger, Kevin Sermersheim, Joey Zettel, Stephanie White, Elizabeth Hunter, and Christina McGee.

To my Shark Week girls, my SnackPack: Rachelle Wood, Savannah Goins, Mackenzie Lauka, Alicia Grumley, Kristin Ungerecht, and Michele Harper. Thanks for being such great friends. And always remember, #ItsStillJustGreg.

To all those who prayed for me, especially my CRHP sisters!

To "the wind beneath my wings" that kept me flying to

write another book: Ashley Zurcher, Laura Goldsberry, Jennifer Goldsmith, Clint Lahnen, Brennan Ward, and Tara Trubela. Thank you all for your help along the way! We make a great team! Literally. Also, please pay special attention to my use of the Oxford comma. Remember to use it wherever you go.

To amazing fellow authors John Green, Brenda Drake, Sarah Cannon, Jay Coles, Sarah Schmitt, and K.M. Robinson, who shared wisdom, advice, and friendship with me.

I couldn't write these acknowledgements without also giving a shout out to a few Facebook groups who have been great supporters of my work: TBR and Beyond, YA Fantasy Addicts, Words & Whimsy Book Club, and Page Turners. Thanks to everyone in those groups for their support, especially T.L. Branson, Melanie Parker, Mireille Chartier, Samantha Mercer, Kristi Housman, Felicia Mathews, Candyce Kirk, Linda Harr, Megan Rogers, Haley Wilson Lemmón, Joanne Wills, Brianna Elaine Coffman, Heather Currie, Hannah Woycik, Kahla Leighton, Jordan Fleming, Stephanie Sarac, Sarah Nelson, Tara Bowering, Leanne Jones, Cheyenne Sanders, Megan Jeong, and Courtney Armstrong Pate.

Another shout out to Julia Byers for the great headshot. I'm still using it, so I hope if you're reading these acknowledgments in public again that you're not crying this time ;)

To my teachers at Peter Panda preschool, St. Pius X, Brebeuf Jesuit Preparatory School, Indiana University, and Butler University.

To Frank Richard Stockton, who wrote the short story "The Lady, or The Tiger?" Your infamous cliffhanger ending inspired me to reimagine your tale. Thank you.

To my English teacher, Mrs. Theresa Desautels. You

introduced me to this story, and without you, it wouldn't exist. I can still remember you asking me, "Did she pick the lady or the tiger?" I raised my hand and said that it could have been either, and I've been mulling it over ever since. And all these years later, I did my best to give it the ending it always should have had.

To my street team: thank you for all you've done and for joining me on this journey.

To some of my most devoted fans: Jordan Edwards and Valérie Pelchat—thanks for your support! And thank you to FangirlPixieJar shop and BookishSignsAndMore on Etsy for creating such lovely pieces of art inspired by my books! Thanks to Elizabeth Sagan (@elizabeth_sagan) for her wonderful Instagram picture of *A Touch of Gold*!

To everyone who liked my author page, shared my blog, or helped in some other way, you have no idea how much I appreciate it and how much you helped me achieve this dream. A special thank you to several people who really helped me along the way: Michael and Nancy Uslan, Sandi Patel, Kathy Lowry, Lynn Ratkey, Chuck Fanara, Valerie Scherrer, Jodi Clark, and Carrie Sukova.

To my readers, thank you for continuing this journey with me. I couldn't do this without all of you. I hope you all find the tiger within!

About the Author

Annie Sullivan grew up in Indianapolis, Indiana. She received her Masters degree in creative writing from Butler University. She loves fairy tales, everything Jane Austen, and traveling. Her wanderlust has taken her to every continent, where she's walked on the Great Wall of China, found four-leaf clovers in Ireland, waddled with penguins in Antarctica, and cage dived with great white sharks in South Africa. You can follow her adventures on Twitter (@annsulliva) or on her blog: anniesullivanauthor.com.

BLINK